ALL PASSENGERS

ALL PASSENGERS

A NOVEL

by
Brenda Foster

RATTLESTICK

TIBURON, CALIFORNIA

Design by Dennis Gallagher/visdesign.com
Book production by Bayside Bookworks
Editing by Elissa Rabellino
Proofreading by Susan Manning
Cover images © 2013 iStockphoto.com/
    LuminaStock /Arman Zhenikeyev
Author photograph © 2013 Elissa Rabellino

Rattlestick Publishing
396 Greenwood Beach Road
Tiburon, California 94920

First printing, 2013
Printed in the United States of America
ISBN 978-0-9854576-0-0

For my beloved family, whose love
has always sustained me.

Thanks to all my supportive and wonderful
friends over the years and their faith in my
ability to complete this book.

CONTENTS

1

Edith

I t wasn't that Edith Sharpe didn't like her hair—she did. It was just that she couldn't make it look big, and her arms ached from the repeated backcombing that she knew she wasn't doing correctly. "It's the eighties," the hairdresser had said the other day as she teased and sprayed, "it's the look!" The girls at the office said that Edith's hair was one of her best features, as was her likeness to Natalie Wood, a remark that Edith had laughed at. "Our hair is the same color—that's all," she had retorted.

Now she didn't know what she looked like—a scarecrow, perhaps? She adjusted the small mirror on the wall above the kitchen sink and vigorously brushed out the knots. Then she scooped and twisted up her curls, anchoring them back from her face with matching combs on either side. Why does one always have to be up to date? she thought. I don't care for the eighties look anyway, with its big hair, big shoulder pads, and gaudy jewelry. Who has time for all this in a morning, and who in Bogmire really cares about fashion? Maybe I would care if I lived somewhere else, she thought—a city, perhaps, a place that teems with life. Not like this town, this street, Slattery Street, where every tired house and garden looks the same.

After swiftly downing a cup of tea, she assembled her mother's breakfast tray before ascending the dark, narrow stairs of the two-bedroom house that led to her mother's room. A cold draft whipped around her ankles, adding to her lackluster mood. When she entered the small bedroom, she was nauseated and overwhelmed by the familiar stench of stale urine and eucalyptus. Her eighty-year-old mother, Ruby, was propped up in bed, surrounded by pillows covered with bits of embroidery and scrappy lace. Around the old lady's knees were layers of crocheted woolen coverlets, unraveling and full of holes. Edith intended to replace these relics one day, along with the yellowing lace curtains and threadbare rugs. In the cast-iron grate, a gas fire plopped and puffed its blue-and-yellow flames, bringing a little heat and cheer to the odorous room.

Edith placed the breakfast tray, containing a plate with two pieces of toast and a mug of tea, on a small marble-topped table at the right-hand side of the bed. "I've been waiting," Ruby said harshly. "You're late!" The old lady's hostile voice and appraising, critical eyes often reduced Edith to tears, at which Ruby would snarl, "You are soft and stupid," a statement directed repeatedly toward Edith since her childhood. Standing by the sink in the corner of the room, she rinsed her mother's brown, ill-fitting dentures in the icy cold tap water. Edith despaired of her unchanging situation and frequent inability to cope with Ruby's excessive demands.

It had been four years since the stroke that had severely affected Ruby's left side, leaving her with limited mobility. Resentment and frustration now replaced any affection Edith might have had for her mother. God knows, for thirty-six years I have tried to love her, she thought, and wondered if, being an only child, she had failed to measure up. She concluded that it was futile to seek any other reasons or justification for Ruby's attitude toward her, just as it had been futile to inquire about the father she had never known. "What happened to him, Ma?"

"He went to war, never came back. That'll be the end of it!" Ruby had said.

She placed the newly rinsed teeth into her mother's claw-like hand. First the upper set, then the lower. She watched as Ruby maneuvered them into her cavernous mouth. Attempting to divert her attention from this ugly morning ritual, she thought of Edwin Meach, her occasional lover of the past ten months. They had met traveling to work each morning on the bus en route to the Bogmire town center. Their association had evolved slowly, beginning with nods and smiles, shared seats, shared comments. They had clasped hands and touched knees, concealing their desires beneath the pages of the *Bogmire Daily News*. For years, Edwin had been unhappily married to Sybil, who said that it was the will of the Lord that kept their marriage together, and they should honor that. He worked at a shoe store close to the insurance company where Edith worked as a claims adjuster. "I am a buyer," Edwin had said—"that is altogether different from a salesman."

Sometimes Edwin had the use of Sybil's car, allowing them to leave town occasionally and therefore avoid local prying eyes and gossip. Edith savored Edwin's unwavering affection. She likened it to a cushion she could lean on, reliable and secure. Because she had never felt truly loved, it had taken courage and time to allow this person into her life, her thoughts, and, ultimately, her body, though she still shuddered at the memory of their first sexual encounter here in the house. Her office had been quiet that day. She took the afternoon off. Her mother was dispatched to the day hospital, a place she now refused to attend. "All them nurses hate me," she said. A brief phone call to Edwin that afternoon, and he was by her side.

He stayed for four hours that afternoon. Edith had prepared a snack. He wasn't hungry, he said. Sybil had baked scones, which he had eaten on the way over. He accepted the sherry that Edith offered him without hesitation. Her sherry gave her a raging headache. Edwin drank a lot of sherry that afternoon and said how well Edith looked, suggesting that they take a bath together. Edith replied, "We don't have time, and there isn't enough hot water." They watched a rerun of *All Creatures*, agreeing that farm life would be wonderful. Edwin droned on about the advantages of leather soles and arch supports. Edith talked about fraudulent claims and flood damage. Their forced conversation eventually faded, but her headache didn't. After their fumbled lovemaking, he called her his "precious little secret" before scuttling off into the late afternoon.

The rasping tones of her mother's voice jolted Edith back to reality. "Not coming today!" her mother said.

"Who isn't coming?" Edith asked.

"That nurse," snapped Ruby. "It's her day off."

"Why is that?"

"It's Tuesday."

"I'll be sure to tell Lil," said Edith.

Lil lived next door. She was a kind, friendly soul who watched over Ruby when the regular nurse had a day off. Lil did this without complaint and was never offended by the old lady's rude and ungrateful manner. For this, Edith was thankful. Lil's caring ways frequently left Edith with feelings of guilt over her own bitter attitude. "How can I love her, how can I feel something that was never there in the first place?" she had said to her best friend, Mavis. Edith had felt somewhat envious when Edwin spoke of the sense of belonging and affection he had shared with his mother prior to her death some years back, though his copious tears that accompanied that revelation disturbed her. Her thoughts were soon disrupted by the sound of the phone ringing downstairs in the hallway. "Who would call at this time?" she said; it was 7:45 a.m. She rushed downstairs, ignoring her mother's calls. "Maybe it's Lil! She isn't coming!" yelled Ruby. "She's having a perm! She's not coming!"

Edith grabbed the receiver. It was Edwin. "Precious, is that you?" he said.

"Yes, of course it's me, Edwin—why so early?" she whispered, hating the word "precious."

"I've found a special place for us," he said. "To be alone for the whole day, Edith! I have Sybil's car. It's a surprise! It's important. Please, Edith, call in sick, please!"

"But Edwin, I—"

"Do it for us, precious."

"I can't just tell a lie."

"Do it for us," he said, "just this once. I love you, please. It's a wonderful surprise for us."

"But, I, how—"

"Get the early bus. Meet me at the Gaumont Restaurant at nine." He clicked off before she could respond.

It wasn't like Edwin to be so insistent. She was puzzled yet a little excited by his sense of urgency. Occasionally, she felt guilty about spending time with a married man, but his marriage was an unhappy one, and she had to admit that she felt a little flattered by their affair. It had caused a shift in the monotonous pattern of her life. She always felt uplifted by their physical closeness but was somewhat relieved when he left and she was alone again. Once in a while, she craved his physical presence, wondering if this meant that she was in love. These feelings confused her, but she didn't really care and just enjoyed being needed, convinced that time would decide the outcome of it all. Now there was a din coming from upstairs. Ruby was summoning her, not vocally, but by a persistent rapping sound. This she achieved by rattling her walking stick between the vertical rails of her oak headboard, using all the strength she had in her right arm. "What is it, Ma?" Edith asked as she entered the bedroom.

"Me teeth," Ruby said, holding them out, "wash 'em again. Biscuits, don't forget! Who phoned?"

"I won't forget," mumbled Edith, ignoring the question. "I'm late, Ma," she said, and held out a chipped enamel mug for the teeth. Ruby refused to use anything else. Sometimes the teeth would stay in there for hours. There were days when Ruby wouldn't use her teeth, moistening her biscuits in her tea.

Edith removed the breakfast tray, propping it against the landing banister to take downstairs later. She took several digestive biscuits from a tin on the dresser, placed them on a small plate, and then filled a glass with water from the sink in the corner of the room. She set the plate and glass down on the bedside table next to the bed. She turned down the gas fire and made sure the curtains were drawn aside, noticing the rain. Edith checked the clock; it was 7:55 a.m. She had enough time to catch the early bus and meet Edwin. Why not, she thought, curious to know what he had planned for them.

"I'm off now, Ma," she said.

"It's Tuesday, the nurse's day off. Don't forget," yelled Ruby, "Lil can't come, she's having a perm!" but Edith was already out of the room. She rushed downstairs, seizing her bag, gloves, umbrella, and raincoat off the hallstand. "Who's coming, then?" Ruby called out. Her thin words were drowned out by the slam of the front door. The old lady flinched and lay back on her pillow.

The bus stop was two houses down from her home. Edith felt

conspicuous taking an earlier bus, knowing that neighbors observed each other's every move, and any deviation from a normal routine was sure to be gossiped about. She held her umbrella low over her face. She anguished over the phone call she would need to make to her office if she was to comply with Edwin's request. Rarely was she absent from work. She was proud of her employment record. She had been with Shield Insurance for eleven years. She had turned down promotions at out-of-town branches—who would care for Ruby if she moved away from Bogmire? The only other member of the Sharpe family was her uncle, Ruby's younger brother, Leon. Leon had left for Australia when Edith was six. Contact with him had been lost, and Ruby declined to speak of him.

The bus cruised around the corner into Slattery Street before groaning to a stop. "Good morning, madam, it is much raining," said Saleem, the regular driver of the No. 9. "Good morning," said Edith. She loved the way Saleem bowed his head when he spoke. His quiet dignity and the soft lilt of his fractured English appealed to her. "You are coming sooner, yes?" he asked as he took her fare.

"Yes," she nodded. Saleem was well built and taller than most of the Pakistanis who had settled in the town. Their dark presence in Bogmire was resented, and their attempts to integrate were frequently met with hostility. "You can't trust 'em," Lil had said. "Not the way they stand about like that, in little groups. They're a shifty lot!"

Edith chose a seat close to the front, where she could watch Saleem. His hands fascinated her. He had long, strong fingers and clean nails. A gold wristwatch encircled his sculptured wrist. When he moved his arms to manipulate the huge steering wheel, the white cuffs of his shirt would slide upward, revealing muscular brown forearms, sprinkled with just the right amount of dark hair. She had the impression that he was in total control of himself. Where did he belong, with that dusky sensuality and polite acceptance of his menial occupation? His head turned and he looked at her.

"You are here, yes?" he said, drawing up to her usual stop, which was a block from her office.

"No, actually, I'm … I need the Gaumont, at Market Square, thank you."

"You are changing?"

"Yes—no," she stammered, struggling to return his gaze. Her hands were perspiring; her body felt too warm. Was this flirting? She didn't care, because she secretly relished these sensual voyages each morning.

"It is much raining for you now," he said, drawing up to the Gaumont stop. "Be having a good day, please," he said.

"Thanks," she said, "I hope I do."

She stepped down into the frenetic morning bustle of the town center. Rain splashed her ankles as she hurried along. The arousing warmth she had experienced was now rapidly diminishing. People dodged one another as they sought their destinations. She was hard put to see any happy faces. It was as if they, too, were trapped here, locked into the dull sameness of the place. She took some pleasure in the fact that today would be different for her, or possibly exciting. She headed across the street to the Gaumont.

2

Edwin

- - - - - - - - - - - -

&dith was perplexed by the urgency of Edwin's phone call so early that morning. He was not a man of surprises; he was all too predictable. Still, he had sounded sincere and earnest. Earnest! She laughed to herself. Earnest, that's what he should have been named. He was earnest about most things. Perhaps he was finally leaving Sybil. I will give him his due and hear him out, she thought. It was raining heavily now, and she was eager for cover. The town square was busier than she had anticipated; then she realized it was market day. Stall owners were unloading produce. Canopies and stands were being erected. Trucks and vans were parked everywhere. She dodged the traffic to cross the road.

The Gaumont Cinema and Restaurant had once been a special place. Its fine columnar exterior was now blotched and streaked from the many pigeons that inhabited its crevices and ledges. Edith remembered her visits here as a child with Uncle Leon holding her hand. He would treat her to afternoon tea in the restaurant. She remembered that potted palms stood amid the white-clothed tables. There were fancy cakes on fancy plates, waitresses in frilly caps and aprons. She recalled treading the thick plush carpet. She had felt part of a family back then, but now it seemed that Ruby, Leon, and she were unconnected.

Soaked with rain, she mounted the steps to the spacious foyer. It had been some years since she had set foot in the place. Movies were no longer shown. A large sign at the entrance read, "Bingo! Here! Big Prizes." The foyer appeared to be empty. The only sound came from the distant droning of a vacuum cleaner and the pings of raindrops landing in a bucket halfway up a wide staircase leading from the foyer. She looked at the layers of dust and grime on the chandeliers that hung from the ceiling. She remembered a cherub fountain in an illuminated alcove in the wall to the left of the main entrance. The cherub was eyeless now, cigarette butts were strewn about its feet, and a bingo card was wedged between its fat legs. The foyer carpet still felt soft beneath her feet; the golden swirls of the fleur-de-lys pattern made her feel dizzy. She knew she should have eaten breakfast. From somewhere behind her, she heard a cough. She turned. A man was placing a billboard at the foot of the stairs.

"You're not daft," he said.

"Pardon?"

"Getting a good seat early. We get big crowds when it rains. Plenty more where that comes from," he said, gesturing to the bucket. "They're open in yonder." He pointed to the restaurant.

"Right," said Edith. "Thank you."

"Could be your lucky day, eh?"

"Well, who knows?" she said, cautiously aware of her reason for being there. She was due at her office in thirty minutes. She went into the ladies' room. I look like a drowned rat, she thought, staring at herself in the mirror. "How do you stay so slim and pretty?" one of the girls at work had said last week. She couldn't remember when she had last felt slim and pretty, if ever—certainly not now. She applied some lipstick and fiddled with her damp hair. Had she been too hasty, too eager to comply with Edwin's plan? Maybe he wanted to end their affair. What if he did? She would cope. She was growing tired of his whining about his miserable wife. She dabbed some blush on her cheeks before heading to the restaurant.

The once-elegant restaurant now functioned as a self-service cafeteria. A few people sat here and there. She soon spotted Edwin sitting behind a pillar, his face partially obscured by a copy of the *Bogmire Daily News*.

"Edwin, I'm here," she said softly.

"Precious." He jumped up to kiss her cheek, his bifocals slipping. The newspaper fell to the floor. He bent down to retrieve it, and his glasses disappeared into the folds of the paper.

"Why so early, Edwin?" she asked. "What is it?"

"Edith, I have Sybil's car, all week," he whispered. "She is away at one of her conferences. I have a special place for us." His voice became louder as his words tumbled out. "A place where we can be alone, away from here, just the two of us today, my precious." He stopped, took a deep breath, and replaced his glasses. "I want you to take the day off." He was flushed as he folded and refolded the newspaper. "I know it is a lot to ask at short notice, but everything had to be done so quickly. Edith, I need you so, and I know how you need me! Call the office. Tell them Ma is unwell. Come with me today—we can be there soon." He grabbed both of her hands and stared at her with wide eyes. If she didn't know him better, she would be afraid of him. "Edwin, this place—what kind of place is it, and where?"

"A caravan, at Baker's Farm," he said.

"A caravan! But Edwin, it's February, it's winter, it's cold, and that place is miles away!"

He drained his coffee. "Precious, when have we ever been cold?" He clenched his cup. His knuckles were white. Crumbs of Styrofoam fell onto the table. Edith had never seen him quite this way before, so agitated and perspiring. Even when they made love, he never became flushed or perspired, just scratched his head a lot afterward. Maybe there was a passion she hadn't discovered, a private part of him she had yet to find. Maybe this time she would experience the ecstasy of sex with love instead of the anatomical groping that took place in the front parlor— even this was frequently interrupted by the rap of Ruby's walking stick on her bedrail.

"Call your office," he pleaded in a loud voice. "Tell them Ruby has had a bad turn; do it for us. It has been so long, Edith, three weeks. Just a phone call, my precious." More tables were occupied now, and people were staring. "I'll get you coffee," he said, and leaped up from the chair, tripping over his umbrella. A woman at a nearby table placed a hand over her mouth and looked away. Edith checked her watch. She was due at the office in fifteen minutes. She was hesitant to call her boss. Lying wasn't something she did readily. What was she risking? Not too much—her job was secure, the most secure aspect of her life. She thought of Mavis, who worked alongside her. "Be good to yourself, Edith," she would say. "If you don't take risks, you go nowhere!"

Edwin returned with her coffee. He put some loose change on the table. Perspiration was beading on his pink forehead. He hunched his shoulders and screwed up his face, and with his mouth wide open he sneezed. He wiped his nose with a white handkerchief that Sybil had ironed. Briefly Edith wondered what had initially attracted her to him. He was a little too thin, perhaps. Apart from his two slightly prominent front teeth, which gave his pale face a look of perpetual anticipation, he looked quite ordinary. It bothered her now that she should think about these things. Mavis would say, "Do it, Edith, just go for it!"

"All right," she said, standing up. He steered her to the public phone, which she felt was too close to the counter. He thrust some change into her hand.

"Don't let us down, darling. I'll be waiting in the car at the side entrance." He kissed her cheek and hurried off. She dialed the office number and waited. Ada, the longstanding receptionist, who knew her well, answered the phone. "Shield Insurance, good morning."

"Ada, this is Edith Sharpe," she said, and related her story. "Mother, she has to be watched closely."

"We do sympathize, Edith. I know when I tell the boss, he will fully understand," she said. "Don't you worry about a thing."

"Thanks, Ada."

It surprised her how easily she had lied. Relieved, she headed for the side exit of the building. Edwin beamed when she stepped into the Ford Cortina. "I'm proud of you," he said, kissing her cheek. She tried to beam back at him, but the heavy rain had chilled her. "Let's just go," she said.

3

Alice

Alice Larkin clicked her front gate shut. She opened up her umbrella and began the half-hour walk to the Bogmire bus depot, where she worked as a custodian of the ladies' toilet block. Alice had resided in Bogmire for all of her fifty-three years. She loved walking to work and enjoyed the strong sea breezes and caterwauling seagulls by the oceanfront. She was used to the rain that smacked hard on her umbrella. Walter was right, she thought, when he said that the town needed a good wash now and then.

Alice lived alone. Her late husband, Walter, had spent his evenings at the pub and weekends at the football club, so she was used to being alone. She never cared for the pub or the football. Five years had passed since that fatal night at the Black Bull Pub. Walter's heart had stopped in the middle of a rousing chorus of "Land of Hope and Glory!" The bartender said, "His voice was never better." At the funeral, Karen, their twenty-year-old daughter, whispered, 'Well, Mum, now we can get on with stuff.'"

Alice wore black for a month; it felt like the right thing to do. Karen soon left Bogmire to be with Lyle, her guitar-playing boyfriend. "Bogmire's a dump, Mum! Come live with us," she said. Alice declined Karen's offer. Lyle was moody, and like Walter, he was a little too fond of the pub. "I'll be fine," she assured them, and she was.

Humming as she walked along, she thought, as she always did these mornings, of her upcoming wedding to Jimmy Jack, the owner of the newsstand at the bus depot. She smiled to herself, thinking how flattered she had felt a year ago when Millie from the ticket office had confided to her, "Jimmy has had his eye on you for a long time, Alice. Everybody knows it." Alice had always suppressed her fondness for Jimmy, not daring to think they were anything more than fellow workers. She thought Mary Lacey, from the tea kiosk, had Jimmy in her sights. "Mary fancies anything in trousers," Millie said. "The thing is, they never fancy her! Is it any wonder, the way she carries on? Her powdered nose is out of joint. She's jealous of you, Alice."

Alice was not sure how their romance had developed after that. Jimmy turned up at the Bingo Club, and she suspected that Millie had something to do with it. They were awkward and shy with each other at first, and then they came to trust and confide in one another. She could still feel the strong support of his arm beneath hers, when last night they had strolled home after a fish and chips supper at the Red Lion.

"Jimmy and I, we fit together like a pair of old socks," she told Karen.

"Phew, Mum, don't be daft."

A gust of wind lifted her umbrella as she turned in to Slattery Street. Tugging it back down, she was startled to see Edith Sharpe at the bus stop. That's odd, she thought—Edith gets a later bus, the one that she herself used to ride. She waved, but Edith didn't notice. Alice had known the Sharpe family for years. They used to attend the same church. Ruby, Edith's mother, had always kept to herself, as Alice remembered—more so after Edith was born. There were some stories going round about the Sharpe family after the war, Alice recalled. Ruby's brother, Leon, had left for Australia after a falling out. She had been a teenager then and hadn't paid much attention to the gossip. I wonder how he is, that brother, she thought. Jimmy would know. They would be about the same age, sixty-something. She had heard about Ruby's stroke some years back. She exchanged greetings with Edith at the depot almost every morning, but Edith never mentioned her mother or her uncle Leon.

The No. 9 bus rumbled past with Edith on board, its wheels spitting up rain. She will reach the depot before I do, Alice thought—funny, that.

She turned from Slattery Street and proceeded up Marine Avenue to the seafront promenade, past numerous small hotels and Victorian houses with bed-and-breakfast signs in the windows. Bracing herself against the biting wind that blew in from the north, she crossed over to a pedestrian pathway. A row of seagulls clamped to a railing watched her. "I don't have anything for you," she said. "Tomorrow, if I remember." Steps led down from the path to the sea and sands below, where a ribbon of flotsam and jetsam stretched for miles. Jutting above the mud flats were some barnacled pylons; they were all that remained of a pier that had burned down during the war. Some said the fire was started by kids playing with matches; others swore it was the work of the Germans.

Over the years, Alice had witnessed the deteriorating face and character of her town. How grand it had all seemed when she was a child. The world was slower then, she thought. People's faces were softer, ready to smile. Margaret Thatcher had promised to restore England's glory, guaranteeing pride and prosperity for all. Well, mused Alice, she forgot about this part of the country, even though the talk around town was of an ambitious plan to tear down the old depot and erect a new streamlined transit center. The plan bothered Alice. "Under one roof," she had said to Jimmy, "with everybody else! Fifteen years I've pushed that mop back and forth over my tiles. I'm not sure I'm cut out for that big a change."

"Likewise," Jimmy said. "I'm me own man, in me own place. Thirty years I've sold them newspapers and the mags," he said. "I'm done with it now. I can keep the betting going on the side—the horses, the dogs. Folks will expect that. You and me, Alice, we've paid our dues; we'll be fine. Perhaps this change is telling us something," Jimmy said with a wink. "This feelin', you and me, Alice. Oh heck," he said, "I'll just say it! I love you, Alice, and I want us to get married. What do you say?"

"Of course I'll marry you, Jimmy, of course," she said.

"I want us to do it proper, church an' all," he said. "I don't want us to wait too long. We'll tell folks only when you're ready."

"All I have to do is tell Mary Lacey at the tea kiosk," Alice said. "Then the world will know—she can't keep anything to herself!"

"That's for sure," laughed Jimmy.

Alice turned from the seafront and headed to the bus depot and the center of town. The rear entrance to the depot was blocked by a delivery van. Alice waited and took shelter from the rain under the eaves of the kiosk. "Mornin', Alice," said Mary Lacey.

"Mornin', Mary." On this wet February morning, Mary wore a white sleeveless blouse over a too-short red vinyl skirt. Her black fishnet stockings did not flatter her long, thin legs or her feet, which were squashed into gold high-heeled sandals. "Mary still thinks she is Miss Bogmire Holiday Queen," Jimmy had said to Alice. "Nineteen-fifty-four is long past," he said. "Mind you, she didn't look so bad then. Now, her painted face would stop a clock!"

"Don't forget them extra bread rolls," Mary yelled to the driver, who was reversing his van from the blocked entrance. "'Bye," she cried, "be good now!" There was a blast from the horn. Mary let out a throaty laugh that degenerated into a coughing fit. Alice moved to the front of the kiosk alongside two of the bus drivers.

"There you go, boys," Mary slid cups of tea across the counter.

"Thanks, gorgeous." They laughed and turned to leave.

"Them fellas!" Mary said. "They're a cheeky lot." Alice nodded. "They're all the same except for him," Mary said.

"Who?"

Mary pointed to Saleem. He was lounging against a barrier reading a newspaper. "He's different, ever so polite and all. Not surly like them other Pakis."

"I wouldn't know," said Alice.

"What can I get yer?"

"Tea, Mary, please—I need to warm up."

"You're not warm-blooded like me, are yer?"

"I need to get going," said Alice.

"Right, just one thing, Alice. Do me a favor—would you ask Jimmy to come and see me? I can't leave the kiosk. I fancy a flutter on the horses today. I feel lucky!" She twisted up her dyed red hair and held it in a clump on top of her head. "What do you think, then, up or down? Of course, me roots need a touch-up."

"Well, I ..."

"Sorry, Alice. It's not your thing, is it, hair and stuff? Did I tell you I'm expecting the bosses?" Mary said. "They want to talk to me about the new cafeteria. I'm in the running for it. I'll be in charge." Ash from her cigarette drifted onto a plate of egg sandwiches.

"Really!" said Alice.

"Oh, and guess who I saw earlier?"

"Who?"

"That Edith Sharpe. She were rushin' off, like a bat out o' hell! She usually comes later. Funny, don't you think? She went 'round the town hall corner. Her office is the other way. She looked ever so bothered. Just wondered—not my business, really."

No it's not, thought Alice. "I have to get on, Mary."

"Will you ask Jimmy, then? He knows what I fancy. Whoops! The races, I mean." Mary smirked.

"Mary fancies a bet," she said to Jimmy later.

"That's not all she fancies," he laughed, and rolled his eyes. "Silly cow, I'll fix her up," he said. "The two o'clock looks promising."

Alice coughed as she walked over to the toilet block. She didn't know which was worse, cigarette smoke or the diesel fumes trapped for the day beneath the canopied roof of the depot. When she reached the sanctuary of her toilet block, she began to sing "True Love," one of her favorite songs. She unlocked her cupboard, pulled out her stool, and hung up her wet raincoat. She finished her tea and put on a clean apron. That was another thing she had heard about the changes: everybody wearing uniforms. That didn't seem right, somehow.

"As I give to you," she filled her bucket with water, tipped in the disinfectant, and swished the mop around, "love forever true," she sang.

4

Baker's Farm

----

dwin and Edith drove slowly along the back streets of Bogmire, leaving the built-up areas behind them. Baker's Farm was a forty-five-minute drive from the town center. It had once been a popular summer resort for the workers of England's industrial north. With the advent of cheap packaged air travel and the guaranteed sunshine of European beaches, the popularity of Baker's Farm and the like had suffered.

"This is so wonderful," said Edwin.

"Yes."

"I feel it's a new beginning for us."

"Maybe," she said, "maybe."

"Dearest Edith, listen to me," he said. She looked over at him. His eyes were moist, his nose twitched, and he looked as if he was about to sneeze again.

"If we are to achieve our ultimate pleasures," he said, his voice shaky, "our souls can board our own private vessel. Sailing free to our passionate destination. Our anchors firmly secured in our bed of intimacy." A car honked; they had drifted too close to the center of the road.

"That's from my poem," he said. "That's from my poem about us. It's nearly finished." Clearing his throat, he reached over and put a cold hand on her knee. "Do you like it, my poem?"

"Oh, of course." She touched his shoulder.

His arduous ramblings continued on; then he began to hum. With the town now well behind them, the road became straight and open, running parallel to marshland and the seashore. The horizon, however, was obscured by rain and mist. "The radio," she said, "shall we turn it on?"

"It broke down," he said. "Sybil didn't want it fixed—too distracting. She feels the same way about the heater. She had it disconnected. One needs to keep a cool head when driving, Sybil always maintains. She keeps a rug on the back seat," he said. "You can also follow the route—there is a map in the glove box."

She reached behind her for the rug. It smelled of mothballs. Neatly folded in the glove box sat Sybil's knitted-string driving gloves. They had palms of chamois leather, and beside them was a small gold-embossed card. She read the black scripted letters.

Yield not to temptation for yielding is sin.
Each victory will help the other to win.
Fight manfully onwards, dark passion subdue.
Look over to Jesus, he'll carry you through.

"Do you ever go with her?" she said. "With Sybil, I mean. To her prayer meetings?"

"Once I did," he said. "She needed someone to help set up the chairs. I felt in the way, out of place. Sybil said my soul wasn't ready to receive. I never went back. My soul is ready for yours, Edith," he said. "Our two souls together."

"Mmmm." Edith stared at the long, flat stretch of road ahead; there were no trees or hedges. Rain lashed across the open fields. Cows stood about in forlorn groups. She checked her watch: they had been driving for only twenty minutes. It felt longer. Her raincoat was wet. She was hungry and had a headache that throbbed along with the slip-slap of the windshield wipers. Traffic hissed past them. A sign read, "No Camping." Who would want to? she thought. The place was viewless.

"Almost there. I'll have you warm in no time," he said, and resumed his humming. If only he knew a structured tune, she thought, and concluded that there was little music in Edwin's life. He'd told her that he had joined Sybil's singing group, the Vestry Voices. He left because he didn't have an ear for that kind of music and preferred romantic ballads and sometimes, for the thrill of it, marching bands.

They drove slowly along the open road, and she wondered, not for the first time, what the extent of her need for Edwin really was. She recalled the early days of their friendship as they traveled to work together. He was a buyer of shoes, he had told her. That was very different than a salesman, he said. He promised her a discount and a preview of sale items at the shoe shop. "Feel that calfskin," he said, slipping her foot into a sleek court shoe. She had felt charmed and flattered. She remembered her other lovers. There had been two or three over the years, but they had been forgettable, leaving her heart wanting. My heart still wants that something, she thought, glancing at the humming Edwin. She felt out of sorts and out of place now. He was driving too slowly to get anywhere, and she wished this journey would come to an end. They were now passing what had been the old village of Bogmire. Her mother told her that fishermen and farmers had worked and walked the many footpaths that linked the small community together. Children had played in the meadows around here and skipped along the once-golden sands. Then the greedy ones came along, her mother said, and everything changed, was ruined.

"Allow yourself to trust me, Edith. We are on a passionate journey, you and I. You understand that?" Edwin said. His enthusiasm was beginning to irritate her. She thought, what is there to understand? It's all about sex, so why don't you just keep quiet till we get there and do it. She looked at his pale hand folded around the gear knob and thought of Saleem's hands. She sneezed. At least the No. 9 bus was warm.

"Almost there, precious," he said as they approached some scrub-and-gorse-covered hills. "Aha." He slowed down to peer at a sign that read, "Cattle Crossing." The road narrowed and was darkened by tall, wet, waving poplar trees. A larger sign read, "Welcome, Baker's Farm. Drive Slowly! Children Playing!"

They followed the signs as they proceeded down an unpaved side road: "Campers Crossing," "Drive Slowly." Edwin braked suddenly and Edith lurched forward. Looming above them on either side of the road-way were two enormous white turretlike structures. Barred windows had been painted on the sides to simulate a castle. Straddled atop one of the turrets was a grinning gnome. The toothless gap of its red mouth revealed a cavity of twisted chicken wire. Its vulgar yellow-painted face stared out at them. The turrets were joined overhead by an archway of rusted wrought-iron letters, reading, "Happylands." Edith shivered. She needed to use a toilet.

"This," Edwin said with a deep gratified sigh, "is it. We shall be cozy in no time at all."

He slowed the car down and kissed her cheek. Peering out from behind a tree was a smaller gnome just as garish, supporting a sign that read, "Office and Cafeteria." Edith quaked at having to register in this place and have their presence acknowledged. The crisp voice of Edwin interrupted her thoughts.

"They know me here," he said gaily and drove past the office.

"You've been here before, then?" she said.

"Didn't I tell you that I was in floor coverings before I was in shoes? I did all the floors here—big job, custom linoleum, color-coordinated."

"Oh well, fancy that," she said.

She looked through the car window. There were several caravanlike structures on a small hill, all painted in different pastel colors. Each structure was surrounded by a picket fence with a gate. Perched on each gate were more gnomes supporting their respective numbers. Crows, their glistening heads cocked, pecked and prodded the wet ground. Seagulls squabbled and strutted around dilapidated play equipment.

Edwin parked the car. "That's ours, the pink one, No. 6," he said gleefully. "They all have views. ... Hold on. I'm not sure where I put the key." He fumbled in his pockets. "Ah, there it is." He then produced and held up a Marks & Spencer plastic shopping bag. Edith heard the clink-clank of bottles. "Something to fortify us with," he beamed.

Needles of rain stung Edith's cheeks when she stepped out of the car. The wind pushed against the two of them as they opened the flimsy gate to No. 6. Inside, the space was smaller than she had anticipated. It was freezing cold, aggravating her need to use the toilet.

"I need to go to the toilet now!" she said. He pointed to a cubicle in the corner. She trapped herself inside and sat on the smallest toilet bowl she had ever seen. This sounds like Niagara Falls in here, she thought as she relieved herself. She cranked the pump to flush, and the whole structure thumped and shook.

The bed dominated the cramped space. It consisted of four oblong foam pieces sitting together on what looked like a plywood tray. The foam was covered by an orange nubbed fabric with gold metallic threads running through it. Three turquoise brocade cushions with buttons in the center had been carefully arranged in the corner of the bed. There was a sink at one end of the space and beside it two small gas cooking rings. When Edith sat down, she felt her pantyhose snag on the scratchy fabric.

"It's full size—the bed, I mean," said Edwin, smiling. Cream lace curtains were gently moving, due to a draft that sneaked through the Perspex windows on either side of the van. "The pillows are my touch," he said, closing the curtains.

"Oh," she replied, and sniffed, irritated by the heavy scent of lavender, or was it hyacinth? She noticed a spray bottle of air freshener next to two bottles of Spanish Amontillado sherry with a lime green sticker on each that read "4.99 Special." A blue plastic vase containing sweet-smelling jonquils and daffodils sat on a fold-out shelf near the toilet cubicle.

"I popped in last night to get everything ready," he said.

Edith shuddered. She felt weak and hollow and knew she should have eaten some breakfast. A bundle of magazines secured by an elastic band sat beneath the window. She glanced at the titles: *Your Guide to Tropical Fish*, *True Romance*, *Holiday Haunts in Britain*. Huddled in a corner, Edwin endeavored to ignite the kerosene stove. There was a gushing noise followed by a loud pop. "Righto!" he said, "she'll warm us up nicely."

Edith kicked off her shoes. Her head pounded. The kerosene fumes were competing with the floral odors. From a cupboard above the sink, Edwin produced two plastic tumblers, and with an affected flourish, he opened and poured the sherry. "We owe it to ourselves," he said, passing her an overflowing glass. Owe what to ourselves? She hadn't expected to be in this claustrophobic place. She couldn't sip the sherry; it was too cold. She gulped it all down, quickly feeling its instant warmth, though it tasted like bitter walnuts. Edwin eagerly refilled her glass and sat next to her.

"Here's to us, then," she said, and gulped it down again easily. They clicked their tumblers. He kissed her hand and slowly removed her watch, laying it on the draining board. He took out the two combs that secured her hair. She shook her head, enjoying the loose freedom of it. Edwin loved her hair. She had stopped shivering and smiled at him. His face looked larger than usual, so she sat back a little. She was beginning to feel warm inside, though her skin still felt cool.

"Edwin," she said, as he fiddled with the buttons of her cardigan. "Oh Edwin, I would love it if you, if you ..." She heard herself laugh.

"What, my love, what?" he asked. His voice was muffled. She couldn't see his head; it was somewhere beneath her cardigan. "I would love something to eat. I'm so empty!"

He pulled a bag of mints out of his pocket. "This is all I have." She raised her legs to stretch a little and, in doing so, caught him off guard. The mints dropped to the floor with a clatter.

"Top me up, then," she said, waving her glass. But he was down on the floor scooping up the mints.

"This bed is only just long enough," she laughed, and stretched out. She attempted to read the camp rules posted above the door, but the words blurred. The jonquils and daffodils drooped in the vase.

"Dammit!" Edith said, as her pantyhose snagged again on the scratchy cushions. She pulled them down, along with her skirt, over her slim hips and tossed them onto the floor. She removed her cardigan, letting it drop to the floor.

"That's better," she said. She thought her voice sounded loud. Closing her eyes, she could still hear the car, or was it the bus? She could see Saleem's elegant neck, his white collar, and the confident turn of his head and shoulders.

"My precious is tired?" Edwin's voice sounded far away. His hand caressed her cheek. She turned her head.

"Ouch, ouch!" she cried, sitting bolt upright. Her hair had caught on the button in the pillow. She stopped still. There was something connected to hair that she needed to remember. She repeated the word "hair" to herself but could not concentrate, and her thoughts soon dissolved. As she disentangled herself from the cushion, she raised her head to see Edwin standing naked before her, his white slender body almost childlike. "I found them all," he said, "the mints." His genitals were almost obscured by a mass of black hair, his lust and longing not yet physically apparent. What's the rush? she thought, waving her empty tumbler at him. He turned to reach for the second bottle of sherry. She noticed his clothes neatly folded in the sink. With his back to her, she observed his sloping shoulders. He didn't seem to have a spine. There was a tuft of black hair at the small of his back. What am I doing here with him? she wondered.

He turned back to face her with refilled tumblers, his gray-green eyes darting all over the place. When she first met him, she thought he might have been handsome once, but now she doubted it. His front teeth looked huge as he came nearer to her. She closed her eyes. I should be somewhere else, she thought, but where? He unclasped the pearls from around her neck and softly kissed her ear. He began to struggle with the buttons of her blouse. His hands were red and hot. "I'll do it," she said. She sat up and felt dizzy for an instant. Thoughts of hair returned. What was it? There was something about Lil next door. She felt dizzy again. "Ah well, I can't recall. No matter," she said. Grinning, she flicked off her blouse, along with her bra and panties, flinging them toward the door. He filled her glass, and she drained it quickly. At least I am not fat, Edith thought, as she lay naked on her back, knowing that if she lay on her side, her small breasts would look droopy. A girl at school once said that if you were breastfed, you would get big tits! She asked her mother if she had been breastfed. "It's none of your business," her mother had snapped.

Taking Edith's glass from her hand, Edwin began to smother her with feathery kisses; she could barely feel them. She listened to the wind and rain pattering on the thin roof. She could smell his mint-and-sherry breath. His breathing was rapid. He said, "I love you, Edith." His voice was far off somewhere. She felt detached from everything, somewhere else, out here wherever she was. She felt free and isolated, as if she were completely alone, until she opened her eyes. His hairless chest and pink erect nipples circled above her head. "You are beautiful, Edith," he said. "Be patient with me."

She closed her eyes. The bed, the walls, and the ceiling revolved, turning faster; she couldn't stop it. She knew that if she opened her eyes, it would stop, but they wouldn't open. She heard a voice—not her voice, a male voice? She felt hands on her body. Were they Saleem's? There were fingers in her hair, a mouth on her mouth. She grew warmer; she was hot. The voice grew louder, then soft. She could hear the wind blowing about her ears; she giggled.

"I think you do love me," said the voice.

"I'll drink your dark secrets," she murmured. She was in full flight; she was soaring. She belonged to something, someone. She heard herself cry out. Edwin groaned and sobbed before shuddering into stillness. The lace curtains moved gently against the windows. The rain pattered on the roof. Edith and Edwin lay still, their intoxicated bodies welded together as they slipped into a senseless slumber.

5

Ruby

Alone, hunched in bed, Ruby Sharpe listened to the sounds of the morning traffic on Slattery Street. The thin, toothless old lady gazed about her small bedroom. She eyed the crumbs of toast that had found their way onto her flannelette sheet and lightly brushed them away. She wiped her forehead with the back of her right hand and then lightly toyed with her hair. Another day, Ruby my girl, she said to herself. Is it a blessing or not? She scratched a bony knee beneath the covers. "That feels better," she said out loud. Ruby often talked to herself when she was certain that she was alone in the house. She was grateful that the stroke that had paralyzed her left side had not affected her speech, hearing, or facial mobility. Hearing her own voice was her way of establishing some identity, a way of keeping herself company until the nurses or Lil from next door visited.

The house felt unsettled now, after Edith's hurried exit. Had the girl heard her? She also wondered who had phoned so early. Edith had fled down the stairs, ignoring her words, slamming the front door. These days, when doors banged and voices were raised, she felt as if the house were growing smaller around her. Fondly, Ruby recalled the big house where her parents had been in service for the wealthy Haslett family when she was a young girl. She could see her parents now. Her mother, in her mobcap and white pinafore, was the housekeeper; her father was the gardener—he tended the huge grounds and wore a leather apron and corduroy breeches. Ruby and her little brother, Leon, had been allowed to visit the big house. She was fifteen when Leon was born. "He's a true surprise from heaven, a gift from God at my age," her mother said. Ruby loved that big, quiet house. She remembered heavy velvet curtains on big wooden rings that rattled as they were drawn across the huge drafty doors. Deep-colored carpets stretched down hallways. Once, Ruby and Leon peeped through a crack in a door and listened to the soft claps of billiard balls amid guffawing choruses of male approval.

Ruby was just seventeen when she fell in love with Ira Goldberg, the twenty-year-old carpenter's son, who frequently worked at the house. Their friendship had blossomed beyond her dreams. "You have to realize," her mother said, "Ira's not one of us, Ruby, love. Him being Jewish and all." Her father said, "There are plenty more fish in the sea." Ruby never saw Ira again after that day; she never had a chance to say good-bye. A new carpenter came to the house, a sullen man called Smith.

"You will always have a roof over your head, my girl," said her father when the Hasletts passed on. "God rest their generous souls. They willed us a house and more. Slattery Street will be yours one day, Ruby." That day came sooner than expected when her mother and father succumbed to tuberculosis. "The curse of consumption," some called it, swept a devastating path through Bogmire and England's northwest coast. Though Ruby was thankful that she and Leon had a roof over their heads, she felt that life's choices and youth had slipped by her all too fast. She became mother, father, and housekeeper over the years, and doubted now if Leon had ever appreciated her labors.

Ruby yawned. Recalling the history of her life was wearying but not without pleasure. She recalled the secret joy she had experienced with the baby Edith and Edith's effortless laughter as a young child. She never understood why Edith wasn't grateful, why there were slammed doors and sulks. And Leon—he too should have been grateful. After all these years, she wondered if he had shed the bitterness that had expedited his departure. It was all for the good that he left, she mused. I did my best for him. It is easy for men, she thought. Men can survive the wretchedness of heartache. They can take that extra stride and somehow walk away from their despair. Anyway, there is no point in stirring things up now—no point in telling anybody anything, she thought. The family coffers are intact, and that's what matters.

Ruby felt safe in her bedroom. It had been three years since she had ventured out of her room. Too much effort was required to maneuver the stairs; she knew what went on out there each day. She listened for the noises that connected her to the house and the street. She liked the tinkling chimes of the clock downstairs. She waited for the snap of the letterbox in the front door after the postman pushed the envelopes through. She listened for the soft thud of the *Bogmire Daily News* when it landed on the front porch.

Sometimes she ached to hear the simple sounds of days gone by, when the rains seemed less frequent and the sun warmed Slattery Street's pavements. It was a time when Wilf White, the fishmonger, rang his brass bell. He trundled a cartload of cod, hake, cockles, and winkles from the then-fertile shores of Bogmire. Tom, the whistling butcher boy, would cycle up to the front gate, brakes squealing. "Fresh bangers!" he'd shout. Life was ordered and tidy back then, Ruby thought. People respected their place in life. "Nothing stays the same," her mother had always said. She thought about that and wondered which substitute nurse would come to disturb her reminiscing.

The clock ticked away on the dresser; she was unable to see its face. Edith had placed it too far back. She had a feeling that the morning was sliding into the afternoon. She was dry-mouthed and hungry. Maybe a nurse had not been assigned? Maybe Lil would appear and show off her hairdo? Ruby wasn't partial to Lil. Her irritating chatter tired Ruby. She listened for the familiar huffing and puffing of Lil as she heaved herself up the stairs, for she was a large woman. The bedroom seemed smaller when Lil was around, tidying the bedcovers and punching the pillows. When Lil sat on the wicker chair, it would creak and groan as she launched into her weekly update of neighborhood activities. Ruby didn't care about such things and was always glad to see Lil's bulky frame disappear through the door.

The noon buzzer from the sheet metal factory two streets away startled Ruby. Could it be this late? The old lady waited. Who would bring her lunch today? Would it be the usual soup that Edith left or a potted meat sandwich with the crusts off? She was hungry; she would make do with anything as long as it wasn't cold rice pudding. She was tired of that. She turned her attention to her beloved crocheted blankets. It was many years now since she had worked them from scraps of colored yarn. She liked to feel the weight of her blankets snug around her feet and knees. The top blanket had many uneven holes in it. She counted them out loud. As she listened to her faint voice, she worried about eventual deafness, knowing that it would diminish her already shrinking world. She stopped counting, hard put to think what came after ten. No matter, she thought, and moved her right foot slowly from side to side, aware of her toenails scratching the sheet. She acknowledged their movement, grateful for the few sensations that remained in her damaged body.

Closing her eyes, Ruby listened to the wind as it chased its cold way around the houses and alleyways of Slattery Street. With strong, defiant gusts, it lifted and smacked down the loose corrugated iron roof of the coal shed in the backyard. The sun will shine when the storm is spent, she thought, and watched the drops of rain trickle endlessly down the windowpanes. Each drop traveled in a different direction. Some drops collided and formed larger shapes, never the same, always changing. Sometimes they shone and glittered on the glass. She loved to watch the rain. As a child, she had spent hours gazing out the windows. "Ruby, come down," her father would say.

"I'm watching the weather," she would call back.

She yawned; concentrating on anything at all was exhausting, and she wondered if Lil would appear before or after her perm. Ruby couldn't recall what she had been told. Thirsty and weak, she contemplated reaching for the biscuits and glass of water on the bedside table but soon abandoned the idea. The task seemed overwhelming. She waited. Her thoughts drifted through rain-swept plains, hillsides, valleys, and winding roads, all meshed within the patterned colors of her blankets. Surfacing occasionally, she could feel the uneasy stillness of her small bedroom. No Edith, no Lil, no one, no human sounds.

The chimes of the clock downstairs interrupted the silence. It was 2 p.m., later than she had realized. Her failure to remain awake disturbed her. She knew that she must fuel what remained of her conscious being. Her eyes journeyed toward the wall and the faded flat lavender flowers, rows and rows repeated on the wallpaper. She sought out the marble-topped bedside table and its white faggoted cloth. In an instant, she could clearly see her pretty mother stitching with her nimble fingers. She heard her mother's voice: "No more biscuits for you, my girl." She looked over to the glass of water. "Time to get up now, Ruby!" said the voice, fading away.

Am I awake now? she wondered. Am I still alone? She stretched her right arm; it felt heavy. She tucked the blankets around her knees and shoulders, glad of their comfort and warmth. She rested her arm alongside her body again. Messages of hunger kept invading her misty brain. She was tired of waiting and wanted to eat; her mouth was dry. She turned her head to the right and stared at the glass tumbler of water and plate of biscuits on the table. They seemed to stare back at her. Their very presence was sapping what little strength she had. She looked at her left arm, withered and dormant, and prayed to … what? She did not know. "For thine is the power and the glory. Thine help me now," she said. Using what power and will she could summon, she delegated orders to her right arm and reached out toward the table. "Drat!" she murmured; she was inches short of seizing the tumbler.

Ruby knew what she had to do: She must shift closer to the side of the bed. If she concentrated enough, she could raise her right shoulder from the pillows and edge sideways, bringing her target within reach. It was a maneuver that she had tried successfully once before. I can do it, she thought. Her breathing was shallow, her movements labored, as she pushed and shoved the covers and sheet down below her waist, relieving her upper body of their weight. Digging her right heel hard into the mattress, she flexed her knee. Her leg and toes barely moved under the heavy hillock of covers she had created. However, she could feel her hip—it gave her some leverage as she pressed her good elbow down, preparing to move.

"Bother," she said. Her head fell back onto the pillow. She sighed, realizing that her flaccid left arm had served as an unyielding tether. She positioned it across her chest and tried again. Here goes, she thought, concentrating hard until her head and shoulder were raised slightly off the pillow. She paused to gasp out her breath—something was pulling and tugging at her lower legs. She looked downward to see that the mound of covers was moving, slithering slowly from bed to floor. She could feel her anchored feet now amid the heavy folds of fabric as her upper torso began involuntarily to turn and twist. "Drat," she whispered, "drat," aware that there was no turning back. Her head began to throb. She needed air and strength. Her feet were twisting and hurting. She could not control the lopsided pull of her body, and with her outstretched hand, she clutched at the tablecloth.

The cloth slid across the marble top, causing it and the plate to fall onto the floor, scattering the biscuits. Ruby eyed the still-standing glass of water and reached toward it. She managed to close her fingers around its base and held on tightly. Just a sip, she said to herself, that's all. She was able to raise the glass a little, letting out a sigh before setting it down again. The process was exhausting. Once more, she thought, and, grasping the tumbler, she raised it a little higher this time, only to feel a chill creeping across her hand and down her outstretched arm; the cold water had slopped over the rim of the glass. "God please help me to—" Her words were cut short by the resounding crack of glass against the marble top; her feeble fingers had failed her.

It was some moments before she saw the jagged triangle of glass lodged in the thin shaft of her wrist. She made a vain attempt to move her arm, but it simply stayed flopped down. She hung over the side of the bed, trapped by the unwieldy position of her body. The floor would have been her resting place, but her feet remained shackled by the twisted tangle of her covers.

Ruby remained suspended and still. Her body felt tight and stretched, but almost painless. There was just a vague throbbing in her head, but this was subsiding. She knew what had transpired. She wasn't angry or frustrated, as these were feelings that required an energy she could no longer muster. Able to look down, she became fascinated as she watched the threadbare patches of linoleum absorb the rich red fluid that dripped steadily down from her wrist and hand. Was this what life looked like, after all? So simple, trickling away? Was she prepared for this exit? Should she give thanks for her brother, Leon, and his baggage? For her mother and father, who had denied her love and happiness in the name of a God she never did understand?

She wanted to be at peace with her memories. She had seen indications of love in Edith's eyes, but not enough for the truth to be told. She dozed for a while and then was aroused by a noise on the stairs. It's Lil, thought Ruby. She waited. No one came. No matter—I'll leave them all be, she thought. "You can be sure, your sins will find you out," her mother had always said. Well, they hadn't. Ruby smiled to herself. Her secrets would travel with her, she thought, and closed her tired eyes.

6

Awakening

T he rain had stopped. A man nailed a wooden sign to a tree, his gray raincoat flapping in the breeze. The sign read, "Happy Lands. Off-Season Rates." A strong gust lifted the lid off of an empty rubbish bin; it landed with a heavy clank against the wall of caravan No. 6. The noise did not disturb the occupants. Matted hair framed a besotted expression on Edwin's sleeping face. He lay naked on his back, his body partially covered by his raincoat. One arm was draped across Edith's thigh. Edith had her back to her lover. Part of the raincoat barely covered her hips and shoulders. Her knees were drawn up close to her body, and her hands were clasped together as if in prayer. She murmured frequently, as if to surface from her deep sleep.

Edith had slid into a hypnotic place where she no longer heard Edwin's faltering voice and amorous exclamations. Soft, warm air had enveloped her body, and she became aware of movement. She was in a carriage. The interior was swathed in a white fabric with the texture of muslin. Cushions were scattered about her feet. She was the lone passenger until she noticed a male figure in front of her. He had his back to her, and his arms were folded. The carriage shuddered, the lights dimmed, the fabric wafted and shimmered, the vehicle gained momentum. They were ascending, gaining speed, twisting and curling as they climbed. The man turned to face her; he unfolded his arms and came toward her, arms outstretched. She trembled, blissfully aware that she was looking into the deep brown-black eyes of Saleem. He wove his tawny fingers into hers, his lips caressing her wrists. He removed her shoes, encasing her slim ankles in his warm, savoring hands before anchoring her feet on cushions. Kneeling, he rested his forehead on her knees. With quivering fingertips she stroked his hair. There were noises, voices; it grew dark, unbearably hot. Then one voice rose above the others: "Edith! Edith!" It was Lil's voice. Lil was standing beside her. "Edith!" she cried. Flashing spirals emerged from Lil's head. "I'm having a perm!" Lil shrieked. Saleem had disappeared. The air grew hotter, the smoke thicker. "Perm! Perm!" Lil cried.

Edith called out but was unable to form the words. Her mouth was dry; her tongue felt rough and swollen. The skin on her face was tight and prickly, as if covered with something. She reached up to remove whatever it was that had restricted her speech. Her hand felt heavy as it explored the damp contours of her cheeks and forehead. She was cold now and rubbed her eyes, realizing that she had been dreaming. She struggled with the mystery of where her dream had taken her. Lying still, she wondered if she really was conscious until the sound of Edwin's heavy breathing, punctuated by an occasional snort, reached her horrified ears.

The window was inches away from Edith's head. Through half-open eyes, she watched as beads of condensation clung to the aluminum frames and then slithered down the windowpanes. Shivering, she wondered how long the kerosene stove had been out of fuel. In her narrow line of vision, she saw water seeping under a rotted piece of weatherstripping tacked onto the bottom of the door. The "Welcome" on the doormat was all but concealed by a puddle of water. Close to the rain-soaked mat sat her crumpled heap of clothes. Her bra, which had not made it to the heap, dangled from a knob on the saucepan cupboard. An empty sherry bottle rested against one of her shoes.

She sneezed, which forced her eyes to open wide with painful abruptness. This movement felt and sounded like small hammers cracking in her skull. The deplorable state of the tiny caravan filled her with revulsion. She was surprised now to see how small this space was—just enough room for the bed on which they were lying.

She felt degraded and raw, her body trembling under the inadequate covering of Edwin's raincoat. "Take my umbrella," she recalled his words at the cafe that morning. "I have my raincoat; it is a good one. It's

Burberry. A Christmas present from Sybil." She looked at him and fancied that this was how corpses looked—thin, white, and still. Alarmed, she saw by his watch that it was 3 p.m. He did not wake up when she lifted his flaccid arm from her thigh; he just sniffed loudly and inhaled, expanding his cheeks before puffing out the air in short spurts. The relentless hammers were working furiously in her head. Another sneeze jolted her into a sitting position. She cringed, sensing a moist, sticky sensation between her thighs. The manifestation of what had transpired appalled her, as did the pervading smell of mildew and stale passion, which caused her to retch noisily. Edwin's raincoat became the closest receptacle for the sour sherry contents of her stomach.

"Oh, oh my goodness!" Edwin sat bolt upright. "My poor precious, whatever is wrong?" he asked, reaching for a cushion to cover himself. "It was so wonder—" His mouth fell open as he stared at the soiled mess of his raincoat. "My heavens!" he said.

"Get me a cloth, anything!" she yelled. Her nose was running, her eyes watering. He reached for a towel hanging by the sink. Tears streamed down Edith's face. "Don't cry, my love," he said, and prattled on about how wonderful it was to be so carefree yet intimate. He said that he understood now what was wrong with Sybil. "She is wedded to God," he said. He talked of passion, food, coffee, the raincoat, and dry-cleaners. Edith put her hands over her ears. Her head throbbed. "I love you, Edith," he said, and kissed the nape of her neck.

"Don't touch me," she said, "I feel dreadful. I can hardly move." She bundled up the raincoat and edged toward the foot of the bed. She bent down to retrieve her clothes, and a bottle rolled out from beneath the pile. "I am so ashamed," she said. "How could I get so hopelessly drunk?"

He put a hand on her shoulder. "You're cold, my sweet—let me make you warm again."

"No!" she screamed. "This is awful!" She gestured to the bottles and heaps of clothes.

"But you were wonderful—that is all that matters," he said, smiling. "Our day isn't over."

"I don't feel well," she said. "I need to get dressed."

"Edith, I have a wonderful idea."

"And just what would that be?"

"They have public showers, next to the putting green. I think they're free." He scratched his head. "I'm not sure if they're in service, though. I can go to the office and check," he said brightly.

"It doesn't matter," she said, "I'm getting dressed."

Edith pulled her clothes onto her stiff, aching body. She wanted to cry and scream. She bundled her pantyhose into a ball and squeezed them hard. He repulsed her as he sat there scratching his head, gawking through the window.

"What's the hurry?" he said. "I'll light up the stove. Make us a pot of tea or cocoa. I can pop out and get some crumpets."

The scent of the jonquils combined with the sour smell of the coat almost choked her as she dumped the sodden garment on the floor. She rummaged in her handbag. "I need a comb."

"In my raincoat pocket," he said.

"Ugh, I'll use my fingers." She stepped into the toilet cubicle to rinse her face. Most of the silver backing had peeled off the mirror on the wall, but it was adequate. Beyond her own image, she could see Edwin's bony white shoulder against the turquoise background of a cushion. She cupped cold water in her hands and sucked it up to rinse her mouth. She splashed her face, patting it dry with a sheet of paper towel. Clawing at her tangled hair with her fingers, she despaired, flicking it this way and that. She pushed the strands behind her ears and stared at herself before letting out a gasp. "Oh no! Oh no!" She clasped a hand over her mouth. "The dream," she said, "it's Lil! She was in the dream. Oh my heavens! Lil is having a perm today!"

"Who is? What dream?" he asked.

"Oh my God. Ma! My mother," yelled Edith, "she's all alone!"

"But, but—"

"Don't you see? Ma's nurse doesn't come Tuesdays. Lil normally does it. I forgot. I never called for a substitute. Ma was calling after me, I remember now. I didn't pay any attention. I ignored her. I was rushing out early to meet you. Edwin, don't you see? Ma has been alone!"

"There could be a mistake."

"There's no mistake. It's Tuesday, no Lil. I never thought. Dear God, I have to get there. Get dressed, Edwin, hurry!"

"Who is being permed?" he said, scratching his head.

"For God's sake!" She grabbed his neatly folded clothes from the sink and threw them at him. She closed the cubicle door and sat on the toilet seat. Her head hammered; her body shook. She couldn't understand how she had been so lax. I must not panic, she thought as she strapped on her watch; it will get resolved. Everything can be carefully explained; Ma will understand. But she knew with a quiet dread that it would not be that simple. It was 3:30 now. "Hang on, Ma, hang on," she muttered as she cranked the toilet pump. She emerged from the cubicle to see Edwin dressed. "When you've checked on Ruby," he said, knotting his tie, "we can come back." He moved toward her but she stepped back.

"Let's get out," she said, brushing past him.

"I've put it in here," he said.

"What?" she asked. He held up the Marks & Spencer plastic bag.

"If I get there in time, they should have it ready tomorrow."

"Get what, where?"

"The cleaners, my raincoat."

"God forbid," she said. "Let's get going!" She winced at the blast of cold air that hit her when she opened the caravan door.

"The sun is trying to break through," he said, peeling leaves off the car windshield.

"Get in, Edwin, it'll be dark in an hour."

The car coughed to a jerky start. Edwin clamped a hand on Edith's thigh. She fidgeted with her clothes, adjusting her collar and buttoning up her coat. Her fingers clutched at the ball of pantyhose in her pocket. "How could I have been so stupid?" she said. Images of Ruby, hungry and desperate, flashed through her head. She clung to the faint possibility that Lil might have turned up later in the day. How will I explain things? Account for my mistake? Edwin was the mistake, she thought, the biggest mistake of the day, of her life. She looked at him and remembered his clinging to her like a leech. She felt dirty and wanted to rid her skin of the dampness and smell of him. She would think up a story for Ma that excluded him. What had happened with him was hardly worth accounting for, anyway. It amazed her that he was oblivious to her anxiety and could not comprehend her sense of urgency.

"Where shall we eat supper?" he asked.

"Eat!" She pried his fingers off her thigh. "How can you think of food now?"

"Don't take on so, precious. Everything will be fine," he said, and gave her bare knee a squeeze.

The late-afternoon traffic increased as they drove along the inner streets of the town. "I'm worried and scared," she said.

He took her hand in his. "I know, but tell me, precious, wasn't it grand? Didn't you feel so special? I know you did, Edith, because you called out. 'Set me free,' you said." She pulled her hand away. "I felt so at one with my manhood, Edith. So, well, like never before," he blubbered.

She felt nauseated and rolled down the car window. The traffic was noisy; horns were beeping. Pedestrians seemed to be staring at them. The driver of a van behind them leaned out his window and yelled, "Hey, you in the Ford Cortina! The light, it's green! Yer dozy moron, move!"

"For God's sake, Edwin," she said, holding her aching head in her hands, "drop me off, anywhere—here will do. Now! I'll get a taxi to Slattery Street. Pull over." To be seen in daylight alighting from Edwin's car would certainly provide fodder for the Slattery Street gossipmongers. Edwin pulled up to a taxi stand. Before Edith had a chance to open the door, he kissed her cheek and grabbed her hand. "I don't want you to slip away this quickly," he said. "I'll get kerosene for the stove; then I'll be off with the raincoat to the cleaners. With a bit of luck, they'll get it done before Sybil gets back. I'll ring you."

"No," she said, slamming the car door. "'Bye, Edwin." There was nothing else to say to him. He was incapable of understanding anything. Ma was alone, neglected and hungry. Heaven knew, she would be cold and suffering. What an ill-spent day, Edith thought. The only pleasure so far was seeing him drive away.

"Pitt Street corner," she told the cab driver as she flopped into the back seat. The Pitt Street corner was two blocks from her home. Once she passed the Pitt Street shops and turned in to Slattery Street, the walk would be discreet, short. She would sneak down the back alley and enter the house by the back door, unnoticed.

7

Discovery

- - - - - - - - - - - - - - - - - -

Slumped in the backseat of the taxi, Edith felt nauseated and ugly. Her coat was creased, her legs were bare, and her tangled hair hung loose about her shoulders. Her head throbbed as she continued to grapple with where she had been and what she had done. "A special place for us," Edwin had said. The place was nothing but a dump, she thought. How could I have been so stupid, listening to his pathetic talk? The day was a disaster! Mavis was right—I do deserve better than him. I am finished with him. Done!

"Pitt Street, miss," said the driver.

"Thanks," she said, handing him a five-pound note. "Do you have the time?"

"Four-thirty," he said. "It gets dark early."

"It does. Keep the change," she said.

"But this is a fiver! Are you sure, miss?"

"Yes," she said.

Pitt Street was busy as usual with shoppers and traffic. She caught a glimpse of herself in a shop window and winced. The belt was missing from her raincoat; it hung loose from her shoulders and flapped against her bare legs. Her hair fell about her face. Her combs and scarf were in her handbag, slung across her shoulders. She took some comfort in the fact that in the diminishing daylight, her disheveled appearance would make her less recognizable to the locals. She walked quickly, deciding that once home, she would make a concerted effort to be kind to her mother. She would apologize to her and tell her that she had been left alone due to a simple misunderstanding. "I honestly just forgot about Lil's hair appointment," she'd say. "It will never happen again." She would make Welsh rarebit for Ma's supper, her favorite. They would both have a good sleep, and tomorrow they'd feel fine. She could request a leave of absence. Take Ma on a trip—why not? She had heard about holiday places that catered to infirm folks. Perhaps get Uncle Leon to join them; she could dig him out from wherever he was. They could move down south, where it was warmer. Why hadn't she thought of all this before? Was it any wonder Ma was disgruntled? A change was needed. Things will be different, she decided. I can and will get everything sorted out. "No use crying over spilled milk," Ma would say.

She breathed deeply, and the cool late-afternoon air blunted her feeling of nausea. "I'm actually coming now, Ma," she whispered, and picked up her pace. At the corner, she waited for the lights to change before turning in to Slattery Street. She kept her head down. Her bare feet slipped in and out of her shoes, and the heels clacked loudly on the pavement. Edwin had sold her these shoes. She shivered and could still feel his grasping hands, smell his mothballed clothes.

"Edith!" someone called, "Edith!" She looked up to see Percy Hobbs, the newsagent, in the doorway of his shop. "I have your weekly—it came early," he said. "Hang on, I'll get it." She waited. Percy returned with her copy of *Woman's Weekly*. "She's a bonny lass," he said, eying the picture of Princess Diana on the cover.

"She is. Thanks, Percy, I—"

"Ma all right, is she?"

"Oh, she's fine, you know, the same. I must be off."

"Bit of a carry-on down yonder," he said. "Ambulance shot by like a rocket! The missus heard it in back."

"That's right," said Doris Hobbs, appearing in the doorway. "You're early, Edith."

"The office was quiet," Edith said. "Anyway, thanks, Percy. I'll be seeing you." She turned, but her shoe didn't. The heel was stuck between the paving stones. "Oops!" she said, and quickly regained her composure. "'Bye." Percy removed his flat cap, stroked his head, and said something to Doris. Doris folded her arms and watched the street from the shop doorway. A short distance away, Tom Lott, the butcher, stood in the middle of the sidewalk, cranking back the awning above his shop. He didn't see Edith, she didn't see him, and she walked headlong into him.

"Oh, sorry, Tom," she said.

"Whoa! Edith," he laughed.

"Sorry, Tom." She covered her mouth. The taste of stale sherry rose from the pit of her stomach. "I'm—I'm so sorry," she said, forcing a smile.

"No matter. What's the fuss about down the street?"

"No idea. Have to be off! See yer, Tom."

"See yer, Edith."

Hair by Hilda was the local beauty parlor. It was the last shop in the row. Edith looked in the window, mindful of the possibility that Lil could be among the roller-headed patrons that stared back at her. Edith didn't see her. Good, she thought, Lil might be with Ma after all.

All the houses on Slattery Street were semidetached and identical, each with a small garden and gate that fronted the street. Edith's house, No. 23, was just half a block from the Pitt Street corner. Thank God I'm almost home, she thought, and then stopped abruptly as she drew closer. A crowd of people spilled over the sidewalk and into the street.

"Excuse me," she said. They stood in groups, some at their front gates, others in the street. The traffic was at a standstill. Darned traffic, she thought, maybe there's a collision. Percy had mentioned an ambulance. She glanced about before heading for the alley that accessed the back gate to her yard.

"Hey!" a male voice yelled. "You can't go down there."

"But I ..." It was dark now and impossible to see where the voice hailed from. "Excuse me," she said, "I need to get—"

"They blocked it off," a man said. "Better stay out. The police did it."

"Why is it blocked?" she asked, and standing on tiptoe, she tried to see what was happening down the street. She saw a rotating flashing light and heard the strident crackle of a radio that she assumed was from a police car. She approached the crowd on the sidewalk. "Excuse me," she said to no one in particular, "but I do really need to get through here!"

"Good luck," a man said.

"What's going on?" she asked.

"It's a fuckin' circus," he said. "They broke in."

"What? Who? I live just down—"

"They found someone," a woman said. "Cops broke in."

"Oh my God! I have to … please!" A boy on his bike edged forward, causing people to move suddenly. Edith was shoved. She tripped. Her foot came out of her shoe. She bent down to retrieve it and was pushed again from behind. She dropped her magazine and the shoe disappeared. "Damn," she said, putting the other shoe in her pocket. After elbowing her way through, she finally got close enough to see the police car that was parked outside Lil's house, its blue light swooping over the heads of the onlookers and scanning the walls of the houses. Next to it was an ambulance, with its doors open and lights flashing.

"Oh my God!" yelled Edith. "Oh no! What happened? What is this? Let me through!" She felt sick. She was shivering and standing in the gutter. Rainwater was washing over her bare feet. "Wait! Let me … wait!" An arm pushed against her neck and shoulders like a huge lever as she tried to step up onto the sidewalk. "Back, miss," a police officer said.

"But I—I—that's my house," she said. All the lights of her house upstairs and downstairs were on. A police officer stood at the open gate, and another was by the porch. The front door was ajar, revealing the hallway, the open doors to the kitchen, and the front parlor. It was as if the very soul of her home had been ripped open and exposed to all. People were muttering all around her. Across the street, people stared out from their upper windows.

"I have to get—"

"Back, miss. Please."

"But my mother! Where is she?" She felt the heft of the arm against her body. She was trapped. Suddenly it became eerily quiet. She watched as two men carrying a stretcher stepped cautiously down the narrow staircase of her house. At the foot of the stairs, they nodded to one another and steadied themselves before proceeding into the hallway. Grim-faced, they walked down the front path and out through the gate.

Edith stared at the formless shape on the stretcher, covered by a black tarpaulin. Her heart beat hard against her ribs. Her legs felt weak, and if not for the restraint of the policeman's arm, she would have fallen.

"Ma," she said, "I was coming, I was." The men slid their cargo into the gaping mouth of the ambulance. The doors were slammed shut. People moved aside as the vehicle made its slow way down Slattery Street. Heads shook, comments flowed. "Poor old thing!"

"It's shocking!"

"Bloody disgusting!"

"Somebody did her in!"

The policeman's arm released Edith. She tottered forward. Cameras were flashing and strangers were in her garden. If I could just get inside, she thought. Her fingers found the cold metal bars of her front gate. She closed her eyes. Her head was spinning. What if I slipped away? she thought. I could just disappear. No one would notice or care. Then a sudden shock of pain went through her foot. "Ahh," she yelled, "my foot!"

"Jesus Christ!" said a man standing beside her, his face inches from hers. "What do yer expect with fuckin' bare feet?" His arm was clamped around his girlfriend's shoulders. She looked at Edith, opened her mouth, and snapped out a balloon of gum.

"I lost one of my shoes," Edith said.

The girl shrugged her shoulders. "Don't look at me," she said, ragged scraps of pink across her mouth and chin.

"Move," said a loud voice. "Show's over!"

Cars started up, and the street began to clear. Images were melting into one another—the trampled flowers under the sycamore tree, a dog roughing up the lawn—as Edith held on to the gate. Then her eyes rested on the faces of Lil and Reg from next door. They stood by the low wall that separated the two properties. Tight curls framed Lil's tear-stained face. Reg had his arm around her shoulders.

"Reg! Lil! I'm sorry, I—Lil—I ... ," Edith said, walking toward them. Lil's hands flew up to her face. They both turned away from her and headed up the garden path.

"Wait!" Edith said, "wait!" Reg glanced back and shook his head before closing the front door behind them.

"I was coming," she said, "I was, I ..." The light went on in their front parlor. The curtains were drawn.

"Miss, please," said the policeman. "We need to shut this gate. This is private property."

"Don't you think I know that?" Edith said. "Dammit! I'm not stupid! This is—"

"Take it easy, miss," he said, "no need to—"

"It's all right, officer, she—"

"Mavis! What are you doing here?"

"It's fine, officer, she's Ruby Sharpe's daughter. Edith, what in God's name?" Mavis looked at Edith's bare feet. She drew the hair back from Edith's face. "Come on, love, let's go inside."

"It was Ma, wasn't it? I saw the stretcher! She is dead, isn't she? Tell me."

"I'm so sorry, Edith. Let's go inside, come."

Mavis guided her up the path. "My God, you are so cold. What happened to your shoes? Oh, never mind, it doesn't matter now, never mind." She steered Edith into the front parlor. "Edith, this is Inspector Crawford. He's in charge." Crawford looked too young to be in charge of anything, Edith thought. "Please, sit down," he said.

"But wh—?"

"Please," he gestured to the couch. He beckoned to two men who were leaning on the mantel. "These ladies need some privacy," he said. Mavis hugged Edith, and then kissed her cheek and rubbed her back. "Sit tight a minute," she said, and patted the couch pillows. "I'll be right back with a cardigan. You're freezing!"

Edith clasped her hands together to stop from shivering. Crawford stood in the doorway. There were footsteps upstairs, voices on the landing. Someone was talking on the phone in the hall. A draft blew in from the front door, which was constantly being opened and closed. She felt oddly detached from all that was going on around her. Vaguely, she knew that at some point she would have to account for herself. Everything about the day seemed shapeless; there was no sense to any of it. Everything seemed exhaustively beyond her reach, out of her hands.

"Sorry, pet, I'm back," Mavis said. "Here, put on these slippers and cardigan. I've put the kettle on." She handed Edith a glass of water. "Drink," she said.

"I was coming, you know," Edith said. "I was. What happened?"

"It's all right, Edith. Don't say anything. Get warm; I'll explain." She placed a hand on Edith's knee.

"Mavis, I just wanted to—"

"Edith, love, hear me out," Mavis said softly. "You see, I called you twice from work. The boss said you were staying home, that your mother was poorly. I wanted to see how she was. I kept ringing, no answer, so I knew something was up. I called Reg. He said Lil saw you leave on the early bus. You never do that."

"Oh my God, I was—"

"Wait. I called again in the afternoon. I tried later, thinking perhaps you must have been at the chemist for a prescription. Then I called Lil at 3:30. She was just back from the hairdresser's."

"I just, I meant to, I—"

"Hush now, pet. Good, you have stopped shivering. Well, no nurse, so that's when Lil threw a fit. She said the nurse hadn't picked up the newspaper. We couldn't calm Lil down. She panicked when she couldn't find her spare key to your house. We called the police. We had to. They broke in."

"Oh my God!"

"Edith, it was all an accident. It was."

"No, no, I caused this, it's my fault. I was responsible, no accident. I'll tell you where I was. I was with him all bloody day! Him, Edwin."

"Wait," said Mavis, glancing at Crawford, hovering by the door, "you don't have to."

"I do," said Edith. "I'll tell you what happened. Edwin, he called early. I rushed to get out of the house. Oh, I so w—"

"Miss, perhaps you'd like to explain at the station," Crawford said.

"No, I need to talk now. I just wanted things to be different. That's all, that's all. One day to be different! I wanted things to change. Just one day to be different from the God-awful routine of my life. I'll spare you the details. Not that I can remember, mind you. We drank sherry. Yes, I was wasted, out of my mind, Mavis, me! Me! That's the pitiful truth.

I didn't think about a nurse, Lil's hair, or anything. I left her. I left her! And Mavis, I lied. I lied to the boss."

"Don't. It was an accident, really."

"How is it an accident when someone is left alone like that? How is that? I saw the stretcher. I, I can't …" Edith put her hands to her forehead. "I'm so stupid. I can't believe I thought for one minute that I liked him—Edwin. He's the accident! I mean, I knew it would happen, sooner or later."

"What would happen?"

"She had an appointment, you know, for her heart. When they came to pick her up, she refused to go. Typical!" Edith picked up the glass of water and began gulping it down.

"But Edith—"

"She wouldn't take her pills and spat them out. I found them all over the bed. The nurse told me she would deal with it. There was talk of a pacemaker. It was her day off, wasn't it? The nurse, I mean. Ma didn't like any of them, you know. Don't think they liked her. How could you, I mean, really? Ma was such a … Nobody liked her—rude, she was." Edith began to shake her head, mumbling, "Damn, God! God help us! Stupid! Stupid! Idiots, drunk, useless!"

"Stop! Stop, Edith. It wasn't her heart. Ruby had a fall! A fall, Edith."

"Fall! Ma? That's not possible. She couldn't even get out of bed. She had nothing to fall from."

"I know. It doesn't make sense." Mavis looked away, her eyes filled with tears. "It—it seems like she sort of, well, twisted out of the bed. She'd been bleeding, cut herself, her wrist, on a glass tumbler. At least that's what they said."

"They said?"

"The police."

"Cut! How? How?"

"It was no one's fault, Edith. They will explain." Mavis dabbed at her tears. "I only know what they told me. I'm so sorry."

"When? What time did she … I was coming home, Mavis, when I remembered: Lil's perm! I remembered Ma calling after me. She is really dead? Isn't she? Dead!"

Mavis placed Edith's hand in hers. "They said they would talk to you when you were ready."

"I left her," Edith said.

"Miss, excuse me, miss," Crawford said. "A phone call, an Edwin Meach asking for Edith Sharpe."

"God save us!" said Edith, "I can't sp—"

"I'll handle him. What shall I say?" said Mavis.

"Tell him," Edith paused, "tell him that Ma's dead and the police are here, just that! Tell him."

Mavis stepped out into the hallway to take the call. "What did he say?" Edith asked when Mavis came back into the room.

Mavis raised her eyebrows. "He said he would wait. He said you would know where he was, and then he hung up."

"He can wait forever, for all I care." Edith sighed. She looked at the detective standing in the doorway. "What happens now?" she said. "What are they doing up there?"

"Part of the ongoing investigation, miss," said Crawford.

"I'm going upstairs." Edith jumped up from the couch.

"No," said Mavis, "I don't think we can. The men are still up there, Edith. How about some tea? I'm sure the kettle's boiled."

"What men?" Edith brushed past Crawford and went to the foot of the stairs. She gripped the banister rail. A man carrying a camera came down the stairs. "I'd wait, miss, if I were you," he said. Edith pushed past him. "Whoa! Hang on," he said.

"Miss Sharpe," called Crawford, "it's best that you wait a bit."

Edith kept going. She stood at the top of the stairs, on the landing. She held her breath and swallowed hard. The smell was rancid, sour and fecal. She stood at the doorway of her mother's room. Kneeling on the floor, halfway under the stripped bed, a man was picking at things with a pair of tweezers, depositing them in a plastic bag. Chalk marks circled dark stains on the wood floor; the linoleum had been cut away. A man scribbled furiously on a notepad. A third man directed questions to the others, pausing now and then to bite his bottom lip. "How long would you say then, Bob?" he said.

"Steady loss, three to four hours. Wound deep, brachial artery severed," said the man under the bed. "Wouldn't have been long, tiny as she was." They seemed not to notice Edith or Mavis, who now stood behind her, a hand on Edith's shoulder, until Edith retched. Saliva caught in her throat. The men looked up.

"Could you open the window?" Mavis asked.

"You shouldn't be up here," said the man with the notepad.

"She lives here, for God's sake!" Mavis said.

"Sorry, miss, we can't touch the window. We have to dust for prints. We're done with the bathroom, though."

With her hand over her mouth, Edith rushed across the landing and into the bathroom, slamming the door. She sat on the toilet, inhaling deeply, the nausea eventually subsiding. It was a relief to be alone. She was warm now, but her head throbbed, and the stale taste of sherry persisted. I should be distraught, she thought; maybe I am. I should cry for something, but what? It was too late. I was too late. It's too late for anything now. There was a knock on the door. "You all right, Miss Sharpe?" Crawford called out.

"Yes." She stood up, rinsed her face, pushed her hair back, and eyed herself in the mirror. I look awful, she thought. She brushed her teeth, spitting vigorously into the sink. "Accident? That's a joke," she said to her image in the mirror. "Nothing's an accident, or is it? I'm an accident! Edwin is an accident!" She rubbed her tongue across her teeth. "Ugh!" She spat in the sink. Toothpaste did not blend with the taste of sherry.

"Edith!"

"Yes, I'm okay, Mavis," she said, and opened the door. They went downstairs, where the inspector motioned for them to go into the parlor.

"Miss Sharpe, we will need more information," he said. "I must inform you, there will be an inquest."

"Inquest? But why?" Edith asked.

"A coroner's inquest, miss. In cases like this, it's routine."

"Cases like this?" asked Edith.

"There are some unanswered questions, simply routine," he said. "We shall need you to identify the victim."

"Victim!" Edith said.

In the backseat of the police car on the way to the morgue, Mavis held Edith's hand. "What are they going to ask?" Edith whispered. "Victim? My God, Mavis!"

"It's all right, Edith."

"No, it's not all right. It'll never be all right," she said.

8

The Coroner

----

lease, take your time, Miss Sharpe," Inspector Crawford said as the steel door to the morgue clanged shut behind them. The smell of disinfectant was strong. Water dripped from a tap somewhere. Edith sneezed. The room was cold. The coroner, his face as pale as the white coat he wore, acknowledged them with a nod and gestured for them to step forward. Crawford's footsteps echoed loudly on the tile floor. Edith shuffled. She was still in her slippers.

They approached the table in the center of the room. The three of them stood for what seemed endless minutes. Get on with it, Edith thought, not knowing what to expect or what was even expected of her. The coroner muttered something. He looked at Edith and slowly drew back the sheet. The old woman's skin was stretched over her high cheekbones like parchment. "Miss Sharpe, is this your mother, Ruby Sharpe?" Crawford asked. Edith stared at the sunken hollow of Ruby's mouth. Her eyes looked as if they had never, ever been opened.

"She took them out again," Edith said in a soft voice, "her teeth. She would do that."

"Miss, is this—"

"Yes," said Edith, "yes, that's her." She turned and headed for the door.

"It didn't feel real in there," Edith said to Mavis as they waited in the interrogation room. "But she isn't real, is she? Not anymore. I feel peculiar. I don't really feel present here. Yet I do know, that was Ma in there. I don't know what I am feeling."

49

"It's okay," Mavis said, "just answer their questions for now." Crawford asked Edith if she needed anything. She had been offered tea to drink, but one sip had sent her retching to the bathroom. Now she kept her hand over her mouth to suppress the smell of alcohol that she knew she emitted.

"Miss Sharpe," Crawford said, leaning forward across the desk, "please tell me, where were you today?" With two fingers, Crawford typed her answers as she gave them.

"Baker's Farm," she said. "It's sort of a holiday place."

"Isn't it closed in winter?" he said.

"Well, no, they're open, actually."

"Who was with you, Miss Sharpe?"

"A friend."

"The name of this friend?"

"Edwin Meach. I was with him all day; then I got a taxi home."

"What time would that be?"

"I am not too sure. Around four, I think."

"Did you speak to or see your mother today since leaving the house this morning?"

"No," said Edith, and went on to explain the misunderstanding about the nurse and Lil. "It's Tuesday," she said, "I just didn't realize that the nurse—she's off on Tuesdays."

"Edwin Meach. Where does he live, Miss Sharpe?"

"I'm not sure of his address, but it's up by the reservoir. Sowerby Street. He works at Simpson's Shoes, in town. I don't phone him; he rings me."

"Earlier, Miss Sharpe, when you entered the house, you were not wearing shoes. Why was that?"

"I was trying to get home. It was dark and crowded. I got pushed and one came off, and—"

"I see." No you don't, thought Edith, watching him withdraw the sheet of paper from the typewriter. "I think that tonight, we are finished here," he said, "for now. I have to tell you that the house—your house, Miss Sharpe—is considered a tentative crime scene. So we would be obliged if—"

"Crime scene! My house? What do you mean?" Mavis took hold of Edith's hand.

"Miss Sharpe, it's just routine," he said. "Some things have to be gone over."

"Gone over?" Edith said.

"Yes. There will be an inquest as to the cause of death. It's routine in cases of this nature."

"Inquest? Really?"

"Yes, the coroner will offer his opinion. Understand that there are some questionable circumstances, Miss Sharpe," said Crawford. "It's important that you stay in the vicinity. As I said, it's routine. We will be in touch. I am so sorry for the loss of your mother. There's a car waiting outside for you both. You must be tired."

"Edith will be staying with me," said Mavis. "You have my number."

"We will be in touch, then," he said.

Mavis's one-bedroom flat had a foldaway bed in the living room. She made up the bed and found a nightgown for Edith, who went to take a shower.

"I still reek of sherry," said Edith, putting on the nightgown, "but I have never felt more sober."

"Here's a glass of water," said Mavis, "and have a piece of sponge cake; Mom made it. You need to eat a bit of something, and stick with water for now."

Edith sat on the bed, took a bite of the cake, and hugged her knees. "I have no idea how much I drank, just that it was a lot. I am so ashamed! I don't remember much about the stupid caravan. Only that it was hot and it stank. It's a blur. Things are running through my head. Edwin's stupid voice, 'Precious! Precious!' The stretcher. The ambulance. The whole thing is horrible, unbelievable! So why am I not crying? Back at the station, they were looking at me like I was, well …"

"Edith, listen to me. You—"

"It's as if I am standing outside of it all. God, I don't know how I feel. I know the way I am supposed to feel, and that isn't the way it is at all. She's dead. Ma is dead! I can't even cry for her. Would she cry for me? I wonder. Good Lord, I mustn't think like that. Look at me. All I can do is stare at my knees. I'm heartless."

"It's the shock, Edith, love. That's all, just—"

"Back there in the street, I was like the rest of them, gawking at a horror show. Except it was my horror show!"

"Stop, Edith, stop. This was an accident. It will all be explained." She put her arms around Edith's shoulders. "See if you can close your eyes for a bit. We'll try and get some sleep. I have a sleeping pill if you need it."

Edith lay back on the pillow and listened to Mavis showering in the bathroom. She heard the thump of footsteps in the flat above. She stared at the scalloped fringe that edged the pelmet above the window. From a gap in the curtains, a column of light stretched across the floor and up the wall. Did Ma call out for me, she wondered, in that croaky voice of hers? Had it been a desperate cry, the voice of someone dying? It didn't make sense; nothing did. She sat up and sipped from the glass of water. Loved ones were informed when someone died, she thought. Who are they? Am I a loved one? Is Leon a loved one?

"I will have to find Leon," Edith said to Mavis when she came out of the bathroom. "Lil and Reg said they had all been good chums once. That creepy solicitor Cyril Leakey may know. He would call on Ma before she had her stroke. The two of them would sit there whispering and shuffling papers around. Ma always said he was the only person she trusted. They kept me out of it. I'll have to call him, I suppose." Edith yawned. "God, where do I begin?"

"Edith, get some sleep." Mavis handed her a pill. "Valium," she said, "take it. We'll deal with things tomorrow, the phone calls—leave them to me."

Around eight o'clock the next morning, the phone rang. "Crawford is on his way over," said Mavis. "He said that some issues have to be clarified. 'Routine,' he said."

"Thank God for Valium," Edith said.

"You look better, Edith, more like yourself."

"Thanks, I washed my hair. I slept, then woke up to a nightmare that I simply can't believe, and I am getting to hate that word routine!"

"I know. I'll get the newspaper from the front porch," Mavis said. She returned and gave the paper to Edith, who read the headline out loud:

"'Pensioner found dead! Possible foul play!' Good God! The gossip—it's seeping through the town. I can hear them now. There were enough people on the street last night getting their eyes full, and now this!"

"It's rubbish," said Mavis. Edith threw the newspaper down.

"The inquest will fill in the gaps, Edith. Isn't that why they have inquests?" The doorbell rang. "That'll be Crawford," Mavis said.

Edith sat on the couch in clothes she had borrowed from Mavis, and Mavis let Crawford in. She set down a tray of coffee and biscuits. "Help yourself, detective," she said.

"Just a few details to be cleared up," he said. "About Edwin Meach, Miss Sharpe—we know you were with him yesterday."

"Yes, what does this have to do with—"

"Edwin Meach was apprehended this morning."

"Apprehended? Why, what—"

"He was attempting to abscond with multiple copies of the *Bogmire Daily News* at the depot newsstand. He was intoxicated, and a scuffle ensued. Your name came up several times, Miss Sharpe, when he was questioned. Of course, you were with him on Tuesday. The office at Baker's Farm confirmed that, but there are still some unanswered questions."

"Is he hurt?" Edith asked.

"No, he wasn't charged. His wife took him home."

"Oh dear God," said Edith.

"Lord save us from the likes of Edwin," Mavis muttered under her breath.

"Is there anything about Mr. Meach that you feel we should know, Miss Sharpe?"

"Not a thing," she said, "nothing."

"I see. We shall be in touch then," Crawford said, getting up to leave. "Oh, the boys have finished at your house. The detective team, I mean. You know, we have to be thorough in cases like this."

"Cases like this," Edith moaned after he left.

"I'm staying home with you today," said Mavis. "I called the office this morning; you were still asleep. The boss offered his sympathy. He said for us to take all the time we need."

"I can't believe I lied to Ada like that," said Edith. "Whatever must they all think of me, and the boss, what can he be thinking?"

"Never mind that now. The girls will gossip and then get over it, and the boss, he'll be fine. He's not one to probe. My goodness, look—it's lunchtime already. I'll pop out to get us some lunch at the local bakery—their meat pies are great. Don't answer the phone, Edith. I'll be about twenty minutes."

Mavis soon returned with the food. "Any calls?" she said.

"No … while you were gone, I was thinking," said Edith.

"What where you thinking about?"

"About my father, among other things. I never knew him. Leon must have known him, don't you think? If and when I find Leon, I will ask him. Ma said his name was Charles. I never, ever saw a photo of him. 'He went off to war, never came back,' she said. 'There'll be no more talk of him.' She simply closed the door on it. I asked why Uncle Leon left. 'He's just a fool,' she said, slamming that door as well."

"Edith, you don't have to—"

"I was about fifteen when I quizzed her again. I asked where my father was buried, him being a war hero and all. She said that it didn't matter. I said it did. I'll never forget, she slapped me and called me a little upstart for meddling in the past. I was lucky, she said, that I was too small to remember him. Is that any way to talk to a child?"

"I'm so sorry, Edith."

"I looked for his name, Charles Sharpe, on the war memorial in the town square, but I didn't see it. I even asked her about that. 'Some weren't counted,' she said."

"It must have been hard for her."

"Hard—that's how she was, Mavis, hard!"

"I know," said Mavis. "After lunch, I'm calling Leakey's office for you. I have his number from the phone book; no point in putting it off. Anyway, he should know that you are with me. Let's eat first."

Edith watched Mavis dial the number. She couldn't remember when she had last spoken to Cyril Leakey. Perhaps he was dead; then what? Mavis shook her head and raised her eyebrows before she put the receiver back down.

"What?" Edith said.

"His secretary said he was indisposed," said Mavis. "Who uses words like that anymore? She told me to call tomorrow."

"I don't trust that Leakey, though I know I have to. He must be ancient by now. Ma's will—there must be one. She inherited property; I know that. I have never given it much thought, really. You see, Ma's parents, my grandparents, were in service to this wealthy family. They had no heirs. They owned cotton mills, I think. According to Reg next door, they adored my grandparents. When they died, Ma was the inheritor. That's all I know. I wish I knew more."

"Well, all in good time. Everything will get sorted out," said Mavis. "It's dark out there already," she said. "I've got shepherd's pie in the fridge for supper, and you, Edith, are going to have an early night."

"I'm so grateful to you for all this, Mavis," Edith said.

"All what?"

"Jumping into my mess like this, I mean really."

"Edith, you were there for me. Remember? My ugly divorce? That other woman? You stood by me, right to the end."

"I know, but this is awful in a different way."

"Listen, pet, we do the best we can for each other—we always have and we always will."

That night, the second night after Ruby's death, Edith slept fitfully. Her brief periods of sleep were replete with images: Edwin driving, Edwin naked, the ambulance and stretcher, Lil standing at the garden wall. When Thursday morning finally arrived, Edith lay still in bed and began to wonder if grief for her mother was a delayed emotion. Perhaps she should be alone, allow it to surface. Maybe she would weep then and mourn as people did. She wanted to feel purposeful, be in charge of herself. In the secluded comfort of Mavis's flat, she felt there was little room for that. I need to be ready for something, she thought—the inquest at least, and a funeral; there would have to be one.

"Mavis, I think I need to go home," she said over breakfast. "To Slattery Street. I love being here—you're a pillar of strength for me—but I think I need to sort it all out. This shame, this—well, you know, grief! I can't keep leaning on you."

"Edith, you have been through hell!"

"I have to stand up for myself, Mavis. I feel guilty. What must I have looked and sounded like in that police station? I'm not being stupid anymore. I'm going to confront Leakey and find Uncle Leon. As for Edwin, I hope I never set eyes on him again, ever! I intend to talk to Lil and Reg next door. Imagine what they think of me now."

"I'll go with you, Edith, just to—"

"No, I have to deal with things myself, Mavis, I have to try. I need to shape up. I'll be all right. I feel as if I have to be ready for something, I'm not sure what."

"If it's any consolation," said Mavis, "Dad's solicitor thinks the inquest will come up with accidental death."

"Yes, you mentioned that last night, but I still feel like I have fallen into a mess of brambles, and I have to clutch and claw my own way out. I'll be fine. I'll get a taxi this afternoon."

"Here," said Mavis, "take this tonight." She handed Edith a Valium. "And promise you will call me later?"

"I promise," said Edith, "I promise."

9

Millie

Millie Jamieson, supervisor of the Bogmire bus depot travel and ticket office, sat on a stool in the stockroom that adjoined the ticketing booths. She fingered the long gold chain around her neck, on which was threaded her wedding ring. For six months, she had concealed the ring this way. It was a secret that had once excited and impassioned her. Now it filled her with a nervous foreboding. "We are not wanting to tell people," her husband, Saleem, had said. "I am different. I am Pakistani; people will make trouble for us." Keeping the marriage secret was a justifiable request, Millie thought at the time; it was just a temporary thing. Now she regretted her compliance and the strings she had pulled to secure Saleem his job at the depot. Last evening she had asked him, "Saleem, why must we keep this marriage a secret?"

"I am not being ready for this," he said, storming out of their house.

Whatever happened to my predictable life? she wondered. Her first husband, Leonard, had been a market gardener. He spent long hours in his greenhouses, tending to his prizewinning vegetables. Theirs had been a marriage of simple resignation, each day resembling the one before it. They purchased a new home in Bogmire Heights with a large garden and room for the family that Millie hoped to have. Just two years later, Leonard's coughing began. He became weak and lost weight. "The fact is, Millie," the doctor said, "Leonard sprayed himself as well as the vegetables. As with the miners, the lungs can't take it."

"Find someone to help you with the garden," Leonard said from his sickbed.

"I know someone," the local butcher said. "He's a Paki, though. Mind you, he knows a weed when he sees one. His name is Saleem Banerjee." Saleem was hired and came once a week. Treatments for Leonard failed. Millie's evenings were spent listening to the flat clap of Leonard's respirator in the hospital.

"He was a true man of God's earth," said the reverend at his funeral.

After Leonard's death, Millie kept the job she loved. Saleem came twice a week, then daily. The roses bloomed as never before, and the lawn was sprinkled with daisies instead of weeds. From her bedroom window, Millie watched out for Saleem each morning. He'd return her wave, along with his dazzling smile. She learned that he was forty-five years old. He hadn't had time to get married, he said. His father had died from a stroke. "I send what money I can to Islamabad for my mother's cancer treatments," he told her one afternoon. Millie handed him a tissue to wipe the tear that had slipped down his cheek.

One late summer afternoon months later, Saleem came to her kitchen door. She recalled the scent of the quivering lilac blooms he held out for her. "I must be leaving here," he said, "I am to be needing more money." She cried and pleaded with him to stay. "Please do not cry," he said as he led her to the couch and gently sat her down. He placed a cushion behind her head. "Close your eyes, my beautiful Meelie," he said as he unfastened the buttons of his shirt and took her hand to place on his beating heart. "You are feeling my soul," he said. She succumbed easily to his seductive charms and sensuous ways. It felt so right when, some passionate months later, he proposed. She had never been happier. The registrar at the wedding had wished them well and praised their courage in a country fractured by racial tension.

Millie yawned; she felt desperately tired. The phone calls had been coming at odd times—early morning, late night. "It is Ali, my foolish brother in Bradford," Saleem said. "It is not being your business!" Millie called Ali's number, only to be told that Ali had long since left town. Saleem's responses to her questions began to frighten her.

"You always come home late now—why?"

"You women are like parasite. Get off my skin!" he said, ignoring her tears.

Who in their right mind would conceal a marriage for so long? She envied her assistant clerks, Julie and Rose, with their simple lives. She wished she had siblings, some family, to confide in.

The door to the stockroom was slightly ajar. She listened to the girls' chatter. "Eh, I like them boots, Julie," Rose said. "Where did you get 'em?"

"At the market. That Paki. Him, with the leather jackets," said Julie. "He had 'em in mind, specially for me—that's what he said."

"Get off with yer, Julie! Bet he had sumthin' else in mind for yer." Julie let out a cackle.

"They like blondes, them Pakis," said Rose.

"Ugh!" Julie rolled her eyes. "Forget it," she said. "Any rate, coloreds don't belong in this country."

"Damn right," said Rose, "it's crowded enough! You should 'ave seen the Paki bloke at the hospital that stitched me Mam's finger," she said. "He said nuthin,' like he was sulkin'. Talk about stink! Garlic, phew! Like a rancid frying pan."

"I know what yer mean," said Julie.

"He stitched it up and everything, the finger, but I don't think he was a proper doctor."

There was a knock on the stockroom door. It was Rose. "Hey Millie, you look all in! Do yer want the newspaper? It's about that old woman, the one found dead. It's all in 'ere." She waved a copy of the *Bogmire Daily News*. "It were on telly last night," she said. "Me and Julie, we think it was—"

"No thanks, Rose. I'm going to take a quick toilet break. I'll be back in a jiffy." Tears came to Millie's eyes as she rushed, head down, over to the toilet block.

"Hello there, Millie," said Alice Larkin. "I've just finished the sinks, all nice and fresh now."

"Mornin'," said Millie, quickly entering a cubicle. Millie listened to the flushing and banging of doors as people whisked in and out. She wished she were elsewhere, anywhere, and shivered from the draft that blew through the building. "Oh dear," she heard Alice say. A ball of red yarn had rolled under the door to rest against Millie's foot.

"Oops, sorry," called Alice.

"I've got it, Alice, here you go." Millie stepped out and handed the yarn to Alice.

"Thanks, Millie, love," said Alice. "I'm clumsy when me hands are cold."

"I wish I could knit," said Millie. "It would give me something to do, take my mind off things."

"Feeling down, are you? Working too hard?"

"No, it's not that. It's just, I …" Millie stepped over to the sink to wash her hands. She frowned as she tossed the paper towel into the waste bin. "Alice, you look terrific," she said, changing the subject. Maybe Alice would listen to her story, her secret. Maybe it shouldn't be a secret anymore. This depot, after all, was, in a way, her family.

"You should come out with Jimmy and me to the bingo like you used to," Alice said.

"You and Jimmy look so happy together—you look, well, right," Millie said.

Alice blushed. "I feel great, Millie. What's more, I feel good about the changes around here. It's falling apart, this place," she said, pointing to the cracks in the wall tiles and ceiling.

"I know. It's about time it was fixed."

"They say nothing stays the same. It's all in the name of progress, I suppose."

"Progress—I could use a bit of progress in that ticket office," said Millie. "Those girls haven't stopped talking about Ruby Sharpe."

"Poor old Ruby! What a sad thing," Alice said. "The newspaper isn't saying much, is it? If you listen to Mary Lacey over there at the tea kiosk, she seems to know." Alice lowered her voice. "Mary reckons that it's murder. She has it on authority, she says, that Ruby Sharpe was stabbed by an intruder."

"Authority, my foot!" Millie said. "It only happened yesterday. Who knows the real story? It's Edith Sharpe I feel sorry for. There'll be talk—you mark my words. She's a nice girl, you know."

"She is," said Alice. "Always pleasant, sort of quiet."

"We were at Shield Insurance together," said Millie. "She still works there. She's a bit younger than me. I see her get off the 9 bus each morning."

"Funny thing," Alice said.

"What?"

"Well, just yesterday, I saw her, Edith, getting the earlier bus! I waved, but she didn't see me. I walk to work now, you see—that's how I noticed. Ah well, it's none of my business, I suppose."

"It'll all come out in the wash," said Millie.

"That's true. Still, it's a tragedy."

Millie stared at herself in the mirror. "My God, I look like a tragedy," she said.

"Time for a holiday, maybe?"

"Maybe. I wish it were that simple, I really do." Millie took the cap off her lipstick. With her face close to the mirror, she slid the color across her lips before turning to face Alice. "If you could run away from here, Alice, where would you go?"

Alice chuckled. "Go on with you. I've not been one to think like that, really."

"I am dead serious: where would it be?" Millie snapped the cap back on the lipstick.

"Well, I am not sure."

Millie blinked several times, her eyes moist, as she stared hard at Alice.

"The Isle of Man is nice," said Alice. "I went just once with …" Tears slid down Millie's cheeks. "Millie, whatever is it? Don't cry." Alice took her into her arms. "Millie, love, things are never as bad as they seem."

"Alice, I feel trapped, like a prisoner. Trapped!"

"What? Where?"

"I can't go on like this, you see. Can't go on!" she sobbed.

Alice took Millie's hands in hers. "Loneliness is hard. We are both widows, Millie. It's God's will. There's light at the end of the tunnel. I'm proof of that."

Millie shook her head. "No, Alice, no. You don't understand. I have to tell someone, I—"

"What is it, Millie, what?" Taps were running; people were coming and going, casting glances their way.

"I can't go on," Millie said. She stood a step back from Alice and took a deep breath. "No one lives like we do, no one!"

"What do you mean?"

"I have to tell you." Millie lowered her voice. "Promise me you will keep it to yourself—for now, that is?"

"Of course."

Millie fingered the gold chain around her neck and held up the ring. "I'm married," she said. She braced herself with both hands on the edge of the sink. "There, I've said it. I've said it. You know him, Alice—he works here. The Pakistani driver, Saleem Banerjee."

"The driver? The Pak—"

"Yes."

"Oh Millie, don't feel bad. Just because he's, you know, not one of us. I mean, he seems so nice and so, well, handsome."

"He's handsome, all right. What he seems is not what he is. I think he's a liar, I really do."

"I'm not sure I get your meaning," Alice said. Millie related her story.

"Now he frightens me. I thought I knew him. I loved him, I did. I have to act around here as if—as if I were someone else."

"I won't say anything. But what are you going to do?"

Millie wiped her eyes. "I don't know—that's the trouble. I'd better get back to the office. Those girls will be wondering. I'll have to decide what to do."

"Go easy on yourself, Millie. Go on now, and don't be running off anywhere!"

"Thanks again, Alice. I feel a bit relieved."

"Trouble shared is trouble halved, yer know," Alice said.

"Mum's the word, Alice?"

"Yes, mum's the word." Alice gave Millie a hug. Alice felt sad as she watched Millie walk back to the ticket office on the far side of the depot. Poor lass, she thought. She looked around and didn't see Saleem anywhere. She didn't feel like knitting anymore. Some folks have it really rough, she said to herself as she assessed the soaps, toilet rolls, and towels on the shelves in her cupboard.

"Oh, you're back, Millie," said Julie. "It's drafty when that door swings open."

"Everything okay, girls?" Millie asked.

"Yeh, we had a bit of a rush on," said Rose. "What's new out there, anything?" Rose spun around on her stool to face Julie. "I still can't believe this!" She stabbed a finger at the front page of the newspaper. "It's awful."

"Give us a closer look," said Julie, her metal bangles clanking on the counter as she leaned forward.

"Here, let's read it," said Rose. "'Daughter questioned.' Poor old sod, left alone—that's awful!"

"'Blood-soaked scene.' Ugh!" Julie said as she screwed up her face. "I bet someone did her in."

"Julie, we don't know that," Millie said. "Let's give it a rest for now."

"I hate death," Julie said. "We lost our gran. It was awful. She tripped over the back step and cracked her head on Bobby's kennel. Out for the count, she was. Out forever! That dog barked for a whole week. I want to die in bed, safe an' all. You had to deal with death, didn't you, Millie? Your poor husband, Leonard—what is it, three years now? Me mam said he was a lovely fella, and he grew the best beans."

"Yes, three years," said Millie, "and yes, he was a good man. Now, let's get on. You have people waiting at your windows."

Back in the toilet block, Alice pulled her stool out of her cupboard. She wiped the perspiration off her forehead, sat down, and picked up her knitting. I'd best get on with this, she thought, or it will never get finished.

About every other row, she stopped. "Fancy, who would have thought it?" she said to no one in particular. "Whoever would have thought it?"

10

Slattery Street

----

*I*t was Thursday evening when Edith waited until dusk to take a taxi back home to Slattery Street after spending two nights at Mavis's flat. Thankfully, the driver hadn't engaged her in any conversation; he just grunted when she paid her fare. I'm common knowledge now, she thought, as she walked up to her front gate. Tongues are wagging. Stories are spreading.

She opened the gate and walked up the front path. Maybe I should have walked down the back alley, she thought, and then realized that it didn't matter anymore. What was the point in creeping around? The damage was done! A streetlamp illuminated a few daffodils that had escaped being trampled alongside the path. Cigarette butts lay here and there; a beer bottle sat under the lilac tree. In the corner of the front porch was a bundle of yellow plastic police tape, along with some newspapers. She pushed them all to one side to deal with later and turned the key to open the front door.

When she turned on the lights, the house seemed smaller, as if it had shrunk. The doors to all the rooms were closed. She went to sit on the couch in the front parlor and switched on the electric fire. What now? she thought. Where do I go from here? She was sitting in the same spot where she'd recoiled from the detective's questions two nights earlier. Where she had heard the words "severed," "blood," "body," "death." She recalled how she had been unable to comprehend the sentences that had connected those words together. With a familiar clarity, images yet again flashed before her eyes. The glaring lights of the police car.

Lil and Reg. The mumbling neighbors. The grim-faced ambulance men maneuvering the stretcher. Will I ever be free of this? she thought. Do I deserve to be? Perhaps Mavis was right: being alone is not a good idea.

She remembered an unopened bottle of Glenlivet whisky that she kept in the kitchen for emergencies. Dusting off the bottle, she poured a generous helping and went back to sit in the front parlor. She sipped the drink slowly, hoping that something would change the current state of things. "It'll all come out in the wash," Mavis had said. It was a phrase she had heard often, but now it didn't mean much at all. "I'm so sorry, Ma," she said, looking up to the ceiling. "I'm guilty, Ma, because I can't … I still can't cry for you today."

Perhaps my grief is rattling around in my psyche somewhere, she thought, waiting for the right moment to land. She had read in a magazine once that before true grief presented itself, a distinct numbness could prevail. Yes, that's it, she thought, and took a big swallow of whisky. I'm numb, but for how long? What's next for me?

Edith had only vague recollections of death in her life: dying grandparents of friends at school, aging teachers who had simply disappeared. Pupils would be informed that so-and-so had passed on; prayers would be said for them, and no more. Her questions on life and death always provoked and irritated her mother. Books were Edith's greatest resource. The local library had become a safe and comfortable refuge for her. She loved the quiet, polite attention and being addressed as "miss." Sitting at the large mahogany table in the reference room made her feel important, as if she belonged. As if she were a member of something. Where do I belong now? she wondered. She had wanted her life to change, but not this way. This way was hideous!

She yawned and took a long gulp of her drink before shifting her legs away from the red heat of the artificial coals. She recalled sitting on the footstool by the hearth on cold winter nights when she was a child, watching the flames leap and lick their way around the uneven nuts of coal. "Chilblains, you'll get chilblains!" Ma had said. Edith would pull her cardigan over her knees, stretching it down to her ankles, to avoid getting the blotchy brown marks that covered her mother's thin shins. She would poke the fire and rearrange the coals so that small eruptions of steam hissed and plopped. She deduced that this was how the earth had begun, hissing and exploding. "Rubbish," Ma said. "The truth of creation is in the Bible."

It had been Uncle Leon's job to fill the coal bucket and chop the wood for kindling. What are you like now? Edith thought. Where are you? He must be at least sixty. Are you handsome still? What will you think when you hear the news? Will it bring you back to Bogmire? Of course, he could be married and I could have an aunt, even cousins—who knows?

There will have to be a funeral of sorts, she thought, but who would come? Who would care? Will Lil and Reg even talk to me again? They've known Ma since I was a baby. "Oh God," she said out loud. "What a mess this is; what a mess I have made."

Edith washed her glass and refilled it with water. Then, fulfilling her promise to Mavis, she took the Valium that Mavis had given her before dialing her number. "I'm here, I'm safe," she said.

"If you need anything, Edith, I can be over there in a flash," she said. "I'll call in the morning."

"Thanks," said Edith, "I think I'll be fine tonight." She turned off the fire and lights and dragged her weary body up the stairs. She glanced at the closed door to her mother's room. I'll go in there tomorrow, she decided, and left the landing light on, the way it had been for as long as she could remember. I should say some prayers for Ma, she thought as she lay in bed. "Dear God, please ... what? Please what? Dear God, dear God, I am so tired ..."

The next morning, sunlight streamed through Edith's bedroom window. Grateful for her dreamless sleep, she stretched out and rubbed her eyes. I am alone in this house for the first time ever, she thought. How strange it feels. How quiet. She listened to the throaty noises of the pigeons on the window ledge. She heard the drawn-out squeal of a braking bus outside, then a pause before it groaned off. There goes Saleem; that will be the No. 9, she thought. She could see him now, his broad shoulders and beautiful neck against the collar of his white shirt. Am I still part of the drudge of it all out there? Going to work, coming home, day after day. The same faces and places fitting together like a well-worn jigsaw puzzle.

Sitting up on the side of the bed, she guided her feet into her slippers, donned her dressing gown, and, ignoring the closed door of her mother's room, went downstairs to make coffee and toast. She opened the back door and dispensed the leftover crumbs to a group of waiting sparrows. She paused, enjoying the fresh air. There was warmth in the sun. Tilly, Lil's cat, stared at her from atop the adjoining wall. "Watch out, birdies," Edith said, and then closed the door and went upstairs to shower and dress.

The soothing water of the shower splashed down upon her shoulders. How was my life before all this happened? she thought. What was it all about? She looked down at her feet and watched the soap suds play over her toes. I must get rid of Ma's clutter, she decided. Now, today. "Start with a clean plate," as Ma used to say, "and God will take care of the rest." She wasn't sure about the God bit, but a clean sweep might bring some clarity. The shower water ran cool, and she felt better. Now she had a plan of sorts.

She dressed quickly, putting on a pair of jeans and an old shirt. She brushed her hair and secured it at the nape of her neck with an elastic band before calling Mavis. "I slept really well," Edith said, looking at the clock on the mantel. "It's already 10 a.m. I have a lot to do. I want to get rid of her stuff, Ma's stuff, all of it!"

"Edith, I can help you."

"I know, I appreciate that, but I want to do it today. I'll be fine, really. I'm really all right. You know what Ma would say—'It's no good crying over spilled milk.' "

"Right. I'll be at the office if you need anything. See you tonight. 'Bye, love."

"'Bye, then," said Edith.

From under the kitchen sink, Edith extracted a bucket, some large rubbish bags, detergent, and a sponge; from a closet she pulled a mop, broom, and dustpan. She hauled it all upstairs. She began in the bathroom. On a shelf beside the sink sat the open tobacco tin that contained her mother's hairpins. Next to the tin was a jar of senna pods. "I have to keep regular," her mother would say. All that is finished now, Edith thought. The rituals are over—the hair, the teeth, the bowels, the meals.

She worked briskly, dumping all the bits and pieces into a plastic bag before scouring the sink and tub. She wondered about her mother's teeth and where they had ended up. What the hell did it matter?

She straightened her bed, and glanced at the neat row of shoes beside the dresser and thought of Edwin. Oh, it's good-bye to you, Edwin—I'm finished with you and your dithering fingers and talk of love. Whatever was I thinking? On the landing, she ran the duster across the banister rail, stopping short at the closed door of Ruby's room. She gripped the doorknob and reminded herself that she was no longer governed by the power that had emanated from behind that door. What price will I pay for this emancipation? she wondered. What price am I paying now? Am I to have a life fraught with shame? Will this be the price of not loving you the way a daughter should?

The knob felt stiff; the door seemed jammed. She pushed hard with her knee and shoulder. It gave way, and she pitched forward into the room. Edith gasped. The smell of antiseptic and ammonia was overwhelming. The bed had been stripped except for two pillows and a brown rubber sheet on the mattress. Chalk marks still circled the stains on the floor. For a brief moment, she questioned her right to disturb these last remnants of her mother's life. The room has been disturbed anyway, she thought, and I have to clean it and clear it so that I can start anew. It's up to me, and only me, to deal with the whole damned mess of it!

Desperate for some fresh air, she tugged at the sash window. It wouldn't move. From the wardrobe, she took one of her mother's old court shoes and tapped around the frame with the heel. The window shifted, and she opened it wide, latching it to keep it from closing. She took the pillows and rubber sheet from the bed and dropped them into the yard below, scattering the pigeons and sparrows. She dragged the mattress off the bed frame; then she levered it over the windowsill and let it drop.

Outside, clouds were gathering and there was a light breeze. Lil's washing fluttered on the line next door. Edith knew that inevitably she would come face to face with Lil and Reg, a dread prospect. Above the sink in the corner of the room, she picked up a saucer encrusted with knobs of soap, a toothbrush, and a facecloth. "Sorry, Ma," Edith said, "all this has to go. With all due respect, Ma, this is not how I wanted things to be, but for now, it is the best way. Wherever you are, trust me on that." She emptied the dresser drawers of clothes that Ruby hadn't worn for years. Bagging them all, she dropped them out the window into the yard.

Under the bed, a shard of glass glinted through the wisps of dust as she swept the floor. She mopped the chalk marks away. Holding her nose, she raised the lid of the wicker commode. The enamel pan was empty. She realized then that Ma in her predicament could not have availed herself of it. She dragged the commode to the window and heaved it out. It fell below with a clatter. The pan dislodged and rolled, clanking to a halt against the drain spout. "Oh my," came Lil's voice from below, followed by the slam of a door.

Edith turned to the wardrobe. Mothball fumes wafted out when she opened the doors. "Oh God!" she exclaimed, jumping back. Something was moving. She looked deeper into the wardrobe's dark recess and saw what looked like a pair of eyes, glinting as they shifted from side to side. She peered in closer. "Shit," she said. The eyes belonged to the fox head of Ruby's fur collar, swinging silently on its hanger. Gingerly she removed it, the tail dangling over her arm. She cringed; her recollections of the collar draped around her mother's shoulders were all too clear. On Sundays when she was a child, with Uncle Leon holding her hand, the three of them would walk to church, where meaningless words like "beseech," "begat," and "Holy Ghost" floated over her head. To relieve her boredom, she would gaze at the saintly figures in the stained glass windows, conjuring up stories, bringing them to life. "Ugh," she said as she drew the remaining clothes together. Encircling her arms around them, she lifted them off the rail. Along with the inanimate fox, she deposited them all into the last rubbish bag. "Done," she said, and hurled it out, watching it land with a heavy thud.

Though her yard now looked like the rear of a charity shop, Edith was pleased, having done what she had set out to do. Tomorrow she would get everything carted away. She would send the furniture to the salvage shop.

She had one task remaining. On the top shelf of the wardrobe sat a mahogany box. The foot-square box had been there as long as Edith could remember. It was brought out only when the solicitor, Cyril Leakey, had cause to visit with her mother and was always returned to its shelf. Edith had once dared to inquire as to the nature of their whispered conversations. "Family business is all. Doesn't concern you," her mother said.

Edith assumed that the box contained Ruby's will, along with the usual records and legal documents that most people acquired over a lifetime. Reaching up, she took the box down and set it on the rug in her bedroom to deal with later. She made a phone call to Sid's Salvage, a local hauling company. "Come tomorrow," she stressed, "tomorrow." She called Mavis. "I've not been sitting around moping," Edith said. "I have one thing left to do: sort out a box of things Ma hoarded, papers and stuff."

"That's good. I'll bring fish and chips later, okay?" Mavis said.

"Great," Edith said.

Back upstairs in her bedroom, she placed a pillow on the floor and sat down. Massaging her neck, she yawned. Her body ached a little; it was the satisfactory ache of having done something worthwhile. The wall supported her back. She felt comfortable. There was a soft thud against the front door, heralding the arrival of the evening newspaper. The whole town knows about Ruby now, she thought, pulling the box closer to her. So be it. She yawned again. I cannot and must not cry over spilled milk; what good would it do? You taught me that at least, Ma, and it is all I can hang on to for now. She released the band from her hair. Her head fell forward, and her hair brushed across her eyes as she dozed.

11

Revelation

----

*I*in mine!" Edith sang out, jolting herself back into the darkened bedroom. Her mouth was dry, and her aching shoulders told her that she must have been sleeping for quite some time. She had been dreaming. She was a little girl at Sunday school. Somewhere a choir of children had been singing "Jesus Bids Us Shine." They all ran out to a churchyard and played hopscotch on the flat, mossy gravestones. They were giggling and squealing; the sun was shining.

Edith looked at her feet resting against Ma's box. This is real, she thought, this is not a dream—this talk of funerals, inquests, and, although no one mentions it, blame. It felt at that moment as if this had all happened to someone else. Was this how people went mad? Maybe it was the dreams that made her feel this way, eager one minute to come to grips with it all, then distant and scared the next. In and out of it all! She stood up, turned on the lights, stretched, walked over to the open window, and looked out on the street. It was dark outside, and the yards and houses of Slattery Street looked almost attractive in the soft amber streetlight. She closed the window, drew the curtains, and sat down on the cushion. She thought about making herself a drink but then hesitated; Mavis would arrive soon. Maybe later they would go to the Red Lion. The pub would be noisy and crowded. What better distraction from all this?

"Let's see what you have got in here, Ma," she said, and began to sort through the jumbled contents of the box. Into a wastebasket she tossed folded pieces of Christmas paper. A necklace of glass beads rattled in an empty eyeglasses case. Small bundles of utility receipts for gas and electricity were secured with string. She picked up a small prayer book; it felt damp. Its once-white leather cover was now yellowed and stained. She looked at the writing on the inside: "Presented to Edith Sharpe on her confirmation, November 12, 1957, at the Parish Church of St. Paul." She hadn't remembered receiving it. There were several picture post-cards scrawled with handwritten messages from people she had never heard of, affirming the joys of mundane English seaside resorts.

It's inconceivable, she thought, that anything valuable is among this junk. She would toss these relics out, but then it was probable that a copy of Ma's will was squirreled away in the mess. She picked up a bundle of small black-and-white photographs secured with a decaying rubber band. The uppermost one depicted Edith sitting in the backyard, her child's face squinting at the camera. A wicker basket was at her feet. Potatoes sat in her lap, waiting to be peeled. Judging by her pigtails, it had been taken when she was about ten years old, when kitchen chores were routinely assigned to her. She had enjoyed those tasks. It had been one way of pleasing her mother, temporarily dispelling her mother's notion that she would amount to nothing.

The rubber band gave way, scattering the photographs to the floor. Scooping them up, Edith saw that they were all images of her, Uncle Leon, and her mother in nearby settings: on a bench, in a park, at a pic-nic on the Bogmire sands. In one photo, they were grouped around the Slattery Street front gate. There was Uncle Leon, tall and handsome. She had loved those picnics, in spite of Thermos cups of lukewarm, milky tea and soggy tomato sandwiches.

She could see Uncle Leon now, laughing and building sand castles for her. She would have been about six when Leon left. His absence troubled her now. She needed him to share her confused grief, if indeed grief was what she was experiencing. Leon was her sole family now—a sober yet freeing thought. She placed the photos to one side.

All that remained in the box were several envelopes, crumpled and torn. One contained her school reports. She put them aside to savor later. She picked up an envelope addressed to Ruby Sharpe. Inside was a picture postcard, a sepia reprint of an old Dublin market scene. She read the message: "The ferry was rough. The trip was worth it. Perhaps you will visit? Please forgive us. Love, Leon and Irene." The date on the postmark was blurred. It intrigued her because she had not heard of an Irene and wondered what there was to forgive.

She checked the last bundle of envelopes. Tucked into one were some crumpled blue airmail letters, bound together with string. She flicked through them. The postmarks covered a period from late 1952 to April 1954. All the letters were addressed to Ruby Sharpe and bore the sender's address on the back: Leon Sharpe, c/o P.O. Box 139, Geelong, Victoria, Australia. Why Australia? Her fingers trembled as she struggled to undo the tight knot of string. Did these letters contain the answers to her questions? As a girl, time and again she had asked, "Where has he gone, Ma? Is Uncle Leon coming home? Why did he go?" There had been no logical answers, and eventually she stopped asking.

She felt uneasy as she picked and plucked at the string. She was invading stagnant areas of her mother's life now. It wasn't her business—or was it? The knot unsnarled, and the letters fell to the floor. She was hard put to think that her mother had replied to these letters. Rarely had she seen Ma write anything, other than shopping lists and the odd Christmas card.

She removed some tissue-thin airmail pages from one envelope. At the top of the page, on the right-hand side, was the same P.O. box number, 139, and the date, January 23, 1952. Edith began to read.

> *Dear Ruby,*
> *It is so hot here. The pay is good. My landlady could do with a few cookery lessons. I have thought a lot about what you said and about what that meddling Leakey had to say! Irene still hasn't made her mind up about things. She wants to visit you.*

Edith read on. There was some insignificant news about the town of Geelong, along with a mention of an impending royal visit, concluding with the following:

> *I have found some good mates here. The lads I work with are a cheery lot. The pay is good. Think about what I said last time.*

It's never too late!
  Your loving brother,
  Leon

Edith reread the letter out loud as if to confirm the authenticity of it. "Where does Leakey fit in? What happened, and who is this Irene?" she said, staring at the letter.

She walked out onto the landing and looked down at the hallway and front door. Her urge to leave was strong—to take a walk, take a break, have that drink. No, she thought, I have to finish what I started. Back in the bedroom, she sat down to read the remaining letters. They all contained references to Irene and expressions of gratitude from Leon for the job Ma was doing. Money appeared to be an issue, and Leakey was to be informed if her mother ever needed more. One letter spoke of Leon's disappointment that an agreement had not been reached. What agreement? she thought. What job did Ma do?

At the bottom of the box remained a single envelope. It bore no address, and it was larger than the others. She withdrew the contents, a torn Kodak folder containing three black-and-white photographs and an official-looking document folded in thirds. There was also a note in her uncle's now-familiar handwriting:

June 1958
Dear Ruby,
    Wish you would change your mind. What is done is done, as they say. Here is what you asked for. Irene has a copy and, just for the record, some photos. She has married and has another baby. Ruby, she was never like you think! We did the best we could have done. Some things just don't work out. I suppose that's it, then. I'd still like the other photos anyway. I do have a right, after all! You always had your own way!

                                                              Leon

Edith looked at the letter that no longer appeared to be from a loving sibling. She turned her attention to the photos in the folder. One showed a picture of a smiling Uncle Leon in work overalls at a building site. The second depicted a nun, standing next to a solemn-faced, dark-haired young woman. Behind them, a sign read, "The Little Sisters of the Poor." The third photograph was of the same young woman, smiling and looking lovingly down at the baby in her arms.

Edith put the photos to one side and picked up the official-looking document. Here is Ruby's will, she thought. As she unfolded the stiff, yellowed paper, immediately her eyes went to the red official seal and words at the top of the page.

Certified Copy of an Entry of Birth

Pursuant to the Births and Deaths Registration Acts.
Registration district: Farmley, Yorkshire.

PLACE of BIRTH: Convent of the Little Sisters of the Poor.
DATE of BIRTH: July 19, 1946.
NAME and SEX: Edith. Female.
NAME of FATHER: Leon Albert Sharpe of 23 Slattery St.,
    Bogmire, Lancashire.
NAME of MOTHER:

Here, someone had attempted to erase the name. Only faint ink strokes were discernable. The address of the mother had also been partly erased, leaving what Edith assumed was a *3* or an *8*, followed by *Terrace, Dublin, Ireland.*

Birth registered, August 1, 1946.
Officially witnessed and registered by the authority of the
    Registrar General, the County of Lancashire.

That is my birthday, July 19, she thought. What does this mean? This cannot be right. She willed the document to be false, unable to still her mind long enough to think through the meaning of the facts before her. Who, what, how on earth? She tried to convince herself that it was just a vague record of a distant event. Leon got some woman into trouble, that's all—simple, really. She could see it all now. Yes, he would have been a charmer, a handsome one at that! Ma would have swept it under the mat, and they would have argued about it.

Edith read and reread the handwritten entries in the document. Slowly the revelations assumed an unbelievable dimension. She held the document up to the light to search for a clue, some detail that would invalidate it somehow. She wanted no connection with this record that had been tampered with, but the dates told a story! This was her story: her name, Edith; her birthdate and the father noted as Leon Sharpe, the uncle she had loved! And what of the scratched-out space that represented her mother? She looked again at the photographs.

"You must be Irene, you must be! Why is the nun smiling? You are not," she said. "Where are you? Where is that place?" Then she saw the sign behind the women at the rear of the picture. She looked at the birth certificate, then back at the photograph. It was clear; there was no mistake. "The Little Sisters of the Poor," she read, and then gasped, "Oh God! Oh my God!" She looked at a third photo of the same dark-haired young woman holding the baby. "That must be! That's me she's holding—she's smiling down at me!" Edith shook her head. "Please, God, help me to understand!"

Her body was shaking and the document quivered. She steadied it with both hands. "My father is Uncle Leon! No! No! How can you be my father?" Her heart thumped. He meant everything to me in those early years and I to him, he'd tell me so over and over. "Why couldn't you be? There never was a war hero, was there, Ma? It was all lies!" The more she stared at the words and dates, the more they danced around the page before settling into their rightful places.

"It's me, it's me on that page. I was the cause of all those letters, me," she gasped. She drew her legs up to her chest and rubbed her eyes, smearing her cheeks with the tears that were forming. She stared at the birth certificate that now lay on the floor beside her. "I was a mistake," she said, "a shameful mistake!"

She let out faint cries at first, wrapping her arms tightly about her legs, her forehead resting on her knees. Her muffled sobs grew louder. "No, no, no!" she cried. "Damn you, Ma, this is your doing!" She caught her breath repeatedly; her chest hurt. She was panting and crying as she spat out words. "Damn! Lies! How? She's not worth my tears!" she cried. "You, Ma, are not worth my tears!" She felt as if she were suffocating.

She inhaled slowly, putting her hands to her forehead before exhaling loudly, "Phew! Good Christ! I—I hardly believe it!" She drew the hair back from her face and looked around. Her eyes landed on the photo of Leon on the rug beside her. "Where the hell are you? Did you run from me, from your mistake? Damn you, Ma—no, you are not Ma, you are Ruby. Damn you, Ruby Sharpe—you can go to hell! Because that's where I am!"

She stood up and walked out to the landing. "All you others, you betrayed me! Who am I?" She held on to the banister.

"This is a godless world! This is an unfair world! Damn you, damn you Ruby! Do you hear me?" Her loud cries rebounded off the walls, echoing their way through the small house. "Whom do I belong to now?" She looked up at the ceiling and clawed the hair back from her face. "I belong to her in the picture, Irene," she sighed. "Did she just lose me, or was I taken? I'll find out. So help me, I'll find out!"

In the bathroom, Edith rinsed her face. Her throat felt raw, and she sipped some water. What can this mean now? she wondered. She sat on the edge of the bathtub. Nothing will ever be the same! Who would want it to be? She stared at the corroded pipes under the sink and the orange streaks in the bathtub caused by the dripping taps. I've spent too many damp winter days in this miserable house, she thought. No more, Ruby, no more. That life has gone with you, Ruby. It's all rotting in your bed of lies.

In the bedroom, she gathered up the photos and certificate. She looked at the photo of Irene and the baby, clutched it to her breast, and went downstairs. She turned on the lights in the parlor and switched on the fire before positioning the photo of Irene on the mantel. "Did you love him?" she said, looking at the photo. "I'll find you, Irene. I'll find you and Leon." She didn't hear the front door open and close, or the footsteps in the hallway.

"Hi there! I let myself in," called Mavis. "There you are. For goodness' sake! Edith, what happened now? You look awful!"

"I had a bad dream, one that turned out to be real. Sit down; see for yourself. It's all here." She handed Mavis the birth certificate. Mavis stared at it and then looked at Edith.

"Go on, read it," Edith said as she pointed to the names on the document, the dates, and the place of birth.

"What does this mean? Is this you? That's your birthday! I can't believe this," said Mavis, shaking her head. "I can't believe this. Is it true? Why didn't someone ever say anything, tell you? Where did you get this, anyway? You don't know if it's genuine."

"Oh, I know it's genuine. Why else would it be hidden in Ruby's damn wardrobe?" Edith said. "She lied. She lied to me, Mavis, betrayed me, for all these years! It's all in the letters. You can read them, here. It all makes sense. See these photos!"

"I … don't know what to say, I'm …" Mavis put her arm around Edith's shoulders. "Is that you, then, with her? I mean that is … she is your mother, you think? You are the baby? Edith, are you sure?"

"Yes I am. I feel it, Mavis. Every time I look at her photo," she said. "I know it. Anyway, it's all documented; it's in the letters—read!"

"You must be flabbergasted, to say the least. Oh Edith, my God." Mavis's eyes were brimming with tears.

"She's pretty, isn't she?" said Edith, pointing to the photo on the mantel.

"Oh yes," said Mavis, her lips trembling, "Oh my, yes, she is." She reached into her handbag and pulled out a clump of tissues, handing some to Edith.

Edith took a deep breath. "They say doors close and new ones open. Well, I've opened more doors than I care to go through, Mavis. But I will." Edith nodded at the photo. "I'll get through them for her sake and mine. Now, I need that whisky."

"Good idea," said Mavis, "good idea."

12

Red Lion

I'll never forget this day, this night!" said Edith. "Imagine, I was kept in the dark all these years! Ruby dies, and now this!"

"I know," said Mavis.

"I wonder what she's like," said Edith. "I wonder what she looks like. Do I look like her?"

"I can't tell, love. We just have that picture, and that was taken some time—"

"I can't stop looking at it now. I'm going crazy with it!"

"No you're not! Look, let's go to the Red Lion. It's past seven. We've hardly touched these fish and chips, and they're stone cold."

As they walked the few short blocks to the pub, Edith stopped every few steps. "So help me, Mavis, they lied to me—Lil, Reg, Leakey. I'm a bastard! How could they lie?"

"We'll make sense of all this, I promise," Mavis said.

"Nothing makes sense. Edwin will never make sense to me." she said. "I'm disgusted with myself."

"Don't be so hard on yourself. He was …"

"He was what? You never met him."

"Yes, I did once, remember? At the shoe store; you introduced me. Remember? I held out my hand to him and he lurched forward, tripping over those shoeboxes, and tissue paper was everywhere? I never did get to talk to him. When we left, he was on all fours, looking for his ivory shoe horn, he said."

79

"Oh yes." Edith rolled her eyes. "I remember that now. What an idiot, or I am the idiot! What induced me to sleep with him I'll never know."

"It doesn't matter now, Edith."

"I'm ashamed."

"It doesn't matter."

"He told me he loved me so often," Edith said. "I suppose I liked hearing that."

"Well, who wouldn't?"

"I never loved him, though. I think I really tried to, once or twice."

At the crowded pub, a darts competition was in progress. Someone was thumping out Tom Jones hits on an upright piano in the far corner. The air was thick with cigarette smoke. "It's packed in here," Mavis said as they made their way to the bar to place their orders. "Of course," she said, "it's Friday night, after all." Edith and Mavis enjoyed a few drinks at a quiet corner table. They didn't talk much. It was too noisy. On the way home, the street was quiet, the air clean and cold after the smoke-filled pub. A cyclist whistled a tune as he pedaled by, the red glow of his rear light weaving in the dark as it grew smaller before disappearing around the corner. Shadows from televisions flickered in front parlor windows.

"What did people do before television? Do you think folks were happier?" Edith said.

"I think they talked to each other instead of at each other, and they listened more," said Mavis.

"She used to talk at me, you know, never to me," said Edith.

"Who?"

"Ruby. Funny, she isn't Ma or Mother anymore. She just isn't. I'm someone else now. Everything has shifted." Mavis gave Edith's arm a squeeze. "I am not who I thought I was. But I do belong to somebody, don't I, Mavis?"

"Of course, love."

A tired-looking man mopped the floor of Stanley's Fish and Chips. An amorous young couple in a shop doorway released their hold on one another as the women approached. The boy tossed a cigarette butt into the street. "I hated being fifteen," said Edith.

"Why do you say that?"

"That girl with the boy, she looked about fifteen. When I was that age, I felt as if I was turning into somebody I didn't know, and I had to try so hard to like her. I can't explain it, but I feel a bit like that now."

The No. 9 bus loomed toward them and stopped close by to drop off passengers. "See yer!" "Cheerio!" "Goodnight," they said. The bus rumbled off. "Huh, that's funny," said Edith.

"What's funny?"

"That driver—he's working late. He's always on my early bus."

"Things change, you know, Edith, even in Bogmire."

"You can say that again! He is just, well, different."

"Who is, Edwin?" said Mavis.

"Nah, that driver. He's nice, you know."

"Edith Sharpe, don't tell me you've got the hots for a bus driver," Mavis giggled.

"What's wrong with bus drivers? Especially if they look like Omar Sharif," said Edith.

"Good to see you smile. That's why you look so dreamy when you come in to work, then." They both laughed.

"Speaking of work, I can't think about it. I have so much to deal with," Edith said.

"Of course."

"I'm not sure where to start."

"Tonight we start by going to bed. I'll be on the couch downstairs," said Mavis.

"Right—the drinks will see me out, that's for sure," Edith said as she unlatched the gate.

The next morning, Saturday, Mavis called Edith. "Hi, I'm here at the office tying up a few loose ends."

"I didn't hear you leave," Edith said. "I slept like a log—must have been the drinks!"

"Good—you were fast asleep, so I tiptoed out."

"I had this dream last night," Edith said. "I was on a train. It was hurtling along, and I was stumbling down the corridor, looking into each compartment. Do you remember doing that when you were a kid?

The passengers stared back at me as if they knew something I didn't. I kept going through carriage after carriage."

"Who were they, people you know?"

"No, just passengers."

"I suppose we are all just passengers, on our way to somewhere!" said Mavis.

"I suppose," said Edith. "This morning, I kept reading the letters and the certificate. It is still hard to believe! I have to know more—about me, about Leon and everything that has been kept from me. Anyway, I will find out, you know."

"What?"

"About her, my mother. And that place, that convent. She's somewhere. I know it. I feel it!"

"I know, but first things first, Edith. I was calling people this morning—the police, the church, and Jack Draper the undertaker. The coroner has released Ruby's body. The funeral will take place the day after tomorrow at 2 p.m."

"Oh my God, it sounds so horri—"

"I know it does. You will get through this, Edith, I promise. I spoke to the Reverend Gormley."

"God, he's been around forever!"

"He sends his condolences."

"Does he indeed."

"I caught up with Cyril Leakey, the solicitor. He doesn't talk with clients on Saturday mornings, his secretary told me. It was like getting water out of a stone with her. I insisted on speaking to him. 'Yes, I'm aware of the tragedy,' he said. 'I am familiar with the Sharpe family.' I told him I was taking care of everything. 'All in good time,' he said."

"Well, you *are* taking care of everything."

"Edith, I have to go to Mum's now. I'll ring later. 'Bye, love."

"'Bye."

The box was still on the floor of Edith's bedroom where she had left it. She spread the letters and some of the photos on the rug, swirling them around like playing cards. Is this what my life stands for? she thought. Pieces of paper boxed away? Hoarded in the memory of a bitter old woman! She went over to the window.

In the backyard next door, Lil was removing her ubiquitous washing from the line, and behind her stood Reg, holding a laundry basket. Lil pried off the clothes pegs, dropping them into the pocket of her apron before placing each item of clothing in the basket. You both must have known, Edith thought, recalling a framed photo that sat atop the sideboard in their front parlor. The photo depicted a YMCA cricket team. Seated in the back row were Leon and Reg, their arms about each other's shoulders. The date was prominently displayed, "League champions 1944." Two years before Edith's birth. No denying it, she thought, you must have known. Lil, Reg, you were here then. When all the clothes were removed from the line, Lil bustled her way back into the house, followed by Reg awkwardly negotiating the back step, hampered by his ample girth and the full basket.

She withdrew the photo of Irene with the baby from her pocket. She stared at it, as she often would in the coming days and weeks. In the bathroom, she switched on the mirror lights above the sink and propped the photo against the tooth mug. She stood back and gathered up her hair, twisting it at the top of her head, attempting to replicate the image of Irene. She turned her head to the left and right, glancing frequently at the photograph. This is stupid, she thought. I am looking, but I am not seeing anything. Clutching the photograph to her breast, she returned to the bedroom, scooped up the rest of the items, and went downstairs.

She put Irene's photograph back on the mantel. "You did love him," she said, "it's all in these letters and pictures, it's here." What happened to all that love? None of it reached this house, she thought, except for him, Leon. I loved him before he ran off. She stared at the picture of the nun and her mother against the backdrop of the convent. What part were you supposed to play, Sister whomever? What did you represent, the all-too-powerful church? Was it God's so-called will, or was it you, Ruby? Did Leon and Irene abide by your rules, Ruby? Oh, I think so. You pushed them both away, you and your puritanical ranting. Well, it is my rules now, my rules. "I'll find you," she said to Irene. "I will!" She returned the photographs, birth certificate, and letters to the top drawer of the sideboard. She placed the photo of her mother in her pocket.

There was a loud knock on the back door and she jumped. She opened the door to see two men in overalls. One raised his cap and scratched his scalp with his thumb.

"Sid's Salvage, miss—I'm Sid," he said. "Yer called yesterday."

"Oh yes, I just forgot. Sorry."

"Not much 'ere," he said, casting his eyes over the yard. "We'll take the wicker stuff. You'll need to call the refuse department about this lot, luv. They'll take it off your hands. They have a way of handling this kind of stuff," he said, gesturing to the mattress. "They chuck it in the furnace down at the corporation yard. Wouldn't have their job if you paid me."

"Right, me neither," said his mate.

"There's a wardrobe and a chest of drawers upstairs—I'll show you," said Edith. They all trooped up the stairs.

Sid looked over the furniture and said, "Can't give you much for this," scratching his head again.

"I don't want anything—just take it," she said.

"Five quid."

"Fine, take it."

Edith made herself a cup of tea and listened to the men as they clattered up and down the stairs. "We're all done," said Sid. "We closed the door up there."

"Thanks," she said, and handed him a ten-pound note.

"Thanks. See yer, miss. We're sorry an' all, 'bout the old lady." He shook his head and removed his cap, giving his mate a shove toward the door.

"Thanks again," Edith said. "'Bye!" Tilly appeared on the garden wall. Lil's door slammed. The cat swished her tail. Lil, you are not quiet enough! Edith wanted to shout. Enough of your nosiness! You'll be quiet enough, Lil, when I tell you what I know!

13

Funeral

Almost a week had passed since Ruby's death. Two days continued to fill Edith with dread. The first was today, Monday, the day of Ruby's funeral. It would be a brief affair, according to Mavis, who, thankfully, had made all the necessary arrangements. Though there would be no church service, as she had requested, Edith was still apprehensive about the whole procedure that would take place outside at the cemetery. At least it's not raining, she thought. The second dreaded day was Tuesday of the following week, the assigned day of the coroner's inquest.

To Edith, the very word "inquest" sounded probing and mysterious. The prospect of answering a panel's questions was daunting. If she was to believe the assurances of Inspector Crawford, that it was simply a question of revisiting the facts, why would they bother with an inquest at all?

As she waited for the iron to heat up, she watched the sparrows on the coal-shed roof devour crumbs she had left out from breakfast. She mulled over the chaos of the last few days. There was no pecking order for her, no simple squabble, no just reward that she could envision right now. During the night, she thought she'd heard Ruby rattling her stick on the bedrail and crying out. From the landing, she yelled at Ruby's closed bedroom door, "What right had you to invent a father, claim me as yours, and abolish my mother?" When she was back in her bed, she asked herself, "Who am I now?"

Soon after breakfast, her stomach began cramping. Nerves, she thought. Even her coffee tasted off. The iron's hot surface hissed when she spat on it. She spread out the collar of the white blouse she had chosen to wear and began to press out the creases. Her fingers brushed against the iron's metal rim. "Ouch! Damn! Ow!" she said, and looked at the seared red skin on her fingers. "Blow on them," Ruby would have said. She took a deep breath to do just that, but her intake turned into a gasp. "It's just not fair, it's just not fair," she said into her cupped hands. "I cannot do this!" she cried. "I cannot get it right! I have to get the creases out, I have to!" She slammed the iron down on the garment the way Ruby used to do. Back and forth she went, ironing vigorously, stopping only when the phone rang.

"Edith. It's me."

"Oh, Mavis," she said, sniffing back tears.

"Do you have a cold?"

"No, I'm ironing; it's the collar, my blouse. It has to look right. It is a funeral after all. And I feel so sickly this morning!"

"Edith you're not, you're not preg—"

"Heck no! I'm on the pill, remember?"

"Well, I'm sorry, I just … you know things can happen."

"Yes, I know. You had every right to think that, I suppose."

"Did you eat anything?"

"I had a bit of toast and some leftover canned apricots with my cereal."

"Okay. Listen, I'll pick you up around 1:30."

Edith dressed as she thought was suitable for the funeral: a black beret, a gray topcoat, sensible flat shoes, and a little makeup. She checked herself in the mirror. I look good, quite respectable, she thought.

The doorbell rang. It was Mavis. "Hi," said Edith. "At least it's not raining!"

"Hi, love. The sun is trying to shine. There's no rush—I'm early," she said, following Edith into the house.

"Good, because I feel so awful," said Edith. "My head's thumping, my stomach is aching." She caught a glimpse of herself in the mirror. The blouse was even more wrinkled than before. A comb fell out of her hair. "Oh hell." She whipped off the beret and sat at the kitchen table, putting her head in her hands.

"I can't do it! Mavis, I can't go. Look at me! This collar's a mess. My face is all red and my hair is tumbling down. Look at me—I'm miserable. I've always been miserable. And you! You are always so happy, I mean. Why are you so cheerful all the time? It's not fair."

Mavis put her arms about Edith and stroked the hair back from her face. "Look at me, Edith," she said. "Happiness doesn't come cheap. But it comes. It does. Today, well, this is the worst of it, the funeral. We'll get through it. Think of it as the final payment. Ruby's paid up, sort of. Look, I've had my rotten times, you know. I was cheated on. You didn't know that husband of mine. You didn't know me then. I know how it feels when everything turns upside down."

"I'm sorry."

"I don't talk about it because it's all past. At least I had my parents to lean on. You must lean on me. I mean that, Edith, I do."

Edith looked up. "I hope you're right! It's just that I keep ..."

"It's going to work out."

"But this collar, this blouse, look at it!"

"Stuff the blouse! Wear the jumper I got you for Christmas."

Edith looked at herself in the mirror. "What a wreck! I need to put a new face on. Ouch! These cramps again. Funny how they just come and go."

"At least they go. We had better get going."

"Let's see," said Edith as they drove to the cemetery, "it will be just you and me and the vicar at this funeral, I suppose. That's sad."

"Of course it's sad," said Mavis. "Funerals are sad."

"What I mean is, it's sad that Leon isn't here for his sister's funeral. He is her brother! And my God, he's my father! Will I ever get used to that? Will I ever think of him as my father? What am I supposed to think? That's the trouble. I want to see him, yet I don't want to see him. Don't be surprised if Leakey shows up. They were thick as thieves, him and Ruby!"

"Yes, you told me," said Mavis. "I must admit I thought he might at least have called you by now out of respect and all."

"Leakey is keeping something from me. I know he is! He must know where Leon is. Ugh, ouch! Here we go, cramps again. I feel sick."

87

"I'll open the window and slow down. It's just nerves," Mavis said. "Breathe, c'mon, deep breaths."

"Ah, that's better, gone now. I wish I could just, you know, chuck up and get it all over with!"

"What, and make a mess of my car?" laughed Mavis. "Look, here we are."

A long, treeless avenue sliced through the broad expanse of St. Paul's cemetery. The weak afternoon sun cast shadows over the rows of head-stones, their regularity interrupted here and there by a monument or statue. A gardener mowed a strip of lawn bordering the avenue. He stopped and silenced his mower as the women walked by. "I suppose we go up there," Mavis said, gesturing to a cleared area where the Reverend Horace Gormley stood close to a mound of brown earth.

"He looks like a statue up there. He fits right in," said Edith.

"Who is that standing behind him?" Mavis said.

"None other then my friend Cyril Leakey."

"He seems ancient! What's he staring at?"

"God knows. He looks ready for the grave himself!" said Edith. "Too bad he had to show up. Still, I'll catch him later, have a word with him, yes. He knows a thing or two, I'm sure. I'll pin him down," she said. "Get some answers."

"Oh dear," said Mavis, "I forgot to get flowers—a wreath or something."

"Doesn't matter," said Edith. "Ruby wasn't one to care for flowers anyway. We'd better shush now. Here we go." A seagull observed them all from atop a statue on an adjacent plot. The women stood close to-gether. Across from them on the other side of the freshly dug grave was Cyril Leakey. He acknowledged them with a slight nod. The reverend looked about him, then peered down the drive, ran his finger around his collar, and checked his watch. "I shall commence," he said, clearing his throat.

He looked up to the sky and closed his eyes. "We, God's servants, are here to honor Ruby Sharpe," he said. "Dust thou art, and unto dust thou shalt return." The gardener had stopped mowing. He removed his cap and bowed his head. Edith had never attended a funeral before. This was far removed from the weepy scenarios she had seen on television. She felt ridiculous wearing the black beret she had compelled Mavis to buy for her. Still, it was the least she could do, to muster some sign of respect. She wished she could be moved in some way, feel something. All she felt was sheer frustration at the events that had propelled her there. I cannot even shed a tear now; I have cried enough this morning, she thought, squeezing the tissues in her pocket, and I'll be damned if I'll start again.

"We must needs die, and as are water spilt upon the ground," said the reverend, "which cannot be gathered up again."

"This doesn't make any sense to me," Edith whispered.

"Shush … I know," said Mavis.

Edith looked at Cyril Leakey's timeworn face. His eyes were shut. She looked at the white silk scarf around his scraggy neck. I would like to give it a good yank, she thought, wake him up. She wanted to scream at him, "You know! You must know where my parents are!" He appeared to tilt as the weight of his long body caused his walking stick to sink into the soft ground. "He looks like he might fall in there," Edith whispered.

"Shh," said Mavis.

The reverend continued. "Ruby Sharpe was a respected citizen, a God-fearing citizen." A breeze fluttered the pages of the open Bible he held. Edith looked at the mound of earth that would soon conceal the last physical evidence of Ruby's earthly existence. Tightening her hold on Mavis's arm, she peered down at the plain wooden coffin nestled in its earthy enclave. She recalled a song about worms eating up the dead. She couldn't remember where she had heard it.

"How did it get there—the coffin? I didn't see," whispered Edith.

"Those two men—standing back there, by the angel," whispered Mavis.

"Oh, right."

"Ruby Sharpe was a loyal Christian," proclaimed the reverend. He droned on about Ruby's contribution to the church and community.

"He's making all this up," whispered Edith. "She didn't give a toss about community!"

The Reverend Horace Gormley was not accustomed to addressing such a small funeral gathering. Normally he flourished at funerals. He felt they lent themselves to his oratory skills. The women here were whispering, and Leakey appeared to be dozing. He was being ignored, so he quickly concluded his pious discourse. "Ruby Sharpe is with our Lord, may God rest her soul. She is in God's hands now." He slammed the Bible shut. The seagull squawked and departed, leaving its slimy trademark on the statue's head.

"May God be with you, Miss Sharpe," he said. "His house is your house." He held the Bible aloft, casting a vexed glance at the lethargic Leakey. "For thine is the kingdom!" Gormley said, raising his voice. "The power! And the glory!" He motioned for the two men with spades to come forward. "Lead us not into temptation," he said, stepping back. Edith had her hand over her mouth. She rolled her eyes before bending over. "Oh!" she said, clutching at her stomach. "Mavis, I'm going to be sick!"

"Hang, on Edith—we'll find a bathroom," Mavis said, "just hang on!"

"I—I'm trying!"

Mavis approached the vicar. "Excuse me," she said. He stared straight ahead, completely ignoring what was going on about him. "I'm afraid, vicar, that Edith—er, Miss Sharpe—isn't feeling well. Would it be all right if—" He suddenly turned from them, waved an arm, and headed off.

"Gosh," said Edith, pushing her hair back from her face. She stood up straight. "That was close."

"Well, he has gone, he just fled!" said Mavis. "What did I do?"

"Phew! I felt dizzy then," Edith said. "What did he say? Whose house? Is it over?" She looked at the grave. "Oh," she said, "the coffin—it's in there. Has he gone?" She turned to see Gormley heading back to the church, the cloud of his white surplice weaving through the headstones.

Mavis tugged at Edith's sleeve. "Edith, let's just go. Before you … ," but Edith's eyes were fixed on Leakey, who was pulling on his gloves and adjusting his scarf.

"Just a moment, Mr. Leakey," Edith called out. "We need to—"

"Ah, Miss Sharpe," he said, "a sad occasion indeed."

"Let's go," said Mavis. "We'll ring him later."

"No," said Edith, and walked toward Leakey to stand directly in his path.

"Miss Sharpe, I must get on," he said, "really. Are you all right? You seem—"

"Yes, I'm fine," said Edith. "We all have to get on, as you say, Mr. Leakey, but first I—"

He planted his stick in front of him, as if to keep Edith at a distance. "Miss Sharpe, this is a sad business. I have to be off just now, a train to catch." He doffed his black trilby and turned away. Edith also turned and faced him again.

"Wait," she said, "I want you to—I need to—ugh … oh!" She doubled over, clutched at her stomach, and, with her free hand, grabbed Leakey's walking stick for support. Her beret fell off as she let out a guttural retch, "Awgh!" The diggers dropped their spades. Cyril Leakey, his jowls quivering, turned bright red as he stared down at the undigested apricots slithering off his polished black shoes.

"Good Lord!" he yelled, eyes blazing. "Good God, girl!"

"Oh, I am so, er … sorry," Edith said, straightening up and releasing her hold on the stick. "Oh, my heavens." She took a deep breath and wiped her mouth with a tissue that Mavis had handed her.

"You all right, miss? Here's your hat," said the gardener.

"Oh dear me! Thanks, yes," she said, and blew her nose loudly.

"Here, sir," said the gardener, handing Leakey a rag.

"Let me," said Mavis, and bent down to wipe the shoes.

"I am terribly sorry, Mr. Leakey," said Edith, "really I am," as she spat into a clump of tissues.

"That will do, miss," Leakey said, giving Mavis a poke with his stick.

"Can we do anything else for you?" Mavis asked.

"Enough has been done," he said, scowling at them. He hunched his shoulders and marched off, stabbing his walking stick into the ground with each stride as he headed for the cemetery gates.

"Good-bye, then," Mavis called after him. She turned to see Edith crouched over again. "Are you okay? He's gone. Why are you shaking?"

"I'm—I'm laughing. I'm sorry, I don't believe what just happened," she said. "It's not funny, really, is it? All over his shoes, oh dear! I couldn't help it. I am fine, a bit messy, but I do feel better after that. Where did the vicar go?"

"You scared him off," Mavis laughed. "I think he saw it coming."

"Perhaps he did; I didn't," said Edith. "What do we do now?" The two men were leaning on their spades, staring. "Are they waiting for something?" she whispered.

"I think we just leave," said Mavis.

"We don't have to tip them or anything?"

"Heck no! Gee, Edith." She started to laugh.

"You gals, are you right now?" said the gardener who had given Edith back her hat.

"Oh yes," they chorused, "thanks."

"Things happen here all the time. Not to worry, lass. It's just another day's work," he said as he cranked up his mower. The diggers raised their caps to the women and resumed their shoveling.

"Well, I suppose it's good-bye, then, Ma," Edith said. "I don't know whether I mean Ruby or Ma. I suppose you did your best, Ma," she said softly. "I didn't do my best today. I'm sorry."

"'Bye, Ruby," said Mavis. "Dear God, what a farewell this is." She took Edith's arm in hers. "I don't like the way Gormley took off like that. They are supposed to stay, aren't they?"

"Gosh, don't ask me. I don't know anything about funerals. He's so creepy! They are a funny lot in this town," Edith said.

"Yeh, well, it's over with. Let's go home. How do you feel now?"

"To tell you the truth, I feel so much better, as if I got rid of a load of rubbish—which I did, of course," she laughed. "Imagine if Ruby had seen what happened. No one will believe us, Mavis. I can't really believe it myself, that we just had a funeral," Edith said.

"I know."

The two linked arms and walked down the avenue leading out of the cemetery. The sun had gone down and the air had cooled.

"Well, it's over now, Edith, time to mend," said Mavis. They walked, heads down, observing the uniformity of their steps.

"There's the inquest to deal with yet," said Edith.

"I know."

"I still keep thinking Ma didn't deserve to go like that."

"They said it was peaceful, Edith—the death, I mean—so what did she deserve?"

"I don't know. A better life, I suppose."

"At least the sun shone for Ruby today."

"She never cared much for the sun, Mavis. I don't know what she really cared about, to tell you the truth."

"She cared about you," Mavis said as they walked up the stairs to her flat.

"Do you reckon?"

"Yes, I reckon, of course."

"I suppose. But she had a bloody funny way of showing it!"

"Maybe it was the only way she knew."

"Maybe."

14

Lil and Reg

S he's out there again," said Lil, alerted by the click of Edith Sharpe's front gate next door. Lil was peering through a gap in the curtains of her front parlor window. "She's by herself and all—fancy, at this time of night."

"Come away from the window," said Reg, raising his voice above the drone of the television. "You've been fiddlin' with them curtains for 'alf an hour." Reg sat in a chintz-covered armchair, one of a matching pair. His slippered feet rested on a cushioned stool. The orange flames of a small gas fire endlessly licked at a mound of artificial coals. The chairs, along with the large television set, all but filled the Palethorpes' small front parlor.

"You know, I like things to look nice," Lil said. "These curtains 'ave to 'ang right."

"Curtains don't shift," said Reg.

"Yes they do, if Tilly is on the windowsill. She likes to see what's goin' on."

"Cat's not t'only one," mumbled Reg, continuing to stare at the television.

"Edith hasn't been to work since, you know," Lil said as she rubbed the windowsill with the sleeve of her cardigan.

"Give it a rest. Sit down 'ere. Watch a bit of telly." He patted the chair beside him. "Soccer highlights. Grand!" Reg said.

Lil's preoccupation with Edith in the aftermath of Ruby's death troubled Reg. He longed for a return to the settled routine of their lives.

"I can't get it out of me 'ead, Reg. It's still all stuck there," she said.

"What? Stuck where?" he asked.

"In me mind, like. All what 'appened, all them years ago! Ruby's passin'! It's brought it all back. I was at the post office the other day and ..."

"And?" said Reg.

"Well, Enid Fairbanks said Leon Sharpe might be on his way back after what has happened."

"He said, she said! Who knows?" said Reg. Lil moved a pot of partly sprouted bulbs from one side of the windowsill to the other. "These need more light; they're struggling! I'm not looking forward to him coming back. I'd love to see him, mind you, but it won't be a picnic, will it?"

"What won't, what picnic?" said Reg. "Leon?"

"Leon comin' back. It won't be easy for 'im, Ruby gone like that and all. And Edith, well!" Lil sighed as she repositioned the pot of bulbs. "Edith was a lovely little girl, Reg. It were nice for us then, being as we never had our own." She turned from the window to look at her husband of thirty-seven years. His eyes were intently focused on the television screen. It had never bothered him, she thought, not having children. She touched the narrow string of pearls she wore around her neck and recalled her mother's words: "There's none to blame, Lilian. It's God's will." I do have things to be thankful for, she thought. I have got my health, Tilly, my plants, and my bingo, and I've ordered the new slipcovers. I should be grateful, she thought, and supposed that she was.

"Edith were only six when Leon went to Australia. Is that right, Reg? She was six, only six?"

"No, it's two! Rangers two, United four!" he said.

"You're not listenin'," Lil said, pulling at a stray thread on the seam of the curtain. She twisted it around her fingers before snapping it off and resuming her gaze through the window.

"Reg, that dog is back in our garden again. We'll have no tulips this spring." She thumped on the glass pane. "I wouldn't mind a little dog, though," she sighed. "I need something to take me mind off things. It's not the same with a cat, is it? They don't care. I don't think you care about what I'm going through, either, Reg. What if somethin' like what 'appened to Ruby happened to me?" she said softly.

"By gum, this team plays dirty," Reg said, folding his arms and shaking his head with disapproval. From the television, a loud chorus of soccer fans sang "Abide with Me."

Tears began to slide down Lil's cheeks. "That's me favorite hymn," she said, and dabbed at her eyes with a handkerchief she had plucked from her sleeve.

"I don't fancy Liverpool's chances this Saturday. Mind you, it'll be a good match," Reg said. He rubbed his hands together and shifted his bulk to the edge of his chair.

"Fancy," she said, "it's Wednesday already, a week since Ruby ..." Lil bit down on her lower lip. "I never got to pay me respects. Not even flowers. Enid at the post office said it was on Monday—the funeral, I mean. She knows the groundskeeper at the cemetery. How can a funeral be private? I don't understand that. I got me good black coat pressed for winter—you know, the one with the velvet collar?" she said. "I were the only one 'round 'ere she'd talk to. Even afore Edith come along. Always kept to 'erself, did Ruby, but then she had reason to, didn't she? Didn't she, Reg?"

"Fan-bloody-tastic, lads!" cheered Reg. "Great tackle."

"We were all in our twenties back then. I wonder what Leon's like now, Reg."

"What?"

Lil repeated her question.

"Same as us, I 'spect, gettin' on, sixty-ish," he said. "It was a long while back."

"That's right," said Lil, clearly recalling the early spring of 1946. Leon was much younger than his sister, Ruby. Maybe fifteen years, she couldn't quite remember. She could picture him so vividly with Irene. His arm proudly around her slim waist, Irene's dark curls bobbing about her shoulders. Leon introduced Irene as his Irish sweetheart. Lil came to know her as a pleasant young woman with a ready smile and always a friendly greeting.

"Irene is a pretty little thing, isn't she?" Lil had said to Ruby.

"She's another o' them flighty Irish mill girls," Ruby had replied. "They are all sluts, if y'ask me." Lil's thoughts of a blossoming romance between Leon and Irene were soon dispelled as Lil and Reg became aware of a growing discord under the Sharpes' roof. Angry voices were heard through their adjoining kitchen wall. Leon dropped out of the cricket team. Backyard chitchat ceased. Irene dropped out of sight.

"What's up, Leon?" Lil had asked, but her inquiries had been met with a disconsolate shrug.

Lil never forgot the knock on the door and Ruby's grave declaration. "Things 'ave to be said. That Irish lass, I knew she were up to no good. She's in the family way! She's now't but trash! It'll be good riddance to her. I'll be takin' it on meself, the bairn. I'll not be raisin' a bastard, I'll be raisin' a kin. Anyway," she said, "who will take care of me when I'm old? For sure not Leon—he has the brains of an ass! It's all right for you that's wed; you take care of one another. I'm lookin' to the future is all! I'll be gone for a spell. Leon is thinking about a trip to the Isle of Man with his mates. Anyway, I don't want him moping around. Leakey'll keep an eye on things; he has the key. If folks say owt, yer know nowt! What's been said 'ere stays 'ere! Am trustin' you both!"

Lil recalled how Ruby had looked that day, the angry tightness of her face and her unblinking eyes, an image and attitude that Ruby would retain for the rest of her life.

Around four months later, life began to filter back into the Sharpe household. The milkman resumed his delivery. Leon trimmed the front hedge, and a pram appeared in the backyard. Lil took to lingering over the washing line, pegging and re-pegging the same sheets until Ruby eventually appeared, holding the infant.

"Well fancy, is it a—" Lil started to ask.

"Fancy nothing! Her name's Edith! Some'll say am too old to care for a bairn, me being t'other side of forty. They can think what they will," Ruby declared. Stories had drifted around the street. Some said the baby was a war refugee from Europe. The butcher reckoned that the baby's father had been lost in Germany and Ruby Sharpe was mourning his loss. "The war is still on for some," he'd said, "and folks should mind their own business!" As the months passed, rumors subsided and Edith's presence was eventually accepted by the Slattery Street community. Leon assumed the role of a devoted uncle and rejoined the cricket team. Ruby carried out her maternal duties with a tight-lipped intensity.

"Whoa! How's that for a save?" Reg cried, slapping his knee hard. Lil jumped back.

"You startled me, Reg." She crossed her hands across her ample bosom. "I was miles away."

"Where were you this time?" he asked.

"I was just thinking. I never told Ruby about the Christmas cards Irene used to send us. Perhaps I should have said something. I don't know," Lil muttered.

"Daft sods! Kick it!" he yelled as he scratched his belly through an unbuttoned gap in his shirt. "Come on, lads, wake up. Call that soccer?" he said, leaning forward to turn up the volume.

A bus rumbled past the house along the dark street. Lil glanced at the clock on the mantel. "The 9:30 is five minutes late," she said. "Oh, that's right, it's Sunday; they run a bit late on Sundays." Her cheek was pressed against the window as she strained to see beyond her field of vision. The yellow beam of the bus's headlights arced over the butcher's shop and the Red Lion Pub. "Sometimes she gets on the bus at the corner; I think she goes down the back entry. She talks to him, you know—that driver, that dark one. That Paki," Lil said. "I saw her once and she—"

"Who's she, fer cryin' out loud? The cat's mother?" Reg said, giving Lil a sidelong glance.

"Edith, of course."

"*Benny Hill Show* is comin' on now, Lil. You like 'im—come on and sit down."

Lil stayed by the window, running her fingers along the sill. "He's ever so mannerly, Reg, and tall—that driver, I mean." Thursday of last week, her shopping finished, Lil had stopped by the depot for a cup of tea.

"Be with you in a jiff, Lil," said Mary Lacey. "Hang on, the boys are here." Mary smeared lipstick across her already-pink mouth. Lil waited, watching the squad of drivers that hovered around the kiosk.

"Cheers, Mary, ta sweetheart," they chorused. Mary leaned close in to Lil when Saleem approached. "He's a real gentleman, this one," she whispered. As she handed him his tea, her low-necked blouse gaped open. Lil wondered if he noticed the safety pin affixed to Mary's once-white bra strap.

"I am thanking you," Saleem said. "You were here first," he said, beaming down at Lil. She had never seen teeth so white.

"It's fine," she said, blushing, "I'll wait."

"Not bad lookin', is he, for a colored bloke?" Mary said as he walked away. "He can punch my ticket anytime," she cackled. "Wouldn't that set tongues waggin', me steppin' out with a Paki! Eh, you heard about Jimmy and Alice, then? Gettin' hitched? What a do that will be! Slattery Street, has it quieted down, Lil? She has a lot to answer for, that Edith, I reckon." Mary turned to another driver at the counter.

"Hey, sunshine," the driver said, "what's fresh, besides you?"

"Go on with you!" Mary said. They broke into gales of laughter.

Lil stood back. "I'll see yer," she said, and hurried off for her bus. She never received her tea or heard the rest of Mary's story. She just thought of Edith and Ruby all the way home.

"Oops!" Lil said when the cat sprang onto the windowsill. "Reg, has Tilly been out yet?" she said, raising her voice above the canned laughter on the television.

"Not yet," chuckled Reg. Benny Hill was chasing a scantily clad blonde through a park as the credits rolled. "And now for the news," an announcer said, against a background of ceremonious music. "That Thatcher has a face that'd turn milk," said Reg.

"Her dad were only a shopkeeper," Lil said, glancing at the television.

"Her and her posh talk! Sounds like she has like a gob full of plums," Reg said. He turned down the volume.

"I wonder if Edith's packed her job in, Reg."

"Yer doin' too much thinking, and it's none of your business," said Reg.

"Yes it is, Reggie. Leon was your best friend, our friend. We know things."

"I reckon he'll just turn up now the old lady's out of the picture. It'd be grand to see me old mate. Good grief, Lil," said Reg, turning to look at her. "Don't start cryin' again. I could fill buckets from yer weepin' these past days."

"That's cruel," she said. Her chin quivered as she sniffed into her handkerchief.

"Now listen," Reg said, "Edith, poor lass, needs to hear the truth, and I am speaking up when she comes around 'ere, and I know she will. It's only right."

"Poor lass!" Lil cried. "There wasn't much love lost there! I don't think you cared much for Ruby, either, Reg. You weren't neighborly." Lil patted the ridged blue waves of her hair with first one hand and then the other.

"It won't bloody fall off, you know," said Reg.

"What won't?"

"Your hair. For God's sake, sit yourself down."

"Yer don't understand," Lil said, her eyes full of tears. "It's ruined this perm for me, this nasty business. The girls at Hilda's put some extra blue in it, to give me a lift. It doesn't matter now, somehow."

"Am only teasin'; it looks fine. Listen, Lil, Ruby Sharpe never bothered wi' folks. She was a bitter old biddie."

"Don't talk about the dead like that."

"Well, she was. It's over. Done with. You saw the paper. The inquest. Accidental death. That's it. Done with!"

"It's just that, well, I wasn't invited to the inquest yesterday either. No one has asked me anything, except the policeman that day." She fumbled with her handkerchief, looking for a dry spot.

"Not invited, not invited! It wasn't a bloody wake, Lil. You don't get invited to an inquest, for Christ's sake! Come on, cheer up. I'll make us some cocoa, a snack. How's that?" He eased himself up off the chair.

"All right," she said, giving the curtains a final stroke before she sat down.

"Chin up," said Reg. "Princess Di's on the telly again. She's a bonny lass."

"She's a bit thin," said Lil.

"Nah, she looks all right to me. ... Do you want jam on yer crumpets?" Reg shouted from the kitchen.

"Strawberry," she called out.

"Coming up," he said.

15

Cyril Leakey

----

dith yawned and turned to look at the clock on the wall. It registered 8:30 a.m. It was Wednesday morning, two weeks since Ruby's death, when her life had been upended in ways she had never imagined. She let out a sigh of relief that the inquest, which had taken place the day before, was now behind her. She could not remember the questions she had been asked or the faces of her questioners, seated around the big table. She knew, however, that she would never forget the slow, deliberate way the magistrate had removed his glasses, setting them down on the table as he prepared to speak. "Not guilty of culpable neglect," he announced. "No proceedings will be taken." Mavis and Edith had hugged one another awkwardly, having to remain seated. The magistrate closed his file and, with a nod to Edith, left the room. A couple seated behind the women shook their heads. Others stepped aside, their eyes averted as Mavis and Edith were ushered out through a back entrance.

A reporter from the *Bogmire Daily News* was lounging by the gate of Edith's house on their return to Slattery Street later that afternoon. "There is nothing to be said; it's over," Mavis said as she parked the car. "Please leave." The women quickly retreated behind Edith's front door, drew the net curtains across the parlor window, and flopped down on the couch. "Did you see that woman who sat near us?" Edith asked, shaking her head. "As if—"

"Stop, Edith, it's over—the ordeal is over!"

"I know, but …"

"Listen. To change the subject, I have an idea. You know how you told me that every night you seem to hear Ruby, her stick rattling on the bedrail, and you can't sleep?"

"Yep," Edith said. "Ma's gone, dead and buried, and it's as if she is still up there in her room. It's horrible! I hate this house, what happened here. I hate it!"

"You can come back and stay with me, Edith, till you get things sorted out."

"But what if I—"

"Look, you can return here each day, deal with all your stuff—phone calls, et cetera—then just lock up and leave. Reg can keep an eye out for you."

"Oh God! Reg and Lil—I haven't spoken to them yet!"

"All in good time, you will. It makes sense that you need to get away from here. It's, well, creepy!" Easily persuaded, Edith followed Mavis's advice later that evening: she packed a bag and moved in with her.

The next morning, the phone rang, and Edith got out of bed to answer it. It was Mavis. "Hi, Edith, it's me—I'm at work. How are you?"

Edith yawned. "I could be a piece of lost luggage," she said.

"What?"

"Oh nothing, I'm being silly. Yes, I slept, I actually slept," Edith said.

"Good. I didn't wake you, then?"

"Gosh no. I still can't quite believe yesterday, that it is over and done with. Officially, that is. I mean, I'm still, you know, responsible. It's my—"

"Don't be worrying now. Listen, I've found out where that convent is, the Little Sisters, or whatever it was called. It's not a convent anymore, so I don't know whether you want to go up there. I doubt whether there will be any records or information to be had."

"That doesn't matter; I just want to see the place, you know. Just see it, where I was born."

"Fine, I understand. I can easily get a day off. We'll drive up. So you will do it this morning—see Leakey, I mean?"

"I will; I have more than a bone to pick with him. I'll show him everything—the letters, the lot!"

"Don't stand for any blarney from him."

"He had a soft spot for Ruby, I know that for sure," said Edith. "Maybe that's why he's been staying quiet. I just want the truth. Anyway, there's a lot at stake. I mean, where's Leon? What about the house? Who knows anything?"

"I know. I have to go. I'll be late home. Mum's got some errands for me to run."

"Right, see you later, then," said Edith, thinking how cozy the word "Mum" sounded when you owned it. Edith stretched and eased herself off the bed. From the pocket of her dressing gown, she retrieved the photo of her mother and traced her fingers over its surface. "What shall I call you?" she said. "Mum, Ma? No, not Ma; Ruby was Ma. Soon the right word will be on my lips," she said, "and yours when I find you. But I am not sure about Leon. I am not sure who he is, or what he has become." She showered, dressed, had breakfast, and ordered a taxi for Bogmire Centre and Leakey's office.

It was 10 a.m. when she alighted from the taxi in town. She walked past the depot and headed across the Bogmire central shopping area, happy to lose herself in the street crowd. She hurried past the shoe shop where Edwin had worked. Thoughts of him sickened her. Mavis had heard that Edwin and Sybil were traveling around the country with her church choir. A good thing he's away, she thought; he was the last person she wanted to run into. Without him, none of this would have happened, she supposed. Ruby's secrets would have stayed hidden away. But then, Ruby could not have gone on forever, she thought, and recalled the days when she had abandoned hope of anything ever changing. Ruby was gone now, and she still felt guilty. Will I always feel like this? she wondered. "Time heals all wounds," Ruby used to say. I hope so, she thought.

She stopped by the town library, where she made copies of her birth certificate and all the letters and postcards. The quiet ambience of the place soothed her. She sat down and leafed through a copy of *Queen* magazine. On the cover was a photograph of Princess Diana cradling her baby. Funny name for a baby, Harry, she mused. Edith isn't much better, she thought, replacing the magazine on the rack. She checked the contents of her briefcase, and her fingers closed over her mother's photograph in her pocket. "Let's go," she whispered.

Cyril Leakey's single-story office was down a side street, off the main town square. Too many frustrating days had passed since Ruby's funeral, when all efforts to speak with Leakey had proved fruitless. But now, this morning, with the inquest behind her, Edith felt confident. She had not seen or heard from Leakey since the funeral nine days before, and now she was more than ready for some clarification of the mismanaged mess of her life. A brass plate engraved with the words "Cyril Leakey Esq. Solicitor" was affixed to a huge oak-paneled door. She rang the bell before entering a hallway. A large cardboard sign read, "Wait Here." Below it was a diagram of a hand that pointed to several cane chairs lined up against a wall. The hallway was cold; Edith shivered.

"One moment," a woman's voice called out from behind a half-open door. Edith waited several minutes, then pushed the door open. She stood in the doorway. "I'm Edith Sharpe," she said. "We have spoken on the phone."

"Oh, I'm Ada Fitch, Mr. Leakey's secretary," she said, and jumped up from her desk. A sheaf of papers slipped from her hand. "Oh dear, Miss Sharpe. Mr. Leakey is not expecting you. Do you have an appointment?" Ada Fitch looked as Edith had imagined: short and thin with a pinched, pale face.

"Who is it, Miss Fitch?" a male voice drifted out from an adjoining office.

"It's, er, it's Miss Sharpe."

Cyril Leakey's tall frame appeared in the doorway. His mouth dropped open, and his bifocals looked as if they were about to slip off his extensive nose. He looked at Edith and then at the dropped papers that had fanned out across the floor.

"Ah, Miss Sharpe. Ah, well ..." He extended his hand to her. Edith kept her hand in her pocket; the other held on to her briefcase. "Miss Sharpe, I—" he said, his glasses barely holding on. They stared at each other. Finally, he said, "Fetch some tea, Miss Fitch."

"You did not respond to my phone calls," Edith said, after Miss Fitch left.

104

He took several steps backward into his office. Edith followed him. A large oak desk dominated the room. Leather-bound books occupied the shelves of one wall. Framed documents were arranged on another.

"Mr. Leakey, I need information. I know you have avoided me," she said.

"I … well … there seems to have been some misunderstanding," he said.

"There is nothing to misunderstand," said Edith, closing the door behind her. "My needs are simple, Mr. Leakey. It's all here. Here, Mr. Leakey. Look! I need explanations." She placed the birth certificate on the desk, and then propped it up against a large inkwell.

"My dear Miss Sharpe." He coughed noisily and pinched his chin with his thumb and forefinger.

"This was among her belongings," said Edith, "Ruby's belongings." She stepped back from the desk, her hands clasped tightly around her briefcase. She was shaking. "I have letters, photographs. Here!" She patted her briefcase and withdrew all the letters, cards, and photographs. "I know you were involved. You assisted Ruby in all of this. I know the truth. You are mentioned in these letters. I know that Leon Sharpe is my father. Where is he? What happened, Mr. Leakey? I want an explanation for this," she said, pointing to the birth certificate.

"Well, now, I, er—" He drowned out his words with a guttural cough. Covering his mouth with one hand, he swayed forward, grabbing on to the high back of the wooden desk chair. "I am afraid it was necessary to …"

"To what?"

"I didn't know how … I was afraid that, well, I couldn't begin to explain—" There was a knock on the door. Miss Fitch entered, carrying a tray with a pot of tea, a jug, cups, and saucers. She positioned the tray at one end of the large desk and gave Edith a consolatory look. "Here we are, dear," she said, as if a cup of tea would diffuse the tension. "The milk isn't fresh," she said, pointing to the jug on the tray, "but I'm sure it will suffice."

"Ah!" Leakey shuffled his feet as if to sit down but remained standing, bent over like a wind-licked tree. Edith looked at the old man. There was perspiration on his forehead and around his blue lips. She wondered if she had said too much too soon. His eyes did not appear to focus on anything, vacant sockets in a gray face. She wondered how old he was, because at that moment he seemed truly ancient. Stay calm, she told herself, let him have his say.

The nasal whistle of Leakey's breathing competed with the tick of the pendulum clock on the wall. Miss Fitch stood silently behind her stooped boss, clasping and unclasping her hands. Why doesn't he say something? Edith thought. Why doesn't she say something? Edith wanted to shout at them both but thought better of it and followed the shadowed movement of traffic as it whooshed past the frosted glass windows. Miss Fitch tinkered with the teaspoons. This is a room full of secrets, she thought. Was this the desk around which Ruby and Leakey had sat and defined my future thirty-six years ago? Or did they huddle in the parlor at Slattery Street? What say did Leon have? And Irene, my mother—was she heard, or was she hustled away, to be duly silenced and then dispatched to Ireland? Edith wanted to knock the tea tray off the desk. She wanted to shock into action this dithering old man before her.

"Oh, silly me," said Miss Fitch. "I forgot the biscuits."

"The file, Ada. Fetch the file."

"Of course," she said. A draft from the door caused the birth certificate to waft across the desk. Edith grabbed it.

"My dear child," said Leakey, slithering down into his chair.

"I am not your dear child," said Edith. She held up her mother's photograph in front of him. "I am her dear child. Her child. Irene. My mother!" she said slowly. "I want to know what happened to her. I fully intend to find her, and Leon, my father." Bolstered by the strength of her statements, Edith had stopped shaking. Miss Fitch returned and placed a plate of biscuits on the tray and a manila folder on the desk.

"I'm afraid I do not know the whereabouts of Miss—er—that would be Monahan. If it's the money ... ," he said, opening the folder.

"I am not here about money," said Edith. "I'm here for the truth. I cannot ask Ruby, now, can I? And Leon, heaven knows where he is. So explain all this to me, Mr. Leakey, please." She pointed to the certificate. "Tell me how I can make some sense of it."

Cyril Leakey raised his hands and turned his palms upward in a defeated gesture. "Some things are better left as is," he said.

"Things!" said Edith. "This!" She picked a teaspoon up off the tray and then dropped it with a clatter. "And this," she picked up the inkwell. "These are things, Mr. Leakey. These are things!" The inkwell felt potent in her hand, and the urge to hurl it was tempting. She set it down with a thud. "The things you speak of, Mr. Leakey, are lives." She leaned across the desk. "Lives!"

He took a handkerchief from his pocket and dabbed at his forehead. "The young Irish girl, she was more than adequately provided for."

"She!" said Edith, "she!"

"Shall I fetch more?" said Miss Fitch. Leakey raised an arm and flicked his hand in a dismissive gesture. Miss Fitch retreated.

"Why the lies?" Edith asked.

"Ruby wanted it that way. It was a difficult time. She had ambitious plans for Leon. She invested in a business for him. Hardware. That sort of thing." Leakey shook his head and stared out the window.

"Please, go on," said Edith.

"I was compelled to honor Ruby's requests. She wanted nothing to stand in Leon's way. Marriage for him, she insisted, was out of the question. Your grandparents' wealthy employers had taken good care of Ruby financially; you do know that."

"I had some idea, yes."

"Ruby threatened to withhold Leon's inheritance if he didn't comply with her wishes. Bogmire was a smaller community then, Miss Sharpe, and the family reputation was at stake. Ruby arranged for the confinement. The nuns cared for everything at the convent. It was Ruby's decision to raise you as her own. That was her decision, and hers only. The young woman returned to Ireland—Dublin, I think."

Leakey lowered his head. "There you have it. I don't know what else I can tell you. Ruby and Leon fought like cat and dog for years after that. His business was sold at a loss. She only wanted the best for him."

"And what about me?" Edith said softly. "Did any of you think about that?"

"Times were hard after the war," Leakey said. "Opportunities were scarce." Edith wondered what the war had to do with her birth, other than the myth forged that her father was a soldier missing in action. As she listened to Leakey's emotionless account, one thing was apparent: that it was up to her to repair what had been broken.

"Thank you," Edith said. She felt weak all of a sudden. She closed her eyes, and an image flashed before her—Ruby's face, determined and defiant. "Miss Sharpe, are you all right?" Edith coughed and opened her eyes. Miss Fitch was waving a bottle of smelling salts under her nose. "Miss Sharpe?"

"Yes, yes, thank you, I'm fine. I'm sorry, I just need some air."

Cyril Leakey spread his hands out on the desk. "There is something else, perhaps, that you may as well know, Miss Sharpe. I was extremely fond of your moth—Ruby. We were friends. A little more than friends, but alas, it wasn't meant to be." He stared into his teacup. "I was compelled to honor her wishes. I am a man of my word," he said.

"Sugar in your tea, Miss Sharpe?" said Ada Fitch.

"Thanks," said Edith.

"There you go, dear. It needs a stir."

Edith looked at the curdled globs of milk floating on the surface of the amber liquid. Leakey dipped a biscuit in his tea and placed it in his mouth before swallowing it with a gulp.

"I have to leave now," Edith blurted out. "It's all about my rightful family, Mr. Leakey. Don't you understand?" He looked at her with an expression of helplessness. Miss Fitch shrugged her thin shoulders.

"I must leave, but before I do, I want Leon's address," Edith said. "I want all the information you have about him."

"Of course. I informed Mr. Sharpe—Leon—by letter when news of Ruby's death reached me."

"'Reached you'? When was that, then?"

"Oh, I can't say exactly … perhaps, er, Miss Fitch?"

"It was the next day, the newspaper report, Mr. Leakey."

"Ah yes, well, following up on the letter we sent, we received a call. Miss Fitch handled the matter."

"I spoke with a young lady in Australia—a secretary, I believe. It was just last Monday," said Miss Fitch. "The overseas post takes a while, you see. She told me that Mr. Sharpe had already left Australia and was on his way here to Bogmire. I asked her where he would be residing on arrival. She said she couldn't tell me that."

Cyril Leakey's body unfolded slowly as he rose from his chair. "Rest assured, Miss Sharpe, the will shall be dealt with accordingly." Edith hesitated before shaking the cold hand he offered. She gathered up the letters, photographs, and birth certificate and put them in her briefcase. Her fingers closed over her mother's photograph, now back in her pocket.

"I am so sorry for all of this, Miss Sharpe," Ada Fitch whispered to her at the door. "Cyril—er, Mr. Leakey—he should have retired. But he is so very good at what he does, you see. People rely on him." She handed Edith a slip of paper with a phone number and an Australian address on it. "Good luck," Miss Fitch said.

"Thank you," said Edith, "I'll need it." She placed the slip of paper in her pocket alongside her mother's photograph.

16

Storm

The wind rumbled and the rain slashed around Edith's house. She watched the 6 p.m. news, which was followed by the weather forecast of storm conditions, heavy rain, and gale-force winds. Her repeated calls for a taxi remained unanswered. When she attempted to phone Mavis to tell her that she would be late, there was a jarring noise on the line, interrupted by an operator who advised her to try again later.

The thought of staying tonight in the Slattery Street house horrified Edith. She didn't belong here anymore. She didn't know where she belonged, but it wasn't here. She was happy staying with Mavis. The arrangement worked well, even though Mavis's flat was small. It was adequate.

It had been a week since Edith's initial visit with Leakey, a week that had consumed her with the tiresome aftermath of Ruby's death. Documents were signed; forms were filled out; and sympathies were offered, some sincere and some disguising curiosity, which Edith accepted gracefully. All of three weeks had now passed since Ruby's demise, that fateful Tuesday. Gossip had subsided; rumors were slowly evaporating. Depot tongues now wagged with exuberant chatter of Jimmy and Alice's forthcoming wedding, along with the anticipation of the new streamlined transport center.

Edith listened to the wind whistling down the chimney. She shivered and switched on the electric fire in the parlor. Maybe I should call on Lil and Reg next door, she thought, but decided it wasn't a good idea.

Lil would be beside herself with this storm; now was not the time. To-morrow I'll call on them, she promised herself, and questioned, not for the first time, why she had avoided them these three weeks since Ruby's death. What am I frightened of? What do I have to lose now? Nothing. They could help me. They knew Irene, and they may know where she is.

I could give it all up, I suppose, Edith thought, this searching. After all, if my mother really wanted to find me, wouldn't she have done that already? She had heard of organizations that helped people to find people. I could walk away from Bogmire, she thought. Begin a new life. Sell this house, now that I know it is mine to sell. The call from Cyril Leakey summoning her to his office that morning had surprised her, as had the news she received.

He stood before her, documents quivering in his hands. "Probate is settled, Miss Sharpe," he said. "It appears the house is to be yours, to do with as you wish. You are the sole beneficiary of Ruby's—Miss Sharpe's—estate." He let out a deep sigh and looked out the window. "There is considerable cash, bonds, and p—" Edith thought he said "property" when his voice trailed off into a nasal groan. "It's all here." He tapped the file on his desk with his bony fingers. His words were cloaked in sadness, as if he were relinquishing a personal possession. "The affection I had for your mother is something I will always cherish," he said. "Ruby was astute," he said, "no less a wealthy woman."

He waffled on about character and loyalty. She heard Ruby's voice loud and clear, her mind racing back to her childhood. "There is no money for that sort of thing, my girl!" They were the sorts of things any little girl reasonably felt was her due. A visit to the circus, clothes for her doll. "Mr. Leakey, I had no idea! Ma was so, well—" She stopped. She wasn't about to launch into memories of Ruby's frugality with him or Miss Fitch, who was fluttering in and out of the room like a trapped moth.

"There you have it, Miss Sharpe." He extended his hand. "As you may or may not know, Mr. Leon Sharpe is now residing temporarily at the Majestic Hotel."

"No, I didn't know that he had actually arrived here," she said. Her head was spinning.

"We will be in touch further," he said.

"Yes."

Now, as she sat in the front parlor, rain slamming on the windows outside, she was still reeling from the news and the knowledge that Leon was close by. Was he aware of Ruby's estate? Does he need money? No, she thought, not if he is staying at the Majestic, the town's premier hotel. The fact that Ruby had been wealthy seemed implausible, and that she, Edith, was the recipient of that wealth was incredible. Affection—that was the word Leakey had used; it was a word she had never associated with Ruby. Still, Edith thought, she fed and clothed me. Maybe she did love me somehow, beneath that impervious skin of hers. I don't think I ever loved her—respect, perhaps, but not love. It wasn't for want of trying! She remembered how as a young teenager she'd wished that Ruby was pretty and the kind of mother who liked to wear high heels and lipstick.

Why was Leon really here? Maybe he is curious and simply needs to see who I am, she thought. See what I have become, whatever that is. Still, she thought, he hasn't contacted me. Will I phone him? If I do, what should I say? You betrayed me and I'm sorry your sister has died. Do I give him a piece of my mind? Tell him what I think? How can I do that if I don't know what I think? I don't have to do anything I don't want to, she thought, and the prospect of starting afresh gathered appeal. I could go abroad; Mavis has a brother in Canada somewhere. I could meet up with his family. It would be a start.

She redialed Mavis's number, only to be told by an operator that some lines were still being repaired. She poured herself a whisky, turned on the television, and began to watch a drama about a philandering football coach. All the while, her mind kept flipping back to Leakey, to Leon, and to the hope that Lil and Reg would be happy to see her tomorrow. Throughout the evening, the storm showed no signs of abating, and taxis were still unobtainable. Around 9 p.m., she poured herself a second drink. There was a distant crack of thunder. I should make a dash for it and head for the bus stop, she thought, finishing her drink. She turned off the television; grabbed her bag, coat, and umbrella; locked the doors; switched off the lights; and headed off.

Outside, the wind pushed and pulled her in all directions. Branches and bits of slate from roofs were littered about the deserted street. She failed to dodge the wings of water that came from a passing car. She pulled the hood of her raincoat around her face, leaned against the metal pole of the bus stop, and waited, the rain stinging her cheeks. After about ten minutes, the No. 9 arrived. Bedraggled and soaked, she boarded the bus, surprised to see that Saleem was the driver. "Good evening, you are in storm," he said. "It is very bad raining."

"Yes, yes," she said as she struggled with her umbrella. The wind had buckled the spines, and it would not collapse.

"Please, I am helping you," he said.

"Thank you." She handed it to him.

"You are changing times, yes?" he said.

"I no longer work at Shield," said Edith. "I am taking a br—" She stopped. Her doings were not his business. Then she realized that he was only being polite and friendly. He corrected the umbrella, folded it, and gave it back to her.

"I am surprising to be seeing you," he said, and smiled.

"Oh, yes, well, I'm staying with a friend," she said, watching his fingers curl over the gear lever.

The bus started up. Edith felt conspicuous and craved the camouflage of more passengers. There was one other person on the bus, a man who whistled incessantly while staring out the window. She took a seat some rows behind him. After removing her rain hat, she shook her head, allowing her dark curls to fall about her shoulders. She glanced up at the rearview mirror and felt a flush rise in her cheeks as Saleem's eyes met hers. She put a cool hand to her forehead, and it felt hot. It must be the whisky, she thought.

The bus rumbled slowly down the deserted streets. Heavy rain danced on the roof and streaked across the windows. The bus paused briefly at the stops and then moved on; there were no passengers to be seen. She wished she had something to read, something to distract her. I'm flirting with him, she thought, and he with me. What's the harm of it? she concluded. Hadn't she engaged in and savored such exchanges en route to work each morning?

The wind's intensity seemed to have increased when they finally reached the depot. Signs had blown loose; rubbish cans and lids had toppled and were rolling about. The bus eased into the parking bay. It was 10 p.m. "End of the road! See yer," said the whistling passenger. Edith could have simply followed him out but hesitated; there were no taxis. The place was deserted.

"You are not wanting to be in rain," Saleem said.

"No, I need a taxi."

"They are not here." He stood to face her. He was broader and taller than she realized. "I am not wanting you to be cold." He pulled on the lever that closed the bus door. He cranked a handle above the windscreen, and a sign rolled into place. It read, "Not in Service."

"Please," he said, "you are to be knowing my name. I am Saleem." He extended his hand.

"I'm Edith," she laughed, and shook his warm hand. Their hands remained clasped as she chattered on about needing to get to Mavis's house. He looked out the window. "Do not worry—I can be taking you."

"But—"

"Please, I drive van, I have time," he said.

"Well, thank you. I don't know how else I—"

"I live just myself, please not worry," he said. The pressure of his hand on her elbow felt firm as they stepped out into the rain. The small van was parked down an alley behind the depot. "I soon make warm for us," he said, as she climbed inside the vehicle. The interior of the van smelled of damp earth. A figurine with arms in a prayer position dangled from the mirror. He drove confidently. The noisy engine and the click-clack of the windscreen wipers prevented any meaningful conversation. Edith shouted out directions while the praying figure swung to and fro as they rattled around corners.

"I am so grateful to you," Edith said when he drew up outside Mavis's flat.

"I am being grateful to you," he said.

"Thank you again," she said, reaching for her umbrella and handbag. "You are living here now?"

"I'm staying with a friend, just for a while. Things have been, rather, er, upsetting. I mean, er, unsettled." She stared down at her knees, aware of her stumbling words. "I no longer work … things have changed. Family things."

"Ah, family," he said. "My family, they are in Pakistan. My mother, she … but you are not wanting to hear of my—"

"Please," she said, and touched his hand, "go on."

"You are not in hurry?"

"Not really," she said.

"My mother, she is very, very sick. The doctors say, unless … ," he turned his head away from her. "She is to be needing money for treatments. You are kind, Edit, to be listening." He took her hands in his. "Being together is to be knowing us," he said. There were tears in his eyes.

"Knowing one another," she corrected. "It's Edith, like *the*."

"Edith," he said, and took a white handkerchief from his pocket to dab at his eyes. "Forgive, please." He rested a hand on her knee. "My mother, she …"

"Oh, I do understand," Edith said, "I do."

"You are being warm now?"

"Yes, I am, and I don't know what I would have done. Thanks for your trouble," she said. "This is not the easiest place to get to at night."

"I am not being troubled," he said. "Tell me, am I not to be seeing you on my bus?"

"Well—oops! There's water on my arm from the window—it's leaking!"

"It is loose; I close again," he said, and reached across her to tug at the handle. She felt the full pressure of his body across hers. She couldn't move, and didn't know whether she wanted to, when his lips brushed against her neck. Oh my God, she thought. She was lightheaded, and it felt as if his whole body were caressing her. "We are the only two people on earth," he murmured as his mouth brushed lightly across her cheek.

"Er, please," she heard herself say. What am I doing? she thought. His hand that had rested on her knee was now firmly on her thigh. She was fully aware of the weight of him and uncomfortably aware of the reaching pressure of his fingers pulling at her coat and her skirt. "Stop!" she

115

said, quickly regaining her senses. "Stop!" Her knee was jammed hard against the door. "My knee, please, please! Get off me."

"You are wanting me," he said. She turned her head away from him.

"No," she said, "no." He pushed her skirt above her knees. His other hand was fumbling with his trousers. "Stop, now!" Her voice came out as a breathless shriek. She felt sick and could taste the whisky in the back of her throat.

"You are wanting, you are wanting," he said with a sneer.

"No," she said, "no!"

"You will have me," he said. No, I won't, she thought, and managed to slide her hand down between her seat and the door.

"I am having you, you are needing. You are giving to me now," he said angrily.

There was barely enough room to move her fingers as she felt for the metal door handle. It didn't take much, and the door flew open. Her bag and umbrella fell out onto the wet street. She planted her foot down hard on the pavement and pushed at him with both of her hands until her other leg was free.

"Shit," she said, "how could you, how could you think of … ?" He glowered at her before maneuvering back into his seat, his unblinking eyes glinting in the dark.

"You are beetch," he said, "all same!" He smoothed back his hair and fastened up his trousers.

"Edith! Edith!" She turned to see Mavis running from her front gate. "Jesus Christ! What the—?" Mavis picked up the bag and umbrella. "I saw the van parked, and I waited. I—who the heck is this? Look at you! Did he hurt you? For God's sake!"

"I got a lift; there were no taxis. It's all right," said Edith. "I'm all right, really."

"You women are like leeches on my skin!" Saleem yelled from the van. "You suck my blood and then—"

"Suck you!" Mavis yelled, slamming the van door. "Sod off, get the hell out!"

"Beetch," mouthed Saleem as he turned on the ignition. The van coughed to a start and rattled off down the street. "I'll get his number," said Mavis, "damn him!"

"No, let him go. I'm all right, really."

Mavis put her arm around Edith. "Thank God you are safe. Come," she said, "let's get inside." She guided Edith through the front gate and into the house. "Who the hell was that, Edith?"

"He's the driver, the Pakistani from the No. 9 I get every morning. Saleem is his name. I thought he was, well, you know, okay."

She sat on the couch, and Mavis brought her a cup of tea. "I tried to ring you," said Mavis.

"Me too," Edith said. "I couldn't get through. I just decided to hell with it and got the bus."

"I'll pour us a brandy," Mavis said. "You need it, love."

"What a night! I learned my lesson," Edith said as Mavis wrapped a blanket around her shoulders, tucking another around her knees.

"And what's that?"

"Don't take chances. Honestly, I thought he was charming. He turned into this, well, beast!"

Mavis took a sip of brandy and raised her eyebrows. "Men," she said, "they can turn on a dime, as the Yanks say. Believe me, I know. My ex, well, I've mentioned him before. 'He's the sweetest thing this side of heaven,' my mother would say. She didn't know half! Neither did I till I opened my eyes. I followed him one day. Into the back door of the Black Bull Pub he went. I saw them, him and the barmaid. Some men, if you open the door a smidgeon, they are in there like a forest fire! Don't ever judge a book by its cover. That is all I'm saying. Come on," she said, "sip on the brandy. Use two hands—you are shaking and shivering."

"I—I suppose I sort of invited it. I did get in his car, but still!" Edith took a sip of the brandy. "I sort of had a plan. I was going to ram my umbrella into him if the door didn't work. It's funny, I wasn't really that scared somehow, at the time. Maybe because of all the other stuff that's gone on today." She told Mavis about the will and Leon. "God," said Edith, "what if I run into Saleem at the depot?"

"The heck with him—who cares?" said Mavis.

"I don't, really. What a nasty piece of work he turned out to be."

17

Reparation

----

*A*fter her experience with Saleem, Edith struggled through a restless night. I'm partly to blame, she thought; still, he is the one who behaved badly. All night long she visualized his dark eyes and heard his threatening voice. She had dreamt that she was in a car crash. There was thunder and lightning. She was in a hospital where an emaciated Leakey was a fellow patient until she woke up perspiring and relieved to hear Mavis pottering about the kitchen.

Over breakfast they talked about what had happened. "I'm kind of proud of myself," Edith said, "for avoiding a worse scenario! I did what I needed to do, for once." Mavis left for work as Edith dressed and showered. She resolved to try to push all thoughts of Saleem and the previous night to the back of her mind. She had enough to think about now, with her forthcoming visit to Lil and Reg.

Edith arrived at the depot at about 11 a.m. She cast her eyes about the place. Drivers hovered around Mary's tea kiosk and Jimmy's newsstand. She boarded the No. 9 and handed her fare to a driver she thankfully had never seen before. She got off the bus at the corner, feeling that the short walk to her house would be calming. A breeze had nudged away the few remaining rain clouds. Mounds of wet leaves and twigs from the storm were lodged in the gutters. A ripped piece of awning flapped noisily above the fish and chips shop window. A dented metal sign was propped against a lamppost. The butcher stood in the doorway of his shop, "Mornin', Edith," he said. "This place got clobbered. That storm had some clout last night. Can't complain, though—we're still in one piece," he laughed.

"That's right," said Edith, and thought, thank God, so am I.

She turned the key to open her front door. I wonder what this house would fetch on the market, she thought. She couldn't remember the last time a house had sold on Slattery Street. People just stay here and die here, she thought. "Ugh," she recoiled, as she entered the small, narrow hallway. The smell of disinfectant still drifted down from upstairs, a rank reminder that something bad had happened here. The house felt even smaller, as if it were shrinking by degrees with each subsequent visit. She walked through the kitchen, opened the door, and stepped out into the backyard. The air smelled clean, and the sun was gathering strength, promising a nice day after a long stretch of relentless rain. Birds squabbled in the sycamore tree, and she could hear Lil busying about in her yard.

"That rain battered me tulips," said Lil.

"These drains are full o' leaves," said Reg.

"I'll check the oven," said Lil. A door closed.

"I'll be there in a jiffy," Reg called.

There is no better time than this, thought Edith. Since Ruby's death, she was uneasy with the growing silence that had formed between them. Edith would catch herself looking out for Lil's furtive glances. Parlor curtains would be hastily drawn, eyes quickly averted. What had they deduced about me, and the mess of Ruby's death? she wondered. She didn't blame them for thinking she was uncaring or ungrateful. They needed an explanation. Lil and Reg need my truth, and I theirs, she thought. Whom had they supported back then when she was born? Was it possible that they had simply turned their backs and closed their eyes and ears? Had Ruby or Leon confided in them? Was her father, Leon, so weak that he dared not oppose Ruby? Had her mother, Irene, simply fled? There was only one way to find out.

She closed the kitchen door and went back into the house. She placed her birth certificate and photographs in her pocket. Here goes, she thought, and walked slowly up the Palethorpes' path, which divided their neat patch of garden. She rang the doorbell. On the porch step, a crate of empty milk bottles sparkled in the sun. Tilly the cat appeared from nowhere and pressed her warm body against Edith's legs.

Amplified voices alternating with blasts of music came from a television somewhere. Edith rang the bell a second time.

"I'll get it!" she heard Lil shout. The door opened halfway, releasing a smell of fresh baking. "Oh, oh my. Edith. It's you," said Lil, peering out. She stepped back, opening the door a little farther. The cat meowed and shot past Lil down the hallway.

"Hello, Lil. How are you?"

Lil stared at Edith. Smudges of flour adorned her flushed cheeks. "Oh, good, we're good. How are you, Edith?"

"I'm fine. Thanks."

"Reg! Reg! It's Edith!" Lil called out. "I was goin' to come round, Edith, I really was. I was wonderin' how you were gettin' on. It's just that, well, things, the funeral." Lil removed a folded tea towel from her apron pocket. She opened it, refolded it, and then placed it back in the pocket.

"I ... Reg!" she called. "It's Edith!"

"I'm 'ere, I can hear yer." A smiling Reg ambled up to the door. "Hello, Edith, luv—nice to see yer. Come in, for 'eaven's sake." He opened the door wide and took hold of Lil's hand, gently drawing her to one side. "It's fine, Lilian, it's okay," he said in a low voice. Then he turned to Edith. "Come on in, Edith," he said. She followed them into their front parlor. Tilly had settled on the windowsill.

"'Ave a seat," Reg said.

"Yes, 'ave a seat," said Lil.

"It smells wonderful in here," said Edith, and sat down.

"It's Wednesday—she bakes on Wednesdays," Reg said in a voice loud enough to be heard over the television. "She likes this program," he said, nodding at the television screen. A fast-talking chef was breaking eggs with one hand into a bowl.

"He's ever so clever," Lil said, her lips quivering. "If I'm quick, I can write them recipes down." She removed the tea towel from her pocket and began squeezing and rotating it in her hands. "Don't know how he does it," she said.

Reg touched Lil's elbow. "Switch it off now, luv, the telly," he said.

"Yes, right, I'll, er—tea, I'll get the pot." Lil bustled out of the room.

"Really, I don't need—" Edith protested.

"No, it's no trouble," Reg said. "Kettle's always on. She'll just be brewing it." Edith could hear a tap running and pots clattering in the kitchen.

"I were checking out the storm damage," Reg said. "It was bad last night."

"Reg, I am really here to—"

"You're in one piece, are yer?" he asked.

"More or less, thanks," she said. "I just came to—"

"It's fine, Edith. You don't have to say anything; we are glad you're 'ere, lass. Aren't we?" he said to Lil, who had returned with a tea tray that she set down on a small table.

"We are, we are, yes. Yer lookin' well." Lil nodded and sat down. "Help yourself, Edith, when yer ready."

"Thanks. Look, I'll just say it," Edith said. "I am really here to see you both because—because—I'm so sorry. About everything, everything that has happened."

"As are we, luv, as are we," Reg said. "We weren't much help to you, Lil and me. It happened so sudden-like. She has passed on, Ruby. We are over it now—the shock, so to speak."

"I want to explain things," said Edith. "I'll get to the point. I never intended to leave her alone that day. It was a mistake. I am so ashamed of what you must think of me. I regret—"

"It's all right, lass," said Reg, "we both know better than to think it was your fault. It was an accident." Reg glanced at Lil.

"Don't mind me," said Lil, dabbing at her eyes with the corner of her apron. "We were so worried about you, Edith. Am just pleased to see you."

Edith explained to them the circumstances that had led up to Ruby's death. They listened attentively. She spoke of the inquest and impressed upon them that even though a verdict of accidental death had been declared, it did not excuse her behavior. For that, she was and always would be thoroughly ashamed, she told them. She went on to explain her absence and her reasons for staying with Mavis. I didn't ever belong in the house next door, she wanted to say. She belonged with her mother, Irene, in her house. But the words seemed to stick in her throat, and she felt one warm tear follow another as they slid down her cheeks.

"I hope you can both understand," she said, "how sorry I am that ..."
Her tears flowed freely now. "It happened in an awful way. I mean, this
isn't coming out the way I meant it to. I—"

"It hasn't been easy for you, has it?" said Reg.

"No, no, I just seemed to shut down." Lil handed Edith a tissue, and
she blew her nose hard into it. "I couldn't, I couldn't think straight
until—"

"It happened. It was nobody's fault," he said.

Lil held her head to one side and folded her arms across her chest.
"Reg is right," she said. "Reg is right. It's not your fault, Edith; you are
not to blame."

"You have both always been so kind to me," Edith said. She wiped her
tears and looked at their faces. They were Bogmire faces, she thought,
faces that conveyed a simple acceptance of their lot in life. It was as if she
were realizing for the first time that Reg and Lil had always been here,
threaded through her life, safely holding it together. How easily she had
taken them for granted—their unfailing recognition of her birthdays,
gifts at Christmas, praise for her achievements when Ruby had offered
so little.

"Thank you both," she said.

Lil glanced at the envelope in Edith's hand.

"There is something else," Edith said. "This was among her things."
She took the birth certificate from its envelope and unfolded it. "You
both may know about this." She handed it to Reg.

His eyes lingered up and down the page. He shook his head. "Bless
you, Edith," he said, and wiped his eyes with the back of his hand. "Bless
you." He handed it to Lil.

"Upon my soul," Lil whispered, holding the certificate out at arm's
length.

"I'll get yer glasses," said Reg.

"There's no need," Lil said, "I can see all I need to see. Ruby should
have told you. She should 'ave. We should 'ave." Tears trailed down Lil's
cheeks. Edith went over to the window. She stroked Tilly's arched back
and gazed out beyond the privet hedge at the endless flow of traffic as
she felt some of the weight of the past weeks beginning to lift.

"Here, give the certificate to me, Lilian, luv. You'll muck it up with them tears," Reg said quietly.

He turned to Edith and said, "We are both so sorry. We knew all about it, this." He held up the birth certificate. "We felt it wasn't our place to say anything back then. 'It's over and done with,' Leon told me, 'Irene's gone.' He was brokenhearted. Hard to see a bloke like that." Reg shook his head and stared at the carpet.

"Go on, Reg," Lil said, "tell her."

"I will, Lil. We lost the darts final that week. I'll never forget it. Then, out of the blue, Ruby said she was going off to visit a cousin in Scotland. Gone for ages, she was."

"She never had no cousin," said Lil, "it were all lies. You were about three weeks old when she brought you home from the convent. The convent was up north, Little Sisters of the Poor. You were beautiful, Edith. I'll never forget yer little fingers—so tiny, nails like pink seashells."

"Go on, you tell her," said Reg, "all of it."

"Well, it was then, she told us the truth. 'My stupid brother, Leon, got that floozie Irene pregnant,' she says to us. 'I'm keeping the baby; it's all arranged,' she said. 'Irene has been sent back to Ireland, where she belongs. That girl wasn't fit to be a mother. As far as you or anybody else is concerned, I'm a war widow left with a child to raise,' she said. We were shocked, weren't we, Reg?"

"We were," said Reg. "I said to Ruby, 'What about Leon? He's the rightful dad, when all is said and done.' 'It will be Uncle Leon from now on,' she said. 'He'd never make a proper father, anyway. He hasn't a lick o' sense!' She made us promise not to say anything. We promised."

"We never said anything to nobody!" said Lil as she shook her head. "There were a lot of babies around after the war. It didn't look out of the ordinary. There were a lot of lads never made it back home."

"It caused a bit of a stir in Slattery Street," Reg said. "Ruby looked a bit long in the tooth to be pushin' a pram. Things settled, though. Folks minded their own business."

"Ruby never had much to do with anyone anyway, always kept to herself," said Lil. "We never saw Irene again. She was so lovely. She sent us Christmas cards for a while, but ..." Lil's voice trailed off. "If only it could have been different, normal-like." Lil wiped away her tears and sniffed. "I've kept all of them, the cards. That's the way I am—I keep things, don't I, Reg?"

"That's right, she hangs on to everything."

"We're ever so sorry, Edith," said Lil. "Whatever must you think of us, telling you all this?"

"You did what you thought was right," said Edith.

"I reckon Leon was always scared of Ruby back then," Reg said. "You were about six, Edith, when they had the big row. 'Can't take it no more,' Leon said. Packed his bags and left. Just like that."

"Remember, Reg," said Lil, "how Ruby would put the pram in the backyard, never out front? I would hear yer cooing, Edith." A smile crossed Lil's face. "When Ruby was busy inside, I would look down from our back bedroom window. Leon would be out there cooing back to yer, fairly beaming, bless him. He was ever so proud." Lil's chin quivered; she crossed her arms and grasped her dimpled elbows. "We knew it would all come out somehow. When she passed on. The truth, I mean. I'm so sorry."

"We were going to say something after the funeral, we really were," Reg said. "Time just passed by and, well ..."

"Can you ever forgive us, Edith? How can we help you?" Lil held out her arms.

"You already have," Edith said as she sank into Lil's soft body. The women hugged and sobbed, releasing themselves into the warm comfort of each other. "I hugged you like this when you were a little girl," Lil said. She wiped her eyes and picked up the teapot. "I think we need a fresh one," she said.

"Please, promise me something, both of you?" said Edith.

"What's that?" said Reg.

"No more apologizing. The truth is, no one should have to die the way Ruby did. However, they say she was lucky. That she didn't suffer. That she—"

"Suffer!" said Lil in a loud voice. She placed the teapot back hard on the table. "Oh no!" Lil said. "She wouldn't suffer, not that one, not Ruby Sharpe. God help us! It was others who suffered—Irene, Leon, and you,

Edith, bless yer heart."

"Now, then, Lilian, don't go getting upset again," Reg said.

"I 'ave to say it, Reg; let me get it out of me system. I'm sorry, Edith, but she dug her own grave. She treated you like dirt from when you was little, and anyone else who offered her a bit o' kindness. We let you down, Edith, we let you down. It's the truth! Ruby appreciated nothing! There, I've said it. And you, Reginald Palethorpe, close yer mouth—you'll be catchin' flies if yer not careful." Lil picked up the teapot and went into the kitchen.

"No, you didn't let me down," Edith called after her. "You did what Ruby asked; you obeyed her. We all did."

"Whew!" said Reg. "I didn't see that coming. You know, Edith, Lilian cried for near on two weeks after it happened. It wasn't for Ruby; it was for you. She was worried about you. She always has been."

"I understand now," she said, "I do."

Lil returned with a fresh pot of tea and a plate of scones. "I've composed meself," she said with a big sniff. "But I meant what I said."

"I'm sure you did," said Reg.

"I intend to find her—Irene, my mother," said Edith. "And I have to see Leon. He is my father, after all!"

"Whatever we can do, we want to help you, Edith," Reg said.

"To be honest, Reg, I am scared about seeing Leon. I know he's staying in town. Leakey told me that much."

"Don't be worryin', Edith. I can vouch for him, cross me heart. He's a good man, he is."

"Have you seen him yet?"

"Not yet, but I'll be seeing him soon."

"What if—"

"What if nuthin'! It will be fine."

"But—"

"Here, 'ave a scone, Edith, they're warm," Lil said. "Help yourself to butter. Reg, be a love and fetch the jam."

"Right," Reg said, and went off to the kitchen.

"I'll go through those cards Irene sent," said Lil. "Who knows, Edith, we might just track her down. It were like a scab on me mind all them years, knowin' the truth," Lil said as she poured the tea. "I knew if I picked at it, it would start bleeding, and that would do nobody any good. But now it's a fresh start. And it's healin' already. I know it."

"I know it, too," said Edith.

"I'm sorry for what you had to go through," Lil said, "Ruby were that mean! I felt so helpless."

"Lil, what choice did you have? You did your best."

"I suppose," she said. "Come on, eat your scone, Edith—there's plenty more where they come from. Reg!" she called out to her husband. "He'll never find the jam; he never does. Men! They are all the same, eh?"

18

Leon

----

il bustled about her kitchen. "You should have told Leon to wear something special," she said to Reg, "so you'd know who he was. People change after thirty years. He could be bent over and bald! We all get a bit bent over when we get old."

"Nah," said Reg, "it'll be great to see him, talk about the old days. We were a force to be reckoned with on that cricket field—me, Leon, and Jimmy."

"I wish I were coming with you," Lil said. "I'd love to see him."

"First things first, luv," Reg said as he kissed her good-bye.

"Right," Lil said, "good things come to them that wait!"

Reg welcomed Lil's optimism after the dark days since Ruby's death. Lil's headaches and tears had been trying. He had grown tired of running the errands and doing the ironing. "I'm so on edge!" Lil had said. "When I iron, the heat sets me head off!" He knew Lil's turnaround was the result of Edith's visit to them. The truth and tears had spilled out between the three of them, lightening their hearts and soothing their souls. "It's like a butterfly, Reggie," Lil had said. "You let it go, but then it'll come fluttering back. That's Edith; she has come back to us, Reg."

Sitting on the bus, Reg wondered what Leon would make of it all, now that the truth was out. How would he account for himself? There had been no love lost between him and Ruby, Reg was sure of that. The forfeited love was between Leon and Edith, his beautiful daughter. Maybe they would find it again. Maybe I can help them pick up the pieces, he thought as the bus pulled up to the stop. It's the least I can do.

Reg looked around the dining room of the Majestic Hotel. His hands were sweating and his collar was tight. Where on earth was Leon? He wished they could have met in the pub, where it would be noisy and dark. "Would you be looking for Mr. Sharpe?" a man said.

"Er, yes."

"This way, sir." No one ever called him sir! Still, he thought, this was the fanciest place in town. "There you are, sir," the man said, pointing, "in the corner."

Leon jumped up from his table. "Reg! Reg Palethorpe, my old mate! I don't believe it, after all these years!" Leon shook his head and threw his hands in the air.

"It's damned good to see you at last, Leon," Reg said. His arm was aching, Leon was pumping it so hard.

"Damned good to see you too, Reg. Now I know I am home!"

"Right, you are home—that you are!"

"You look the same, Reggie, just the same," Leon said, smiling.

"Go on with you! I could do with less of this." Reg patted his girth and laughed. "And more o' this." He touched the top of his balding head.

"Sit yerself down," said Leon. "Who'd have thought? Here we are, at long last!"

A waitress approached the table. "Here we are, gentlemen," she said, setting down a tray with glasses of beer and sandwiches.

"I took the liberty," said Leon. "I ordered two pints of bitter and ham sandwiches, just like the old days. I remembered no mustard for you."

"That's right," laughed Reg, "no mustard for me. I still can't stand the stuff!" Reg saw that Leon hadn't changed much, just a little older. Mature-looking somehow. He was still well built in an athletic sort of way, and he hadn't acquired that tired look that a lot of men around Bogmire had. His eyes were still the same deep blue, and the lines on his tanned face gave him a worldly look.

"I'm thrilled you decided to come back, Leon," Reg said. "Jimmy will be pleased. He's getting hitched, you know! Alice is her name. You'll like her, she's a good sort."

"I know," Leon said, "I rang him straight after I rang you. I'll be meeting with them tomorrow, all being well."

"Good," said Reg. "Jimmy's the same; he's happier than ever."

"Well, my good mate, here's to you." Leon raised his glass. "Cheers, Reg."

"Cheers," said Reg. "Here's to you. Welcome back, Leon. You have been missed."

Leon took a long drink of his ale. "Thanks for coming, Reg. And how's Lilian?"

"She's good, Leon. She made me wear this white shirt and tie. You know how she is? To tell you the truth, Lil was thrilled when she heard you were coming back. She was after me to fix up the spare room. I told her you were booked in here. 'He needs to be private just now, till things get sorted, anyway,' I told her."

"I appreciate that, mate." They sipped their ale and chatted about local news. They talked about the Australian sun and the English rain. They spoke of aging and the slippery, swift passage of time and their inability to reverse it. Reg wondered when they would get to the things that mattered most—Edith, Ruby, the house on Slattery Street. He remembered what Lil had said: "Tread lightly, Reg; it won't be easy for him."

"I'm really sorry about Ruby," said Leon.

"Right, me too."

"You kept an eye out for her, you and Lil—I know that. I'm not proud of anything I did, Reg." Leon looked into his drink. His lips trembled.

"It's okay," said Reg.

"No, it's not. Not a day goes by when I don't think of her."

"She was your sister, Leon."

"No, no, not Ruby! I mean Edith, Reg."

"Edith is just fine, Leon, she's well. It was pandemonium back there for a while. Ruby's passing, I mean, the circumstances."

"I know, I heard all about it from Leakey."

"She stays with her friend Mavis. She can't face the house, being on her own and all."

"I don't blame her one bit."

"She is all right, Leon. We were worried for a while, but then she came to see us, and ..." I might as well just tell him, thought Reg. "Edith found her birth certificate, Leon, and Irene's name had been scratched out! There were letters and photos that Ruby had kept hidden."

"Cyril Leakey filled me in, more or less," Leon said. "Leakey said, 'Matters needed to be clarified to save Edith from being more confused.' That's how he put it. Sounds simple enough. I wish it were that simple. What must you think of me, Reg? All this time! What must she think of me? How can you forgive someone who goes off halfway across the world to live a lie?" Leon dabbed at his eyes with his handkerchief.

"You did what you thought was right back then. Eat your sandwich, Leon. Come on, they taste good." Reg drained his glass, and Leon ordered two more pints. "What's done is done," Reg said, "so let's try and make the best of it."

"Ruby would write to me, early on," Leon said. "She kept me up with the news. Edith's schooling, things like that. Then she stopped writing, no reason. I wrote to Leakey see if anything was wrong. He's been in charge of all the legal stuff since way back when. You know, Ruby had quite an inheritance. I washed my hands of that when I left. I didn't want anything from her, ever!"

"I can understand that," said Reg.

"Leakey wrote back to me. 'Some things are best left alone,' he wrote. 'The child is satisfactory.' The child! I was so angry. It was Ruby and Leakey's idea in the first place, you know, to pass off the baby, Edith, as Ruby's daughter." Leon looked up to the ceiling and wiped his eyes with the back of his hand. "Damn! I'm sorry," he said.

"Don't be sorry; you have to let it out, lad," said Reg.

"All these years it's been eating away at me, Reg, like bloody maggots!"

"Sir, are you going to finish?" The waitress pointed to Leon's uneaten sandwich.

"No thanks." Leon cleared his throat. "Did you know, Leakey fancied Ruby back then? I felt like they were gangin' up on me. The thought of Edith living in a house with that scarecrow! I wanted to come back and wring his scraggy neck! I bought my ticket to come back; I was making good money in construction. When the day came, I couldn't do it. I got to thinking how everybody was getting on all right without me. And Ruby and me, we would be at each other's throats again. Years later, I tried again, same thing. I couldn't go through with it. I wrote letters to Edith but never heard a thing back. That was about the time Irene stopped writing."

"Irene?"

"Yes, we kept it going for a while, but she lost interest, I suppose. Don't blame her, really. Her folks never knew about the baby, of course. She said her dad would have killed her. I never could settle and moved around a lot."

"But you did okay, you found work?" Reg said. Leon handed him a card that read, "Sunshine Builders, Leon Sharpe, proprietor."

"You did well," said Reg.

"I taught myself, brick by brick. I just worked and worked. Hey, I have money in my pockets but not much else!" Leon said. "There was nobody there back then."

"How do you mean?"

"Well, you know, I wanted to have that somebody, to count on. Oh, I know you were my good mate, don't get me wrong. I needed somebody to put me on the right track. Some people have that, Reg, they do. I never had the feeling that I was doing the right thing about the baby—Edith, I mean. I never had the feeling that I was doing the wrong thing, either. Hopeless, I was hopeless. Ruby reckoned it was God's will that I should leave. Good riddance, more like! I hope Ruby didn't suffer when she died. I know being here now is right."

"Yes," said Reg, giving Leon's arm a slight squeeze.

"I want to see Edith, but only if and when she is ready. I have to make it up to her, Reg. Don't laugh at me, but when I was on the plane, I started praying. Praying that Edith would understand. I haven't prayed before, ever!"

"I am not laughing at you, Leon, and you are not hopeless. She's tough. Edith is tough, and she'll come round. I know it. Now, just hang on, I have to find the phone box. I promised Lil I'd give her a ring."

"It's in the lobby," said Leon. "Give her my love."

When Reg returned, the restaurant had all but emptied. "Lil's baked scones," said Reg, beaming, "and she'd love you to come home with me. Just a quick visit, you know."

"Sounds bloody marvelous," said Leon, "why not!"

As Leon and Reg walked to the bus depot, Leon said, "I tried to be happy, Reg, I really did. Almost got hitched a couple of times. Wasn't to be, though. Wedding bells will be ringing for our old mate Jimmy Jack soon."

"Alice is a great girl," said Reg.

"Did I tell you Jimmy's asked me to be his best man? Over the phone, mind you! How's that for loyalty? I'm really honored. After all this time, he sees fit to have me stand up for him."

"Of course he does," said Reg.

"He just wants a quiet affair," said Leon.

"Some hopes!" Reg said and laughed. "Half the bus depot is going!"

"You know, I'd hoped one day that you and Lil might make it down there to Australia."

"Lil were never a traveler," said Reg. "She was pukin' on the ferry all the way to New Brighton! She'd never make it." He pointed to the No. 9 bus. "This is ours."

19

Mary

Alice Larkin swept debris off the toilet block floor. She had to keep moving; a large tarpaulin replaced part of a wall on one side, and the draft made it too cold to sit for long.

"The bricks in there are loose!" a woman said, exiting one of the cubicles, "and what's more, the seat wobbles!"

"It's the demolition," said Alice. "This whole block, it'll be gone soon."

"Good," said the woman. "It's a mess and it smells off!" She pulled a face and left.

"I'll be gone, too," Alice muttered under her breath. The woman was right. The air was tainted. Dust was everywhere, and people who never coughed, coughed. Alice had taken to peeling and eating an orange with her first cup of morning tea. It helped with the smell, she thought.

She pushed her stool as far away from the draft as she could, sat down, and thought about last evening. "I want you to meet my old mate Leon Sharpe," Jimmy had said to her.

"That would be Ruby's brother?" said Alice.

"Yep, he's back in Bogmire. He wants to buy us supper at the Majestic."

"The Majestic Hotel!" Alice said. "Ooh! That's posh!"

"Leon's not short of a penny," said Jimmy. "He's done well for himself down under. Leon and me, we were like brothers in the old days. I hope it's all right, Alice, that I have asked him to be my best man at our wedding. That's not the reason he's back, mind you; it's a little more complicated than that," Jimmy said, offering a meandering version of

Leon's ill-fated courtship with Irene. "Talk about Thatcher being the iron lady—I reckon that was Ruby Sharpe's forte!"

Alice had drawn her own conclusions for Leon's return, based on the current gossip and the gossip that had drifted by her teenaged ears back in the fifties.

Alice took to Leon straightaway. She liked his easy manner and pleasant face; it was an honest face, she thought. "I'm really so happy to meet you, Alice," he said, and she knew he meant it. Throughout the meal, their talk was mainly about the wedding. "I'm honored," he said. "The last time I was in church was for Edith's christening. I just hope she'll give me a chance to say I am sorry. Secrets can weigh heavy over time," he said, "till something triggers, and they collapse under their own weight. It becomes too much for anyone to bear. That's what's happened, I reckon—it's all just collapsed."

"You are right," she said to Leon. Now Millie's secret is collapsing, Alice thought. Again this morning, she had watched tears slide down Millie's pretty face. "I'm really worried now, Alice," she'd whispered. "Saleem hasn't been home in two days. Calls are coming from Pakistan, and I can't understand the language. Something is really wrong! I'm scared to tell the police or anyone anything now."

"I haven't seen him around here, either," Alice had said. "Don't worry, it'll probably be nothing." Still, she thought it strange that Saleem insisted on keeping their marriage a secret. It wasn't fair to Millie. Weddings were supposed to be happy and joyful occasions, as she hoped hers would be—if she could keep it simple, that is. It was only two weeks away, and time was flying by. Two days ago, her daughter, Karen, had called, telling Alice that her boyfriend, Lyle, was bringing his band up from Putney to play at the reception.

"Lyle doesn't drink like he used to, Mum," she said. "I'm not coming if he doesn't come. I really do luv him. He's between jobs now, so we—"

"He's always between jobs," said Alice. "I don't think—" There was a loud sob, a pause, and more sobs. "Well, all right then," Alice relented.

"Thanks, Mum, I knew you would. We'll come in the van with the others." Karen rang off before Alice had a chance to ask about the others. Keep it simple, she thought, that's a laugh.

Earlier that morning at the tea kiosk, Mary Lacey had said, "Hey Alice, guess what? I've got me outfit for your weddin'. It's gorgeous."

"I'm sure it is," Alice said.

"Shot silk," said Mary, "magenta and green, bolero jacket. It's a Dior design—well, a copy, sort of. The frock is strapless with a flared skirt for dancing."

"Good," said Alice, "it sounds lovely. Would you get me a tea please, Mary?"

"Hey, here's your groom comin' for his tea," Mary said. Jimmy was walking toward the kiosk.

"Mornin', ladies," he said. Mary slid his tea across the counter. "Thanks, Mary," he said. "Gotta get back," he whispered to Alice. "Leon's stopping by. See yer, love." He kissed her on the cheek. "There he is now. Thanks again, Mary," he said.

"Who is that?" asked Mary, "that bloke who waved to you?"

"He's Jimmy's old friend, Leon Sharpe. Poor old Ruby's brother; he's been in Australia."

"Wait a minute! I know him from somewhere. Hang on, it'll come to me." The cigarette clamped in the corner of Mary's mouth twitched, and ash fluttered onto the counter. It always amazed Alice how Mary could talk and smoke at the same time.

"About the music for the wedding, Mary," Alice said, "I—"

"Oh, it's all arranged. Like I said, my gift to you. They sound like a real band! Wait till you hear the two of them."

"But I don't think—"

"Christ Almighty, it's him! Les Sharpe."

"Leon," said Alice, "it's Leon!"

"I'll be damned! He was my dancing partner, and we was fantastic together. You were too young to remember, Alice. We won the silver cup, foxtrot and waltz, 1950. It's him for sure! Ooh, I'm all of a shake just rememberin'! It's all coming back to me, Alice. There were a bunch of us dancers. We went everywhere. We had a bus an' everything."

"He's Ruby Sharpe's brother, Mary. He—"

"Yeh, that's right, he cleared off! The old girl kicked him out, didn't she? He stopped dancing and took up with someone from the mattress factory. He's come back 'cause she's dead—his sister's dead, right?"

"Well, yes, but—"

"What about that stuck-up niece of his? She's a lot to answer for, huh?"

"Mary, about the wedding—"

"Is he here on his own? I mean, is he marr—"

"He's on his own, and no, he's not married."

"Fancy that! Can't wait to speak to him. My God, he'll have a fit when he sees me! I know what, I'll surprise him." Mary winked at Alice and whipped off her apron. Tucking her blouse into her too-short skirt, she said, "Keep an eye on things, will you, Alice? There's plenty of hot water in the urn." Mary rummaged under the counter and produced a plastic bag bulging with lipsticks and bottles of makeup. "I'll 'ave to go and fix meself up a bit." She spat on her fingers and pulled on several strands of hair, spiraling them down in front of her ears. "What's me hair like at the back?"

"It's fine," Alice said.

"Now, where's me high heels? Here they are. I'll just be a jiff, Alice." She tottered off to the toilet block.

I give up, Alice thought. First Karen and now Mary. No one listens to me. Who does Mary think she is? She'll turn up at the wedding looking like a trussed-up turkey, shoving her sixty-year-old body into a dress made for a twenty-year-old. And now she's hell-bent on grabbing poor Leon. Alice looked over to the newsstand. Leon was sitting on a stool with Jimmy beside him. Jimmy's hand was on Leon's shoulder; they were laughing. Ah well, she thought, I suppose Mary means well, as does Karen. The wedding will sort itself out.

Alice was finishing the last of her tea when the shout rang out. "The toilet block," someone yelled, "it's on fire!" Alice turned to see the toilet block obscured by a cloud of gray smoke.

"Quick," someone said, "get the fire brigade!"

Jimmy and Leon, followed by some others, ran up to the scene.

"Jimmy!" Alice shouted, "Mary's in there!"

"That's not smoke!" Jimmy shouted. "That's cement dust. The wall is collapsing!"

"The tarp's coming down," said Alice. "Oh, poor Mary!" Mortar and bricks were spilling out onto the pavement.

"Jesus!" said Jimmy. "The whole building is crumbling."

"Don't panic," said Leon, "we'll get to her."

"My heavens!" cried Alice. "What a mess!" The gap in the wall was now only partially covered by the blue tarp.

"Hey, I'm stuck!" Mary cried. "I can't get out. I can't move me arms!"

"We're here, right here. We'll get you out—hang on!" said Jimmy.

"The prop has given way," said Leon. "She's wedged in. The bricks must have been loose. Are you hurt in there?"

"Don't know. I can't budge!" Mary said.

A fireman appeared. "Stand back," he said, "we need to shift that prop slowly. Me mate was here a minute ago, don't know where he went."

"No worries," said Leon. "I can lift this bottom end. Jimmy, you hold the top."

"Right, then," said the fireman, "I've got the middle. I'm going to lever it slowly away. Hang on, missus!" he called. "Better close yer eyes. Are you ready, boys? One, two—" There was a crunching sound.

"Help! God in heaven!" Mary's muffled cries came from beneath the rubble. Bricks and mortar fell all over the place.

"Missus, are you hurt anywhere?" said the fireman.

"How do I know?"

"Hang on a minute—we'll just get this tarpaulin off you."

"Alice, Alice!" Mary called.

"I'm here, Mary, what?"

"Pssst, Alice, don't let them move the thing yet. Me knickers are 'round me knees," she said.

"Right, lads," said the fireman.

Alice reached under the tarp, but she couldn't see Mary's face, just her knees.

"Pull 'em up quick," Mary said.

"I'm pulling! They're full of stones," Alice hissed. "Hang on, I'm tipping them out!"

"Alice, what yer doin'? Get back," Jimmy said.

"Shhh," said Alice.

"Get back here, miss," said the fireman.

"Mary, they're up now!" Alice said, moving back as she launched into a series of choking coughs.

"Careful now," said the fireman. "Boys, stand clear!"

The tarpaulin was slowly raised like a stage curtain. Grasping the fireman's arm, Mary emerged, covered in white dust from head to toe. The crowd of onlookers that had gathered applauded.

"Thank Christ," Mary said, tears tracking down her white cheeks as she was ushered to a waiting ambulance.

"I'm coming with you to the hospital," said Alice. "This is Leon. He and Jimmy helped get you out."

"You were very lucky," Leon said.

"Oh," said Mary, and looked away.

"I wanted to surprise him," Mary said to Alice on the way to the hospital. "Leon, I mean."

"You did, sort of," said Alice.

Later, Mary told reporters, "I looked death in the face," as she posed for photos. "Tea Lady Trapped in Toilet" read the headline in the *Bogmire Daily News*.

"It will never be the same for me," she told Alice a few days later.

"What won't?"

"Going to the loo—I'm traumatized! I freeze up! I have to 'ave a smoke before anything happens. And I don't like them portable things they've put there. Everyone sees when you go in and when you come out!"

"I know what you mean," said Alice. "Nothing's the same round here."

"That's fer sure. Where's he staying at?"

"Who?"

"Leon Sharpe."

"The Majestic."

"Ooh!" Mary took a long drag on her cigarette. "That place isn't cheap—nothing's cheap, I suppose. These smokes cost me an arm and a leg. Still, you gotta do something to stay happy, don't yer?"

20

Rhonda

- - - - - - - - - - - - - - -

&dith sat on the edge of the bed, still in her nightgown. She tossed the morning newspaper to one side, having read about the collapsed building at the depot yesterday. Oh dear God, she thought, is my world on the verge of collapse now, or has it already? She was worried about Alice Larkin's wedding, which was less than two weeks away. Lil wouldn't stop talking about it. "I want you to be there," Lil said. "You are part of the family."

Just what family was she part of? The groom, Jimmy, had been one of Leon's closest friends, according to Reg. If she was invited, wouldn't she have been asked by now? First things first, she thought, and gazed at the piece of paper in her hand. On the paper was a phone number, the numerals of which Edith knew by heart, having repeated them to herself throughout her night of fitful sleep.

In one of Irene's old Christmas cards to Lil, there had been a reference to pupils and a school. Irene had once taught primary school in Dublin, Lil recalled. Edith tracked down and called schools in the Dublin area. She knew she had hit the jackpot when finally the response on the line was "Monahan, Irene ... Oh yes, Irene taught here, many years ago. Irene's sister, Rhonda, helps out once in a while," the person said. "She's younger than Irene; she lives in Dublin. I can give you her number if you like."

"This number feels different, as if it carried weight somehow," she told Mavis. "It's promising me something—I can feel it." Edith called the number three times before she went to bed last night, but there was no answer. Now she pondered whether to hold off calling until she got to Slattery Street later that morning. How can I wait? she thought. I have turned a corner. I've peeled back the first layer. It's 7:30 a.m. Someone is bound to be home at this hour. She dialed the number, holding the receiver firmly against her head to steady herself. Her breathing echoed back to her from the mouthpiece in amplified gasps. She held the phone away from her face. She was perspiring.

"Hello, hello?" a female voice answered.

"Oh, I'm sorry," Edith said. She had rehearsed what she would say, intending only to clarify Irene's name and perhaps obtain an address. "I'm looking for someone. Er … sorry to bother you at this early hour, but I …" Her thoughts were tumbling over each other, and nothing was coming out as she had planned. She knew she wasn't making much sense to this person. She took a deep breath. "Is this, er, I'm looking for an Irene Monahan. Do you happen to know her?"

"Well, that I do. As God is in heaven I know Irene," the woman said. "This'll be Rhonda, her sister, yer talkin' to. Who is this? What would you be wantin'?"

"My name is Edith Sharpe. I'm calling from Bogmire in Lancashire. I'd really like to, well, if possible, talk—I mean, find her," Edith said. "I sort of knew, er, know her."

"Oh, I see. Well, she's Irene O'Reilly now, Sean's wife. She has a brood to show for it an' all," the woman laughed. "They live out in the country, near Dun Laoghaire. I'm up there at the weekend. Was it Bogmire you said?"

"Right," said Edith.

"Ah yes, she was there. But that's a long while ago. I'll give her your number anyway, but first, can I tell her why you called?" The woman spoke quickly, and her brogue was hard to follow. Edith's pulse was racing; this was Irene's sister, and speaking about her mother, who was real. She was close!

"I …" Words caught in Edith's throat. She looked at Irene's photo on the bedside table.

"Hello, hello? Are yer there, love? Are you with me?" the woman said.

"Yes, yes, I am," whispered Edith.

"Wait a minute now. Just wait a minute," Rhonda said. There was a pause. "Bogmire, you say?"

"Yes. Bogmire."

"Could it be that—I mean, can you tell me why? Why yer really would be wantin' our Irene?"

"Well, it's because—I think—I think that she is my mo—" Edith wiped tears from her cheeks with the back of her hand. She had not intended to be so direct with this stranger. "I'm sorry, it's just …"

"Don't cry, sweetheart. Don't cry now. Let me ask yer something. Tell me, how old are you, love?"

"I am thirty-six."

"Jaysus, Joseph, and Mary! Dear God in heaven! Now, listen to me, am I right in thinkin' that Irene doesn't really know you?"

"Well, no," Edith sniffed back her tears, "it's a long story, really."

"I know the story, dear child. I do, as sure as I am standing here. God knows I do! It is you, isn't it? Really you?"

"Mmm."

"You are Irene's baby girl. Her baby. Oh my, I'm cryin' meself, but there'll be tears a-plenty afore this is out! Tell me, darlin', are you well, are you all right?"

"You do know? Who I am, then?"

"Of course I do. Me heart is doin' somersaults. This is a day our Irene's been prayin' fer, all of her life. I don't know what to say, except me sister's prayers are answered. How did you find us? Well, never mind, youse can tell me later. It was just between us sisters back then, you understand. Our da would 'ave killed her! Believe me, I am the only one here that knows. Oh, I'll be breakin' the news to her when that old fella of hers is out of the way. Mind you, Sean is a good man, and he is a good father to those four kids of theirs—three boys and a girl they have."

"I felt as if I really knew her, after we talked," Edith said to Mavis immediately after the call. "She was lovely. I was able to tell her things. All about Ruby and Leon. She said that Leon weighed heavy in Irene's heart for years, even after she married Sean. We talked for ages. She wants me to go over to Ireland on the ferry. We talked about that. She's going to talk to Irene today—today, Mavis! She's calling me back tonight. Oh my God, Mavis. What if she doesn't want to—"

"What if nothing! Take it easy, Edith. This is wonderful. Now, go and water the bulbs on the windowsill. Feed the goldfish, do something simple, let your head settle a bit. This is big news."

Edith looked at the goldfish. She watched them gulp at their meager ration. She gave the box an extra tap, showering the flaky crumbs into the bowl. She watered the bulbs, slopping water into the saucers. She brewed herself a cup of tea and got dressed. A shoe was missing. Hopping around the flat, she waited for her toast to brown. The shoe was under the bed, and her toast burned. Her tea was cold. "Bother," she said, and called for a taxi.

"Slattery Street, please," she said to the driver.

She wondered what her mother's house in Ireland was like. Rhonda had said it was in the country. And what of those four children—three boys and a girl, Rhonda had said? And their father, Sean, what kind of a man was he? She took the photo of her mother out of her pocket. "Now I have found you," she said to her mother's image and held the photo to her breast. "I've found you," she said. "Please like me—please, all of you, like me."

"Pardon, what's that, miss?" asked the driver.

"Oh nothing." She smiled, closed her eyes, and kissed the photo before putting it back in her pocket. Where would Leon fit in now? "You'll never meet a better man," Reg had said. She had tried to imagine what he looked like. "Mavis, I see nothing," she said, "and that scares me. I'll have to face him sometime soon!"

"As your uncle, Leon was good to you, right?" Mavis said.

"Of course," said Edith. "But he left me. Gone!" she said. What if I don't like him? she wondered. What if he doesn't like me? There was no order to any of her fleeting thoughts. What would Ireland be like? She tried to envision the family: all smiles, arms open, ready to love her. A farm, green trees, and space. Rhonda's tears flowing as she introduced them all. She envisioned her beautiful mother with shining black hair and laughing blue eyes.

"Miss! Miss!" said the taxi driver, "this is your stop. This is Slattery!"

"Oh, thank you." She paid the driver and stepped out of the taxi, waving to Lil, who was at her front window, fiddling with the curtains. Reg popped his head out the front door. "Hiya Edith, coffee's up," he called.

"Be right there, Reg," she said.

Morning coffee was a regular occurrence now. There were no more secrets between them, and Edith didn't mind Lil's gossip or Reg's mundane comments about the weather and the football team. This chatter always led Edith to where she wanted to go, into their stream of memories, their cherished recollections of times with Irene and Leon.

"Mornin', Edith, love. Sit yerself down," said Reg. "Black with a little milk, right?" he said, snapping the lid back on a can of coffee.

"Right," she said.

"Scotch pancakes—here you go," Lil said, and set a plate down. "I made these when you was little; you loved them. They're still warm."

"Now," said Reg, "how did you get on with them phone numbers?"

She told them about the call to Rhonda in Ireland, about Irene and her husband and children, whereupon Lil began to sob and then disappeared into the kitchen. "She's off again," said Reg, rolling his eyes. "I'll just be a minute. I'll set her right, don't worry." Edith helped herself to the pancakes; she was hungry. Lil came back into the room and wiped her hands on her apron.

"I knew something would come of all them cards I kept," she said. Reg winked at Edith.

"There's something I didn't mention before," said Edith. "Did you know that Ruby was wealthy? Did you have any idea? Because I didn't," she said.

"I knew it," Lil said. "I knew it all along."

"Knew what?" said Reg.

"That she had more than she'd ever let on," Lil said. "I always knew."

"You never said anything to me," said Reg.

"Well, it wasn't my business, was it?"

"That's a bit daft, coming from you," he said.

"It's that family her mother worked for, the Hasletts," said Lil. "They were rich; it came from them. She was old Miss Scrooge, that's what

Ruby was. She'd patch up the bed sheets till there was nothing left to patch! I'd see 'em on the washing line, raggy old things."

"None of that matters now," said Reg.

"On the way over here, I was thinking," said Edith, "well, I was thinking a lot of things. I can't live in the house again. I'll need to sell it, and I shall visit Ireland. I also want to go to the convent, to see where I was born."

"Edith, are you sure?" said Lil.

"I'm sure. And now that Leon is here, I don't know where to start with him. I can't bring myself to phone him. What will he think about all this, the will, his sister leaving him out of things? I'd hate to think he'd be upset."

"Nah, not Leon. It's you, Edith. He's come back to see you," Reg said. "Leave it to me. I'll set it up. Just between you two—a little meeting, cozy like. It'll be fine. He's worried about you. As for the house, Edith, Frank Thacker, the estate agent, he is your man. He'll take care of things for you, and he'll see you right. He's reliable. Still, it's one thing at a time, I suppose."

"That's right," said Lil, squeezing Edith's hand, "we'll help you. Whatever we can do."

"Thanks," said Edith. "When I called Ireland this morning, I was so excited! I'm finally on the right track."

21

Meeting
----

dith remembered she had been six years old. She was hiding behind the pantry door when Ruby yelled down at her brother from the top of the stairs, "Be sure your sins will find you out, Leon Sharpe!" She watched as Leon, without a backward glance or pause, opened the front door and slipped away. Her memory of him was formless at times, but aspects of him were easy to recall, such as his constant whistling and Ruby's annoyance at that. "He was ever so nice, your uncle Leon. Did he die, then?" Edith's young friends asked when he ceased to pick her up after school.

"He's gone abroad," Edith had been told to say.

"He's far away!" Ruby affirmed. "There'll be no more talk of him. It's good riddance to bad rubbish!"

It had been arranged by Reg that she was to meet Leon at 11:15 later that morning at the Majestic Hotel. Her own attempts to call him had repeatedly dissolved into her stammering utterances of "Sorry, wrong number."

"I can't do it!" she had sobbed.

"Of course you can't, lass," Reg said. "You can't expect heavy doors like that to swing open after all this time. There's rust and dust," he said. "A little bit o' grease is needed here and there, to ease it along, so to speak. Call it patience, if you like."

"And what if the door slams back in my face?" Edith asked. "What then?"

"That'll never happen—leave things to me."

145

From her bedroom window, Edith observed the people and traffic in the street below. She felt envious all of a sudden. They are all connected down there, she thought. All of them, intertwined with their kids, families, pubs, and pastimes, darting in and out of each other's lives. Will that be me one day? she wondered. Will I ever be a true loving part of something?

She closed the window; it was time to get ready. She had set her clothes out the night before: a gray straight skirt, a white blouse, and a pair of marcasite earrings. The earrings had been a gift from Edwin. How long ago that all seemed—being with Edwin in that hideous caravan. She wasn't sure whether to feel resentment or gratitude that her fateful time with him had brought her to this place of uncertainty and discovery.

"My feelings are so mixed up," she had said to Reg.

"Some folks go to church to sort them things out," he said. "Me and Lil, we'll sit quiet in the backyard of a morning. Birds singin', sun tryin' to shine. He is up there, is God, behind them clouds, fixin' stuff, I reckon. You'll be all right, Edith, trust me."

She gathered up her hair and coiled it above her head, securing it with clips. Her favorite red coat completed the picture she wanted to portray for Leon—one of confidence, of knowing and looking as if she knew what she was about. "You'll knock Leon's socks off!" Lil had said when Edith told her what she would wear. Knocking Leon's socks off wasn't exactly what she wanted to do. I don't know this father of mine, she thought. I just want to meet him. Then again, he may leave again—who knows?

"I want to let him know," she'd said to Mavis, "how rotten it was to abandon everything like that, to hide from me and lie! I do want to like him, though," she'd said. "I really want to like people from now on."

The Majestic Hotel was in the center of town, a short walk from the depot. She crossed the street, tottering slightly. It had been a while since she had worn high heels. She pushed hard against the hotel's revolving door and was gently steered inside. Briefly, she thought how easy it would be to keep going full circle, back into the street. This thought was soon dispelled when a lurch forward spilled her and other patrons into the vast lobby like fish from a net.

A desk clerk gave her directions to the ladies' room. On entering, she was greeted by a haze of tobacco smoke. Leaning against a sink, a woman smoked. The name Rita was embroidered on her uniform breast pocket. "Hi there, got the time?" she asked Edith.

"Ten after eleven," Edith said.

"Thanks. Nice coat. I can't wear bright colors like that," the woman said and turned on the tap, swishing her cigarette down the drain. "I have to get a move on," she said, and entered a cubicle, slamming the door behind her.

Edith looked at herself in the mirror. She felt overdressed. I look so old all of a sudden, she thought, and removed the clips from her hair. She shook her head, and her curls fell about her shoulders. She removed the earrings and dropped them into her handbag. I should just get this over with, she thought. He's probably out there waiting. A toilet flushed and the woman stepped back out. "I know you from somewhere?" the woman asked.

"I don't think so," Edith said, toying with her hair.

"Wait! Aren't you Ruby Sharpe's girl?"

"No, I'm not."

"Huh, funny, I could 'ave sworn. See yer, then," the woman said.

"See you," said Edith. "I am not Ruby's girl," Edith said under her breath as she headed to the dining room. "I never was!"

The dining room was long and narrow, making it difficult to get an overview of the tables. She looked around but could not see anyone that she thought resembled Leon. "What will he look like?" she'd said to Reg. "You'll know," he'd said. She would leave, she decided, if she didn't spot him soon; no sense in wasting time.

"Excuse me, madam." She turned. A uniformed man was at her side. "Your party, madam," he said, "this way." He pointed to the rear of the room. "Mr. Sharpe has table twelve."

Edith followed him through the maze of tables. How does he know who I am, she thought? The man tut-tutted and fluttered his hands, moving chairs to clear a way for her. Darn it, I stand out in this red coat, she thought. She kept her eyes down, watching the man's footsteps in front of her. The feet stopped; she stopped. There were voices: "Yes" and

"Thank you."

Edith looked up. There he was, standing about three feet away from her—Leon, her father. He was taller, more tanned than she remembered, but as handsome as he appeared in his early photographs. He still sported a full head of dark hair, except that now there were streaks of silver at his temples. He wore a tweed jacket, a fine-checked shirt, and a wool necktie. His brow was furrowed, and his eyebrows appeared to meet in the middle. Edith stared, taken aback by a strong sense of elegance about him, a dignity she hadn't expected. She placed a hand on the table to steady herself. As she looked at him now, she saw Ruby—the high cheekbones, the long nose, the same contracted brows that had fostered Ruby's unrelenting frown. Why wouldn't they be alike? she thought. They were siblings!

Leon looked at Edith, and then he blinked and put a hand to his mouth and blinked again, as if to challenge the credibility of the moment.

"I—I hope I am not late," she said.

"No, no, of course not. Thanks so much for coming. Please, have a seat." He stepped forward and touched her elbow. She placed her handbag on the table, catching the rim of a saucer. It tipped, sending a teaspoon clattering to the floor.

"Oh gosh, clumsy me," she said.

"Never mind, I'll get it," he said.

"No, I can—" Their words collided. They fell silent, staring at each other.

"It doesn't matter, leave it," he said. "You look wonderful, Edith."

"Thank you very much. I mean, thanks," she said. "So do you." She knew she was blushing.

"Here, please." He pulled out a chair for her and sat opposite her across the small table. "I would have completely understood if you had decided not to come," he said.

"Oh, goodness no," she said. "I am just so, well, I am so relieved—"

"'Scuse me! 'Scuse me!" Edith looked up to see Rita, the woman from the ladies' room, wagging a pencil. She took a notepad from her breast pocket, flipped it open, and said, "Just so yer know, the lamb chops are special today, but the soup's off."

"Thanks. Hang on, we need a minute, Rita," he said.

"Right, then." Rita wedged her pencil behind her ear. "Take all the time you need, Mr. Sharpe. I'll be back." She flashed a smile at Edith and flounced off.

"Sorry about that," he said, "and that fellow, the one that led you to the table—he insisted on watching out for you. I've been here a week now, and they can't do enough! There's not much they don't know about me already!"

"Ha! That's Bogmire," said Edith.

"True," he laughed. "I hope you didn't feel, well, you know, too conspicuous?"

"It's fine," she said. "I mean, here we are. It's quite an amazing thing!"

"It is," he said. He clasped his hands together, placing them on the table. "Edith, I have to say this before you go, and before I say anything else." He looked down.

"But I am not going anywhere," she said, slipping her coat over the back of the chair. "I'm not." Maybe he is the one who is going, she thought. I will wait for the small talk to be over, before I get down to what really matters. Find out what his plans are. I just have to be patient.

"Tell me something," he said. "The letters I sent—they never reached you, did they?"

"Letters? No, I never, ever saw any letters," she said. "Ruby would never tell me where you were."

"She knew where I was living from my letters. I had told Leakey to always maintain contact. I had to know where and how you were. When I heard nothing back," he said, "I felt as if, well, Ruby wanted to deny my existence! Maybe I deserved that." He looked down at his hands. "She wanted you to herself, you know. She felt she had a claim on you. Leakey threatened me. He kept track of me somehow. He said you were in the best hands, and if I ever returned, he said, your young life would be ruined. He called me irresponsible and unfit to be a parent. The pathetic thing is, I believed him!"

"But wasn't it mostly all Ruby's doing?" Edith said. "According to what Lil and Reg told me."

"Yes, I know, but that's no excuse. I was a coward."

"About Ruby," said Edith. "The way she died, it was so—"

"Stop! No one could account for that, no one. Reg explained everything to me. I think it was a blessing, God rest her troubled soul. We can't go back. I mean, here we are, you and me. Things happen for a reason. Maybe we should drink to that, to us, together. Some wine?"

"Yes," she said, "wine would be nice. Can I ask you something?"

"Of course, ask me anything, anything at all."

"Did you love her—Irene, my mother?"

He sighed. "I think maybe I always have," he said. "She never did come back from Ireland as she said she would. Our letters trickled to a halt. We were so young! Reg, he told me that you traced her whereabouts, that you have found her," he said. His face brightened.

"Yes, I have."

"That's wonderful. How is she—is she well?"

"Yes, she is, I think, according to her sister. I am going see her in Ireland."

"Really, Edith, that's wonderful."

The waiter brought the wine and poured it for them. "To us," Leon said.

"To us," said Edith.

"Edith, I say this to you in all sincerity," Leon began. "First, I'm truly and honestly, deeply sorry. For everything, everything you have had to go through. You mean the world to me. I know that sounds strange coming from someone who has been, well, gone from your life. I'm so ashamed." He looked down at his hands, still clasped on the table. This isn't small talk, thought Edith. He's jumped right in! He's opened the doors. She took a long sip of wine.

"Wait," she said, "I have to say something before you go on." I am going to say it, she thought, because if I don't now, I never will. "I felt betrayed," she said, swallowing hard. "By you, by Ruby, by Cyril Leakey, I was betrayed." She took a deep breath and sighed. "What happened to Ruby, well, I am ashamed of my behavior—"

"I am so sorry—"

"Please, I'm not finished," she said. "I was so angry when I realized that I'd been, well, duped. All those years, I just dallied along, I suppose, following the path laid out for me. I was on a spiritless treadmill, if you like. I don't want ever to go back to that. To tell you the truth, this is a day I never thought could happen. I was led to believe that my father was dead! Days like this happen to other people. Just knowing I belong. What has happened to me—to us—is, well ..."

Leon cleared his throat and looked up to the ceiling. "I want to make it up to you, Edith," he said.

"I believe you, but I don't really understand why people do what they do. If they love people and ..." She stared at the lumps of sugar in the bowl, the monograms on the cutlery. Why can't I look at him? she thought. It's because he is going to cry, that's why, and so am I. I don't want to cry, not here. I hadn't expected this. Why can't I just say what I wanted to say and be done?

The dining room was filling up. Her hands were clenched under the table, her fingernails digging into her palms. "I don't want to lose anything else," she said, her voice trailing to a whisper. "Please, tell me the truth! Are you going to leave again?"

"I belong here, with you, Edith, if you will have me. I'm not leaving." He leaned across the table, his voice barely audible. "I love you," he said. A tear slid down his cheek. The only man Edith had seen cry was Edwin, who had sniveled into his sleeve whenever he spoke of his mother. This was different—this was pain, years of it, and now she was crying, too. She couldn't stop.

"I never should have left you that long," he was saying. "I was weak. I know that. I'm so sorry. All those years, I thought about you." She took the hand he extended across the table. It was warm and firm. The hand he held was the only part of her body not shaking. He closed his other hand over hers as if to steady her.

"I'm blessed," he said, smiling through his tears, "truly blessed. I'll never leave you, Edith. I know this is so hard for you."

No, she wanted to say, it's not hard, not now. She wanted to tell him of the relief she felt at that moment, "I ... ," but her tears drowned out her words. She sniffed loudly. "Oh God, I ..."

"Here." He handed her a tissue from his pocket and took one for himself. They blew their noses.

"What a racket," Edith said, and laughed. A broad smile crept across Leon's face. He was as she remembered him now, with no trace of Ruby's frown.

"People are staring at us," she said.

"Who cares?"

"I don't," she said, and shook her head. "I'm just glad we are here."

"So am I. I want to be what you want me to be, Edith."

"Just stay, be here," she said, "for now."

"You deserve more than that," he said. "God willing, I want to help you in any way I can. Can we start afresh, get to know each other, you and me?"

"Yes," she said, wiping away fresh tears, "we can."

"I'm sure you will love her, Edith, your mother—you deserve each other. I want Irene to feel as happy as I am right now, you here with me. She deserves that. Nothing in the world is, or can be, better than this." He raised his glass. "To us," he said, "and may we—"

"'Scuse me!" Rita was hovering, tapping her pencil on her chin. "There's only steak pie left," she said. "Soup's back on, though—pea."

"Fine." They smiled and clinked their glasses.

"Maybe it will make some sense, bit by bit," Edith said, "why things happen the way they do."

They ate their lunch. She told him about Mavis and what an incredible friend and support she had been. "I am staying with Mavis for as long as I need to until things settle," she said.

"I understand," he said. "Do you have any plans?" he asked.

"No, nothing beyond Ireland, that is. I feel awkward mentioning this," Edith said. "It's about Slattery Street. It's really your house as well as mine. Ruby, well, she left it to me, but—"

"I know," he said, "I heard from Leakey that Ruby willed you the house and more. I'm glad—no worries."

"I want to sell the house," Edith said. "I can't live there anymore."

"Of course, it's your decision, Edith, and rightly so. For all those years, Ruby kept her deep pockets a secret," he said. "Only Cyril Leakey had privilege to that information. I never, ever expected anything from her, anyway. She always resented me, Edith. After our parents died, she had no choice but to look after me; we had no aunts or uncles. I was a noose around her neck, me being so much younger. There was a young fellow, she told me, a carpenter, who took a shine to her. His name was Ira, and he was Jewish. I don't know what happened to him. I cramped her style, maybe."

"What did they die of, your parents? I suppose they are my grandparents."

"TB—consumption, they called it then. I was too little to remember much."

"People don't succumb to that these days," Edith said. "Thankfully, things have changed."

"My friends haven't changed," said Leon. "Jimmy, Reg and Lil, salt of the earth they are. I'm to be Jimmy's best man at his wedding."

"I heard. That's great."

"You'll be there, won't you, Edith?"

"I don't know Alice that well; she asked Lil to ask me. The invites aren't formal, so yes, I'll be there. I'll tag along with Reg and Lil."

She asked Leon about Australia. "I did all right for myself," he said. "We'll talk about it all one day, but not today. That's the past; it's the present that counts."

They finished their lunch and got up to leave. Leon helped Edith on with her coat, and they hugged and laughed and hugged again. "She's my daughter," Leon whispered to Rita, who was standing at the exit.

"I know," Rita said.

She watched the two of them walk across the lobby. Leon's arm guided Edith, who stumbled and laughed as they entered the revolving door. Back out on the street, they linked up again. "I was right all along," Rita said to no one in particular. She fished in her pocket for a cigarette. "I love happy endings," she said, and headed for the ladies' room.

22

Frank Thacker

----

dith boarded the No. 9 to Slattery Street, relieved to see yet another substitute driver. The bus picked up speed; so did the chattering voices of her fellow passengers, especially two women in the seat in front of her. "She takes her hair off every night, you know," said one. "She puts it on a stand!"

"Who does?"

"Margaret Thatcher."

"Who says so?"

"They do."

"Well, you could be right, Doris; her hair always looks the same!"

"I wouldn't like her job, anyway."

"Me neither—she looks fed up all the time!"

The woman who sat closest to the window rubbed the glass with her sleeve as if to clean it. It was a gesture that reminded Edith of her childhood. When she arrived home from school each day, the click of the front gate alerted Ruby, who would appear at the front window. "Wipe your shoes! Mind them milk bottles!" Ruby would mouth, as she rubbed a sleeve-covered fist across the pane. Why don't I remember pleasant things about Ruby? she wondered. There had been a time at school when she was about twelve years old, and the teacher requested that each pupil stand up in turn and state what he or she wanted in life. "I just want to be ordinary!" Edith had related, "and have a dad at home and a mum that's pretty!" Before Edith had a chance to sit down, the teacher yelled, "Next!" over the stifled giggles of her classmates.

Maybe now these things will finally materialize, she thought. Reaching into her handbag, she removed an envelope; inside it was her ferry ticket to Ireland two weeks from now. She stared at the itinerary; it amazed her that she taken the positive step of purchasing it. She had told Leon of the fear that crept in sometimes when she thought of Ireland—fear that she was pushing her luck. She told him of her plans with Mavis that afternoon, to find the convent where she believed she had been born—just to see if it still exists, she told him. "Don't worry," he said, "I'm proud of what you are doing." His easeful smile and laughter had helped dispel those fears. They now spent time together, walking and talking, laughing and crying, as they learned more about one another each day. "Hard to believe he kowtowed to Ruby," she said to Mavis. "He's so sturdy and genuine."

As the bus wended its way through the suburbs, Edith pondered her blessings, closing her fingers over her mother's photo in her pocket. Not everyone is blessed, she thought. She hadn't meant to eavesdrop the other day at the depot when she purchased her ferry ticket to Ireland. The dismayed expression on Alice Larkin's face was hard to ignore, as were the words uttered by a distraught Millie Jamieson. "The police are looking for Saleem," Millie had said, "they are questioning all the drivers. I'm spilling the beans, Alice! I have to."

"Just tell them the truth," Alice said. They were oblivious to Edith washing her hands at the sink until she interjected, "Any paper towels, Alice?"

"Of course. Shopping, are you, Edith?" Alice said.

"No." Edith told them about the ticket she was about to purchase from Millie for Ireland. "You won't miss the wedding, will you?" Alice said. "Jimmy's so excited about Leon being back—it's soon, a week Saturday."

"No, I won't miss the wedding," Edith said. "Congratulations to you both."

"Millie will be there. Won't you, Millie?"

Millie appeared to have calmed herself. "God willing, yes," she said. "It'll do me good."

After completing the ticket transaction for the ferry to Ireland, Edith and Millie chatted about their time together at Shield Insurance, agreeing that the years had gone by too fast and vowing to keep in touch.

"Something's up!" Edith said to Mavis later. "And what about those beans about to be spilled?"

Edith arrived at the house to see Reg standing on his front porch. She checked her watch. "Thacker will be here soon," she told him. "I know I'm doing the right thing, selling this place. You were right about Leon, Reg. He doesn't care about the house or the money. Anyway, I'd better get on. Mavis and I are going up north this afternoon. The place, that convent, where I was born."

"Good luck," said Reg. "I hope it's still standing, Edith. Them little sisters is not so poor," he said. "They run that posh school over in Yorkdale."

"The butcher's girl goes there," Lil said, appearing at the door. "Hi there, Edith. That school cost them a pretty penny!" Lil craned her neck to peer at a bus cruising past the house. "Different driver," she said. "That Paki has gone. Mary Lacey says the cops are looking for him."

"Heavens, Lil!" said Reg. "You can't believe everything Mary spouts off."

"Reggie, I'm just telling you what she said." She glanced up at the sky. "We could be in for a shower. I'll see yer later, Edith; I'm ironing just now."

Edith let herself into the house and went to the kitchen. She looked out the window at the gathering storm clouds. We'll get wet today, she thought. Maybe it's not a good idea, searching for a place that may no longer exist. Am I chasing dreams? What if it all goes horribly awry? And Ireland—is that another dream? She envisioned herself wandering the streets of Dublin, hopelessly lost and alone. "Don't fret about it, lass," Lil had said, "God will be with you." Lil uttered the words with an ease that Edith envied. She wondered if this God would give her the courage she needed. "Hear me, God," she whispered, "guide me today!" Yes, that was the word, guide. It crops up all the time in prayers, she thought. I need guidance! She closed her eyes. "Whosoever you are, God, hear me."

The doorbell rang. Edith took a deep breath, buttoned up her cardigan, and opened the door. Before her stood a middle-aged man dressed in a suit. He looked like a sentry. He carried a wooden post supporting a large sign that read, "For Sale, Thacker & Sons Estate Agents." "Mornin'," he said. "Frank Thacker—we talked on the telephone."

"Yes," she said. "I didn't expect you so soon."

"Didn't want to keep you waiting," he said and turned from her to drop the sign in the middle of the lawn alongside a mallet he fetched from the back of his car.

"Good morning," said Edith. She showed him inside. After looking around the kitchen and parlor, he went upstairs, knocking on walls and tapping on windows.

"Keep the windows open in here," he said. "It needs to freshen. Oh, and you might put a rug or two in that empty bedroom. Give it some life."

"I will," she said. "Do you think …" Thacker was already on his way downstairs, heading for the front garden. "It's rained; she'll sink in nicely," he said, digging his heel into the lawn.

"Mr. Thacker, maybe the gate would …" He was twisting and forcing the post into the earth; then he slammed it repeatedly with the mallet.

"There's a new estate up where the old slaughterhouse used to be," he said, "if you're looking for something smaller."

"I'm not sure—"

"They've knocked it down, of course." He stamped his foot, pushing the sod back into the ground around the post. "You'd never know— stink's gone. Lovely gardens they 'ave up there. I can see you like gardens." He flicked sweat off his brow with a finger.

"I don't really, er …" She looked up to see Reg on a ladder clearing leaves from his gutter.

"It's leanin' a bit," Reg called out.

"Right," Thacker said, and gave the post a hard thwack. He stood back and appraised it. "Bingo," he said, tossing the mallet aside. It landed on a clump of crocuses. "Here today, gone tomorrow." He winked at Edith. "I'll soon shift this for you."

Standing at her front parlor window, Lil wiped away tears with the corner of her apron. She was to cry even harder some weeks later, when

Thacker, briefcase in hand, emerged from Edith's front door accompanied by a bearded Sikh and his sari-clad wife. They shook hands and posed for pictures with the sign that now read, "Sold."

"It's just not right, Reg," Lil cried. "It won't be the same!"

"Nuthin' is the same, luv," he said, "nuthin'!"

23

Convent

----

dith and Mavis had been on the road for almost two hours. "We
have to look for a sign," said Edith, "'Crags Corner,' and then we
turn left. According to Lil, it was a big stone place. She thinks
it's a teachers' college now. 'Homes for wayward girls'—that's what they
called those places then."

"Ugh, awful," said Mavis. "What about the wayward boys, then? I
suppose they got off scot-free! It's so isolated up here. Your poor mother—how must she have felt?"

"I know. Well, I don't know, do I?" Edith said. "How can I really
know? That's why I am coming up here, to help with that, to get a feel
for her. Thanks for doing this, Mavis, taking the time off."

"I'm happy to do it. I understand your reasons, Edith, love. I really
do."

"Reg said the trains came up here," said Edith. "I bet that's how they
traveled here."

"Who?"

"Ruby and Irene."

"Oh, right. Of course they would have."

"Imagine, Mavis, the two of them. Thirty-six years ago, two women
on a train: the older one firmly resolute as to the path to be taken, the
younger one pregnant, fearfully resigned to her fate. Lil remembers
when they left. Ruby was gone about four months, she said. She never
saw Irene again. Irene went back or was sent back to Ireland. Ruby came
back to Bogmire with her arms full of me, didn't she? Too bad her heart

wasn't. Do you think that made Ruby happy? Did my arrival make any-body happy, then?"

"Edith, look, we can turn back, you know. It's pouring down now. It's dismal out there. There's no one around, and not much of anything."

"No, it's fine. I want to keep going. I really do. Anyway, I want to see where I began, so to speak. Sounds daft, but I do."

"No it's not daft at all. Hey! Look over there. Isn't that the sign?"

"Yes, that's it! 'Crags Corner.' We should turn there. Look, Mavis, see that big stone building over there by those poplar trees? There's the driveway. That's it! Turn here; it starts here," said Edith.

"Right. I don't see a sign telling us to keep out. There's nobody around. Maybe they've gone for the Easter break. It's coming up, after all."

"Pull over when you get closer," Edith said. "I want to walk up there. I want to know."

"Know what?"

"Know what she felt. She carried me, Mavis. My mother carried me all the way up here. She carried me."

"Wait, Edith, you'll get soaked!"

"I don't care, I'll just be a few minutes."

Edith stepped out of the car. Rain sliced through the cold air, and the wind whipped at her scarf. She pulled it around her head and knot-ted it under her chin. She thrust her hands into her pockets and closed her fingers around her mother's photo. She walked slowly, the gravel crunching under her feet. Some sheep huddled under a tree and stared at her before skittering off when she quickened her pace. The drive led into a cobblestoned yard. "Staff only" was painted on what remained of a crumbling brick wall that bordered it. Edith stopped short to catch her breath, almost slipping on the wet moss that dotted the shiny cobble-stones. An arched gateway led into another, larger, courtyard. The gray building now loomed in front of her.

The building was four stories tall, and its bleak blackness seemed to suit the wind and rain, as if no ray of sun had ever graced its seasoned walls. Pigeons circled before landing in and around a dilapidated bell tower that rose from the center of the slate roof. Edith scanned the rows of identical gabled windows. Some lights were visible from between thick-looking curtains. A weathered statue of the Virgin Mary cast a pious eye upon the faithful from a lintel above huge oak double doors.

"Edith, hang on, wait!" called Mavis. "I'm coming. Here, I've got the umbrella. Phew!" she said and looked up to the roof. "It's been a while since that bell tolled! Do you want to go in? I'm sure they would—"

"No, no, it's awful."

"Edith, look!"

"What, where?"

"A graveyard! Look, those are tombstones! See, they're small!"

"Oh my God! You're r-r-right." Edith's teeth were chattering. "I w-wonder who? I mean, my poor mother." She drew the wet hair back from her face and moved away from where Mavis was sheltered beneath the archway.

"Edith, it's dry here. Don't go over there," she called. "It's raining harder now. Let's go, let's get out of this."

Edith looked straight ahead, walked to the center of the yard, and stood by what appeared to have been a fountain, a crumbling structure that stood about five feet high. It consisted of a circle of winged angels. Their arms were raised to support the bowl of the fountain. Edith leaned against it, placing her hands on the bowl's rim for support.

"Edith, come over here!"

Edith watched the raindrops splattering into the brackish water. She drew her hand across the blotched stone face of one of the angels, her fingers lingering across the cherubic cheeks and mouth.

"Edith!"

Edith looked at the other figures, at their blank eyes and mottled bodies. How cold they are, she thought. She looked up to the windows, then over to the Virgin Mary above the door. This was all she was left with, she thought. This was all my mother was left with, morbid memories!

"There are no angels here!" Edith called out. "They are all dead! Dead babies! That's all there is! There is no God here. No! No! Never!" Her cries reverberated through the yard, over the sound of the rain and wind. Her hands slithered off the edge of the bowl, and her legs buckled under her. "She didn't belong here! Not with them! My mother didn't belong!"

"Edith!" Mavis screamed. The wind tugged at her umbrella. She let it go and ran to Edith.

"It's all right, Edith. It is!"

"It's nothing but a prison, it's so cruel," Edith said and threw her arms around Mavis's knees, almost toppling her. "We didn't belong," Edith said, burying her face in her hands. Her body began to heave with deep sobs. Mavis's eyes filled with tears, and she stroked Edith's head and shoulders. "It's all right," she said. A light went on in the doorway of the building. A man carrying a large umbrella was hurrying across the yard toward them.

"It's going to be all right," Mavis said, and looked up to see the black canopy of an umbrella shielding them from the rain.

"Is she hurt?" the man asked. "Did she trip?"

"No," said Mavis, "she is just upset and—"

"Oh God," Edith said, and put a hand to her mouth. "I'm so sorry. I'm so—"

"Easy now," the man said. He helped Edith to her feet.

"Thanks, I'm sorry."

"It's no bother," he said. "You'd best come inside, lasses." Huddled together under the umbrella, the women followed him into the building and then to a small room off a cavernous hallway. "Get warm, sit by the fire," he said. "There's no one here but me." He produced dry towels from a cupboard. He grouped some chairs around a wood stove. "I'm just the caretaker—I'm Jack," he said, "of all trades." He laughed. "I noticed your car earlier; then I heard a shout. It gets a bit rough up here in winter. Never mind, spring's around the corner. Here," he said, passing them mugs of hot tea.

"We are truly grateful to you," said Mavis. "We were just sort of visiting around, and … well … not a good day to be out!"

"I was born here," Edith said in a firm voice. She sat up straight in her chair. "That's why we came up here: I was curious. I have never seen the place before. I didn't expect to get—well, look at me, I'm shaking."

"Ah, I see," said Jack. "You'll get warm. My old mum used to clean and cook for them up 'ere," he said. "She'd tell us some stories—some good, some not so good. Some of them bairns, well, they wasn't so lucky, eh?"

"Right. I guess I was one of the lucky ones," she said softly.

"That you were," said Mavis.

On the way home, Edith said, "What a nice man. I made such a scene! I was embarrassed, but he didn't seem to care. Honestly, I really thought the place would be different, nicer. I felt for her, Mavis. It all crept through me, the horror of it, what she went through. I felt it back there. I walked in my mother's shoes, I did." She sighed. "Everything gets so tangled! It's all so ... I keep thinking how wrong it is that anyone should have to be pregnant and then banished, so to speak. Stuck up there with those nuns, and Ruby, for God's sake!" She rubbed her eyes and sniffed back her tears.

"Never mind. You went—we went—and I am proud of you," Mavis said.

"They say what you don't know doesn't hurt," said Edith. "Well, it did hurt, it still hurts, but it's less painful—bearable, if you like."

"You had to go through that," Mavis said. "You were brave. My grandma used to say, 'If we don't feel the pain life throws at us, we will never heal.' Edith, with those tears you are healing, love, believe me. You cry all you want; I'm just going to keep driving home, okay? Tell you what."

"What?"

"We'll have hot soup when we get home."

"You know, I never really enjoyed the comfort of that word," said Edith.

"What word, 'soup'?"

"No, 'home'! It has a warm sound to it, doesn't it? Going home. Here's home. Come home. Hmmm ... Slattery Street was never like that. It was just a place. Somewhere to keep my bike, do my homework. Do my time."

"Cheer up, Edith, those days are gone. See, it's stopped raining. We don't have far to go now."

"I'm just so tired."

"Close your eyes. See if you can sleep." Mavis drove slowly. Edith eventually dozed off. There was little traffic. They reached the main road about an hour later, and Edith woke up.

"You know, the worst part of my story is back there. Goodness knows how many stories lurk within those walls. I had imagined a lawn, trees with blossoms, a verandah, fat smiling nuns with red faces, you know."

"I know," Mavis patted Edith's hand.

"Fancy, Leakey and Ruby never saying anything! Keeping it all to themselves," Edith said. "I suppose Ruby did what she thought was right and proper."

"Yes, God rest her soul. She's happier where she is, Edith, really. They owned your secret. When Leon left, they couldn't let go of it. That's Bogmire. Little pockets of deceit everywhere. My mum says that half the town still sails under false colors. Take Millie Jamieson, for instance—who knows what's going on with her?"

"Who knows? Anyway, thanks for doing this, Mavis."

"It's the least I can do. Now think good thoughts about this wedding you're going to!"

"Yes. God bless Alice and Jimmy," said Edith. "Bless them, they deserve each other."

24

Wedding

On the Saturday morning of Jimmy and Alice's wedding, Edith appraised herself in the full-length mirror. Her moss-green fitted suit felt loose because she had lost weight in the seven weeks since Ruby's death. It still looks nice, she thought. She centered the pleat in the skirt and slipped on her beige high heels before checking the combs in her upswept hair. Dusting some blusher on her cheeks, she smiled at herself. Not bad, she thought, applying a final touch of lipstick, not bad at all.

She had arranged to share a taxi to the church with Lil and Reg. The sun was shining when she rang their doorbell. Thank God we are off to a good start, she thought. "Come in, come in, Edith," said Reg. "Don't you look a smasher! Leon will be proud."

"You look a treat, Edith," Lil said. "I'm almost ready—got me brolly, just in case! Help me with me zipper, Reg." Reg zipped up Lil's dress with such zeal that the zipper jammed, so they were late getting into the honking taxi waiting outside in the street.

They eased themselves into the rear seat of the taxi. The front seat was piled high with newspapers and magazines, on top of which sat a huge boom box.

"St. Cuthbert's Church, please," Reg told the driver.

"I'm Lenny. This traffic is crap thick," the driver said, and cursed under his breath.

"I haven't seen this driver before," Lil whispered to Edith. "Shouldn't he be wearing a hat or something?"

165

"Stop fussin', Lil," Reg whispered. Edith patted Lil's hand.

"St. Cuthbert's, is it? I don't recall that one," Lenny said.

"It's near Marshside," said Reg, and proceeded to explain the route.

"Okey-dokey! Jimmy Jack's weddin'—that would be Jimmy from the depot, right?" Lenny asked.

"Right," said Reg.

"I've known Jim for years—the bettin'! The horses. He's lucky for me, is Jim."

"Nobody calls him Jim," Lil whispered.

"Hush," said Reg.

"I've never been much for churches," Lenny said, flipping a cigarette butt through the window. "I only pray when I have a bet on!" He laughed hard, swerving too close to the curb. A pedestrian jumped back and stared after them.

"Oh my!" Lil said, clutching at Reg.

"It's not far now," said Reg, checking his watch. Lil's frown deepened. She smoothed the skirt of her green crepe dress. As she did, one of her gloves fell to the floor.

"I'll get it," she said to Reg. Edith heard her gasp. "Ah! Pssst!" Lil said, "look!"

"What? What is it?" said Edith.

"Under there!" The glove had landed on a half-empty bottle of Gordon's Gin under the driver's seat. Lil retrieved her glove and then, wheezing out her breath, straightened up. She dabbed at her damp face with a handkerchief. "Oh my!"

"I have a tenner on a horse," Lenny said, turning up the volume on the radio. "Maybe it's me lucky day!"

"They're off," boomed the announcer. Lil kept nudging Reg and pointing to the bottle under the seat. Reg shook his head, frowned, and looked up at the sky. "That rain will keep off for the match," he said. "The sun's gettin' through."

They hurtled on through the traffic. "Stupid nag got left behind," Lenny said. He turned the radio down, narrowly missing a cyclist before coming to a screeching halt at the crossing. The pedestrians glared at him as they dawdled across. He held up his hands. "Dopey sods," he said.

"Bingo," said Reg, "that's the church, over there, on the corner."

While they waited for the crossing to clear, Edith's attention was drawn to the opposite side of the street. Parked beneath a tree, a short way down from the church, was a small gray van with a spare wheel mounted on the back. She recognized it instantly. It was Saleem's van. What was it doing here? The foot traffic cleared, and Edith turned to look as they drove past. Saleem, staring straight ahead, was in the driver's seat. A scarf was around his head and neck, covering his ears and mouth. He looks like the cad he is, she thought, not the charmer I believed in. "A seductive sod!" Mavis had called him.

Was Saleem waiting there for Millie? Was Millie in the church? Just what were the beans she had threatened to spill? She might be with the depot crowd. I should mind my own business, Edith thought; there is no crime to sitting in a car.

The taxi pulled up in front of the church. "Reg, the bells have stopped," Lil said. "We're late!"

"Hurry up, then, out yer get," he said.

"What are you looking at back there, Edith?" Lil asked.

"Oh, nothing; thought I knew someone," she said.

"See you all later, then," Lenny said. "I knock off at two. I'll see yer. I want to meet Jim's new missus. Check out the damage. Ha-ha!"

"They're off!" the radio announcer yelled. Lenny smacked the steering wheel with his hand. "C'mon, c'mon!" he shouted, and held out his other hand to collect his fare.

"I don't trust him," Lil said as they walked up the church steps. "He's not invited—I'm sure of that."

"Never mind that now," said Reg.

A solemn-faced man greeted them in the church vestibule. He checked his watch and gave each of them a leaflet. He put a finger to his lips before standing to one side.

"This way," whispered Reg as he steered them into a pew. Heads turned to stare. Edith saw Leon standing head and shoulders above everybody. He turned and smiled at her; she smiled back and wished she were sitting beside him. He looks magnificent, she thought, and he belongs to me and I to him. No Ruby and no schemes will ever change that now. Thank God, she thought. Feeling tears well up, she closed her eyes. Forgive me, God, but I want this wedding to be over soon, she thought. I want to be away from here, get on with the life I've started.

"We are gathered here today," the vicar began. Edith opened her eyes. The church was packed. There were people from the depot whom she recognized, and many she didn't. She spotted Millie and thought, good for you—to heck with the gossipmongers.

"Alice was right," Lil whispered to her.

"About what?"

"Her little wedding has turned into a big do!"

The organist launched into a hymn. Mary Lacey, sitting in the pew in front of them, turned around and grinned. As she did so, her perfume came at them in sickening wafts. Lil sneezed repeatedly, and Edith handed her some tissues.

"Phew!" said Reg.

"It's California Poppy! That smell." She sneezed again. "I can't help it."

"Hush," Reg said, "it's starting."

Lil kept sneezing, and by the time Alice Larkin said, "I do," she had sneezed her way through the ceremony, and the pew was littered with balled-up tissues.

"I feel a bit lightheaded," Lil said. "Perfume does that to me."

"Take some deep breaths," said Edith. "You'll be fine."

"I now pronounce you man and wife," said the vicar.

"That was quick," said Reg. The organ played the wedding march. The church bells rang. Handkerchiefs fluttered, noses were blown, and conversations started up. All eyes were on Jimmy and Alice as they beamed their wedded way back down the aisle. Mary Lacey pushed people aside to plant her bright red mouth on Jimmy's cheek.

"Got ya!" she said, ignoring the bride. "Smile now." With that, she ran ahead of them with her camera. Outside the church, everyone was hugging. "Don't be shy," said the photographer. He was laughing and dancing up and down the church steps, stooping and clicking. "Kiss the bride—she's all yours now," he said to Jimmy.

"Isn't he a scream?" Mary Lacey said, hugging Lil in a cloud of perfume. The photographer pushed them all together. "C'mon," he said, "everybody happy now!" Confetti flew everywhere. "Hiya Edith! Remember me?" a voice rang out. It was Karen, Alice's daughter. Spikes of bleached hair sprouted from Karen's head, and she wore a tight pink blouse tucked into a black leather miniskirt. Edith didn't remember her. "This is Lyle, me boyfriend," she said. Lyle looked to be in his early thirties. A thin braid of hair dangled over one ear. The rest of his hair was tied into a stubby bunch at the nape of his neck. He wore a black T-shirt with the words "Do it" written on the back.

"Pleased t'meet ya," Lyle said, fingering his earring.

"Likewise," said Edith, stepping back from his breath, which smelled of beer and tobacco.

"He's here with his band," Karen said, giggling. "They're really good. We came all the way up from Swindon on his motorbike!"

"Great," Edith said. "See you inside, then."

"Yeh," said Lyle, "see yer."

"See yer," said Karen.

"Edith—Edith—got a minute?" Lil came up close. "I feel faint," she said. "I'm never any good with smells and crowds."

"Over here," Edith said, guiding Lil to a stone bench away from the crowd. "We'll sit under the eaves; it looks like rain. Put your head between your knees, Lil."

"I can't," she said, "me girdle won't let me. I'll just have to sit." She fanned her face with the wedding program.

They watched the goings on from a distance. Children ran about, scooping up confetti; one bounced a ball off a headstone. "Give us a turn," another said. Through an open door in the parish hall at the rear of the church, they could see several women in aprons busying about, readying for the reception. Edith looked beyond the gravestones to the street. She saw the police cars first, two of them, parked under the trees. About fifty yards in front of them was the gray van, but it was empty. Where had he gone? She looked around for Leon. He must be in the hall with the others, she thought.

"Edith, Edith."

"What? Sorry, Lil, I was ..."

"I feel better," she said. "I needed to cool off. Ah, here's Reggie."

"C'mon you two," he said, "the reception's up and running. Let's enjoy ourselves."

They followed Reg into the hall. "Aren't the decorations wonderful?" said a woman at the door as she handed them glasses of champagne. "We always do this for our weddings." A huge silver horseshoe dangled above the head table, which had been set in front of the stage. Streamers crisscrossed the ceiling. White-clothed tables bordered each side of the room, leaving space in the center, Edith presumed, for dancing. Edith, Lil, Reg, and Leon sat with the newlyweds at the head table in front of the stage. Next to Alice sat Karen and Lyle.

"You look lovely," Leon said to Edith, reaching over to squeeze her hand. "I'm so proud of you," he whispered.

"Thank you," she said, "I'm so happy you are here. It's quite the occasion!"

"Yes," he said. "You and me, together—nothing tops that!"

From the stage, an announcement was made that all the guests must avail themselves of the open bar, courtesy of the Red Lion Pub.

"Whoo-hoo!" yelled Lyle. People cheered.

Edith glanced down the table to see Jimmy kissing his bride's hand. Karen was retouching her lipstick. Lyle was picking his nose. There were multiple toasts, but the speeches were brief. Jimmy was bashful; Alice looked radiant. She kissed her daughter after tearfully thanking and welcoming everyone, especially those who had traveled a fair distance. "Hey, you're welcome! No fuckin' problem!" Lyle responded in a loud voice. He waved his glass in the air. Beer slopped over, narrowly missing the tiered wedding cake in the center of the table.

"Lyle, for God's sake!" Karen hissed.

Leon proposed a toast. "I am honored to be back in Bogmire for this special occasion," he said. Tears slid down Lil's pink cheeks. "He's a dream come true," she said. Jimmy got up from his seat. "Friends, it's time the music started," he said. "Enjoy yourselves."

Mary Lacey was soon on the stage, adjusting the microphone. "Give us a song!" someone yelled.

"Show us your tits!" Lyle shouted.

"Watch yer mouth, young fella," said Leon.

"Just 'avin a bit of fun; I don't mean nuthin'." He laughed and kissed Karen on the neck.

"If you please, a bit of quiet," Mary called out. Two men in matching green waistcoats and red bowties stood in the wings. "A big hand, please," she said, "for Harold Snipe on the accordion and Jerry Bloggs on the keyboard." The musicians stepped to center stage, bowed, and launched into a loud rendition of "The Anniversary Waltz," drowning out the rest of Mary's introduction. Alice and Jimmy took to the floor. Millie Jamieson was whisked onto the floor by the head of the Transport Office, Ralph Peebles. Leon took Edith's hand, and they stepped around to the music, occasionally tripping, only to laugh and give up after a short while. The accordion blasted, the streamers quivered, and the suspended horseshoe began to swing. Mary Lacey tottered back down the stage steps. "C'mon, everyone!" she shouted, hitching up her skirt and kicking up her heels.

Women dashed about with platters of food. Glasses were speedily refilled. It occurred to Edith that the scene looked more like a Christmas party than a wedding. She watched the dancing couples. I'm not really part of this depot crowd, she thought. I'm just a passenger here, meandering in and out of all their lives. She thought of Dublin and her mother. She wished she could to talk to Leon, take a stroll, be with him now, just the two of them, but it was pouring outside and she couldn't see him anywhere.

Mary Lacey had her head thrown back as she danced in the middle of the group. Edith strained to see who her partner was. "Oh my God!" she said to Reg. "Look, it's Lenny! That taxi driver!"

"Cheeky devil," Reg said.

Suddenly the lights went dim and the music stopped. "Stay where you are, dancers," said Harold Snipe. His face was as red as his bowtie, and his head jutted forward from the weight of his accordion. "Now for some real romance," he said over the whistling microphone. "Listen, if you please, to the velvet voice of Jerry, the crooner's crooner!" Jerry Bloggs affected a drum-roll for himself. "This is for the happy couple," he said, looking around the room. "I know yer there," he said with a wink.

"Where are they?" Edith asked Reg.

"They've gone. Leon took them to the train station. They didn't want any fuss. He'll be back shortly."

Jerry Bloggs began to sing. His warbling baritone filled the room. "Some enchanted evening ..."

Mary Lacey's eyes closed as she and Lenny swayed to the music. Lenny's head was buried in her neck. His hand was struggling to find its way under the waistband of her too-tight skirt.

"That Mary, she's disgustin'," said Lil. "As for that Lenny showin' up, who does he think he is?" Couples trailed onto the floor, circling awkwardly to the music, stopping now and then to embrace. Millie was still dancing with Ralph Peebles. At least she's not sitting on her own, Edith thought. Cheers to you—don't let the Bogmire gossip get you down! As Edith reached for her champagne, the tablecloth shifted and a glass toppled. Lyle had leaped to his feet. "This isn't bloody music!" he shouted, slamming a fist on the table. "C'mon, lads, get the amps up there. It's time for them old farts to piss off!"

"Lyle!" Karen yelled.

"Sit down, mate, or else," said Reg.

"That music stinks!" Lyle said. "We're fallin' asleep down 'ere."

"... across a crowded room, and somehow you'll know," sang Jerry Bloggs. Suddenly, at the rear of the hall, someone yelled, "Hey, watch it, fella!" A door slammed.

"Oh no, look who it is!" Edith said. Saleem was coming through the room, pushing people aside, making his way past the tables toward the dancers. "What's he doing in here?"

"Who is he?" said Reg.

"It's him, from the No. 9," gasped Lil. "Don't let him shove people like that!"

"Stop him!" said Edith. "He looks mad; he'll hurt someone. Where's Leon?"

"Get the police!" Reg shouted.

"He's after Millie—I know it," Edith said. "Somebody, stop him! Stop that music!"

"Leave him to me," Reg said, flinging off his jacket. "I'll get him!"

"Reggie, no!" Lil jumped up. "Stay out of it, Reggie!" she said, holding on to the table. "Ooh! I'm dizzy ... the horseshoe is spinning up there."

"Beetch! You are a beetch, Meelie!" Saleem yelled.

"Lil, hang on a minute," Reg said.

"Get the police!" said Edith. Saleem was on the dance floor, his angry eyes inches away from Ralph Peebles's frightened face.

"Get out! Clear off! Leave 'em alone!" Reg yelled. Saleem put his hands around Ralph's neck and Millie screamed. There was a clattering sound. Lil had slithered to the floor, taking the tablecloth, plates, glasses, and cutlery with her. The music had stopped, and the dancers clutched one another, frozen in place. Others had backed away to stand behind the tables.

"Stop!" Millie screamed, cowering behind Ralph. "Stop, Saleem, please!"

"Someone, do something!" Edith yelled. "Get the police!"

"Fuck the police," Lyle said, and leaped onto Saleem's back, wrapping his hands around Saleem's head and covering his eyes with his fingers.

"No, Lyle! No!" yelled Karen.

"Get into him! Bloody Arab!" someone shouted. Saleem grabbed Lyle's wrists, easily throwing him off. Lyle crashed onto the floor just as Lenny stepped up and crunched his fist into Saleem's right eye. Back on his feet now, Lyle jumped around like a boxing referee. "I was trusting you, Meelie!" Saleem shouted, a hand covering his bleeding face. "I was trusting!"

"Fuck off, yer slimy bastard," Lyle growled.

"Don't tell me what to fuckin' do," said Lenny, his bloodshot eyes blinking rapidly.

"Am not talking to you, yer prick. Him, the Paki," Lyle said, but Lenny pushed him backward against the head table. Lyle dropped to the floor, and the top tier of the wedding cake flipped over. Everybody scattered as bits of cake and sugared flowers spilled onto Lyle's inert body. A miniature bride and groom rested sideways on a plate of chicken bones.

"It's about time," Reg said when four policemen marched into the hall. They ran after Saleem, who was heading for a rear door. The door crashed open. There was a scuffle. The lights came on. The police escorted the bleeding assailant across the room and out the main door, followed by gasps, then cheers and applause. Karen sobbed as sirens wailed outside.

This is bedlam, Edith thought. This is Bogmire bedlam! She moved to comfort the shaken Millie. "Stay with me, Edith, please," Millie said, clutching Edith's arm. "This is terrible!"

"Can someone give us a hand here?" Reg called out. He was kneeling next to Lil, who was under the table, tugging at the tablecloth that all but covered her.

"What happened, Reggie?" she asked.

"I think you fainted," he said, wiping crumbs off her face. The police helped him get her back to her feet.

"You missed the pandemonium," he said.

"Oh dear," she said, "I had such a funny turn. Is he gone?"

"Don't worry, he'll be in custody," said the policeman. "We've had our eye on him for a while now."

"Goodness," said Lil, "who's crying?"

"That's Karen. Her boyfriend got into the fight," Reg said.

"He's not dead, is he?" Karen said, standing over the limp Lyle. The police officer nudged him with his foot, and Lyle rolled to one side. "Fuck off," he said.

"We'll put him in the tank for now," the officer said. "As for Lenny, he has a knack for trouble. He'll never learn." They called an ambulance for the trembling Ralph Peebles. He declined it, preferring to sit outside, smoke a cigar, and sip on whisky. The aproned women peeked out from behind the kitchen door. The musical duo had disappeared, as had most of the guests. Mary Lacey sat on the stage steps. Her skirt zipper gaped open as she poked at her nest of red hair. "I've lost an earring," she said. "It's a pity; they were good ones."

Lenny brandished a cigarette, but he was having trouble finding his mouth. "Anybody got a light?" he asked.

"You're already lit, Lenny, you're drunk again," one of the policeman said. Leon arrived just as Lenny was ushered into the paddy wagon. "What on earth?" he said. Reg attempted to describe what had happened. "Where is Edith—is she all right?" Leon asked.

"She's fine," said Reg. "She's going with Millie to the police station."

"I'll go with them," said Leon.

At the police station, Millie held Edith's hand. "I'm glad it's all over, really," she said. They learned that Saleem and his brother Ali were in the country illegally, operating a dubious scheme arranging loans for immigrants. "I feel such a fool," said Millie. "I believed Saleem's every word!" So did I, thought Edith. "I'm scared to go home now."

"Stay at the Majestic," said Leon.

"You'll be fine there," Edith said. "Mavis and I can get what you need from your house tomorrow. I promise."

"He's slipped through our fingers before," the inspector whispered to Edith while Millie was in the washroom. "They all look bloody alike, these Pakis."

"Are we finished here?" said Edith.

"We are. Nesbitt is my name, Richard," he said. "You can call me Dick. I'll have a car outside for you."

"Right," said Edith. "We'll make sure that Millie gets settled."

Later that evening, Leon and Edith joined Reg and Lil in their front parlor. "Them police took their sweet time, and I know why," Reg said.

"Why?" asked Edith.

"Manchester United scored in overtime! They couldn't tear themselves away from the radio!"

"I don't believe that," said Edith.

"I do," said Lil. "Men! They're football mad! Poor Millie. I don't know her that well, really."

"Me neither," sighed Edith.

"There's a lot we don't know," Lil said.

"Right," said Edith.

25

Aftermath

----

*I*t was more like a pub brawl than a wedding!" Edith said to Mavis at breakfast the next day. "I think Saleem had scared Millie into keeping quiet. I never imagined him to be married; I never seriously thought about what his life could be like. Why would I? I just flirted with him, I suppose, more fool me! I knew Edwin was married, but he never lied to me. He just said that Sybil didn't love him—she never had. Pathetic really. Saleem didn't notice me yesterday. Not that he would have cared. Whatever would Millie think if—"

"Edith, keep quiet about that night; it's our secret."

"I hate secrets. They get pried out of crevices in the worst ways."

"You're right," said Mavis. "Think of the good things now. Cheer up. Let's get a move on—we have to get Millie's things."

"Right. I have her key; she lives up at Bogmire Heights on Willow Avenue," said Edith.

"Supposed to be nice up there."

Edith and Mavis drove along the quiet Sunday morning streets. "There were some nice moments yesterday," Edith said. "You should have seen Leon and me dancing! He said to me, 'When you see your mother, Edith, give her my love. There's plenty of it for both of you.' I know he loved her. I bet he still does. She's so pretty in those photos. At least I have them. What if I get to Ireland and I—"

"Hey! What's all this?" said Mavis, braking sharply. Several people were standing in the middle of the road. As they drove closer, they saw that it was a contingent of the Salvation Army. "Well, it is Sunday," she said, stopping the car. "We have to be respectful."

176

"Look at them," said Edith. "They look exactly as they did when I was a kid. Those uniforms!" Bonneted women were handing sheet music to the band members. The sun glinted off their brass bugles and silver triangles. Forming a large circle, they gradually filled the street. Traffic was backing up on either side. Mavis's car was first in line. "We have a front row seat," she said. "We'll listen." She rolled down the car windows. A man with a baton nodded to the euphonium player. Then, with an introductory boom, the group launched into "Onward, Christian Soldiers."

"Marching as to war," sang Edith, a smile spreading across her face.

Mavis joined in, "With the cross of Jesus, going on before." Doors and windows opened. People ambled out to lean on their front gates, yawning and exchanging nods. "Christ the royal master …" Mavis and Edith sang every verse and chorus before dissolving into laughter when they realized that they had an audience. Behind the car, two smirking teenaged boys astride their bicycles faked applause.

"I remembered the words," Edith said.

"Me too," said Mavis.

A Salvation Army woman approached the car and rattled a can through the open window. "Hello," she said. "Anything is appreciated." Edith dropped some change in the can.

"God be with you," the woman said, handing Edith a leaflet that read, "The Salvation Army cares for the needy. Support our shelter."

"Do you think he is?" said Edith.

"He is what?" said Mavis, turning on the ignition. The traffic began to move.

"With me, God?" Edith asked.

"Are you serious?" Mavis said.

"Yes, I am."

"Well, it would be nice to think so. But I—"

"Ma always said that God would find me out. I never knew what she meant, really. That just scared me. Keep going along here, Mavis, to the end; then we turn right. Oh heck!"

"Heck what?"

"Oh nothing, I was thinking out loud. My head is spinning. Sometimes I think I'm going mad!" Edith said.

"Maybe you should hold off."

"Hold off what?" Edith said.

"Going to Ireland, to see your mother. It's days away, right?"

"Yep," said Edith. "I can't wait, I simply can't, though I am exhausted. Turn left here. Go up the hill; this is Bogmire Heights. Willow Avenue is at the end, No. 7."

"It's beautiful up here," Mavis said. "Nice gardens."

"Here we are. Willow Avenue, one, three, five, seven." Edith pointed, "There, seven. Her name, Jamieson—it's on the letterbox. Nice house."

"Edith, I promised Mum I would ring her about lunch later. I'll go and find a telephone box while you get Millie's things together. There's bound to be one around here somewhere. I won't be long."

"Don't worry," Edith called out as Mavis started up the car. "God be with you."

"What?" Mavis asked.

"Never mind," Edith said, "never mind."

She watched the car turn the corner. All was quiet except for the sounds of wind rustling through a beech tree by the gate and bells from a nearby church. She closed Millie's front gate and dawdled up the path to the front door. What a heartbreaking kettle of fish this is, she thought, and sat down on the front steps. She rubbed her eyes with the heels of her hands and yawned. The sun had gathered strength, spreading its warmth through the sheltered garden. A few clusters of daises relieved the flat green of the well-mown lawn. She tugged at some weeds lodged between the step stones and pondered just how many vulnerable souls Saleem had sucked into his sham world. That includes me, she thought; it was a world she had ventured into and thankfully emerged from unscathed.

Birds hopped about, loudly chattering within the privet hedge that bordered the property. Edith realized that the church bells had stopped ringing. The congregation will start shuffling about now, she thought. The women will be taking their inventories of who's present and who's not. The men will clear their throats as they prepare to mouth hymns next to their warbling wives. What is it they find in that church, as they sit in their pews each Sunday? Something I've never found, she thought.

The truth is, it's something I never bothered to look for.

It's peaceful here, she thought; this place doesn't feel like Bogmire, where everybody seems to be falling over each other like the disordered mess of the wedding yesterday. She removed her mother's photo from her pocket, a gesture so familiar to her now that it was comforting. She traced her fingers across her mother's image. "Soon," she said, "soon I will see you, soon." She recalled Rhonda's flippant reference to Irene's children and wondered if she would ever be part of the brood, as Rhonda had called them. Will I be intruding? Will I ruffle settled feathers? "One thing I know," she said to the photo before putting it in her pocket, "I'll not stay in Bogmire. Bogmire, where you are judged before you are born, when word is out that you are coming, and God forbid if you don't stay within your assigned pew!"

Edith opened Millie's front door. The hall led off to a large sitting room with a bay window that looked out onto the front lawn. How cruel life is, she thought, with its missteps, pitching us into voids that leave us floundering. At the top of the stairs was the master bedroom. "Everything on the list is in there," Millie had said. Edith stared at the bed, a king-sized plateau of quilted ivory silk with satin pillows. She opened the mirrored wardrobe doors to see, hanging alongside numerous coats, dresses, and jackets, three saris in scarlet, emerald, and gold. She ran her hands along the cool silken folds of the fabric. Did Millie wear these for him?

She chose a warm coat, as Millie requested, before moving to the chest of drawers. Neatly arranged in the drawers were layers of delicate garments, camisoles and slips. She looped the straps of a nightgown over her thumbs and held it close to her body. The cream satin folds of the garment flared out from a pin-tucked bodice bordered with tiny rosebuds. It was the most beautiful thing she had ever seen. She felt gorgeous and giddy posing this way and that, until a noise downstairs startled her. The gown slithered down, resting in a creamy heap at her feet. Someone was coming up the stairs. The bedroom door was pushed open.

"Anyone home?"

"Er—"

"Ah, Miss Sharpe, it's me, Richard Nesbitt, the police officer from yesterday." He was smiling. "Long time no see," he said, and laughed.

"Oh, right, I was just …"

"It smells fancy in here," he said, and took his hat off. "Huh, it's nice," he said, looking around the room.

"Yes, I suppose it is."

"The front door was left open," he said. "Bit dodgy, that."

"I didn't think."

She scooped up the nightgown and collected the rest of the items. "These are things Millie needs," she said, and held up the list. Had he seen her little display? She didn't care; he looked stupid, lounging and grinning in the doorway. What was he doing here?

"By the way," he said, "they got him, the brother. They picked him up last night in Bradford, and it turns out our Mr. Banerjee has a wife and kids in Islamabad."

"Oh, that's terrible!"

"They come 'ere, these foreigners, and they reckon they can get away with anything! Anyway," he said, "I still have to watch this place, keep an eye out." He looked at his watch. "Is there a telly around?" he said. A car horn sounded outside. Edith looked out the window. Mavis's car was at the gate.

"What? Sorry, I didn't catch that," said Edith, grabbing more things from the drawer.

"A telly," he said. "There's a big match on," he said, "a repeat. I missed most of it yesterday, dammit!"

"I wouldn't know," said Edith. "My friend's out there waiting," she said, and rushed down the stairs, almost tripping on the porch steps.

"Whoa!" said Mavis. "I saw the police car. What's the rush?"

"Yes, that policeman, Nesbitt, he was at the station last night. He just got here. He's supposed to keep an eye on the place. He's a bit of an idiot. He tells me they've picked up Saleem's brother," she said. "I suppose that's a good thing—who knows? And," said Edith, "he tells me that Saleem has a wife and children in Islamabad!"

"Phew! That'll be another rude awakening for Millie, poor woman!"

"Do you think she knows?" Edith asked.

"No idea. Did you get everything on her list?"

"More or less."

"Let's go," said Mavis. "As soon as we are finished, Mum has a roast waiting for us."

"Heaven," said Edith.

26

Ferry

----

dith, Leon, and Mavis stood close together at the Holyhead ferry terminal. They stomped their cold feet, their misty breath evaporating into the frigid early-morning air. Leon picked up Edith's suitcase and handed it to her. "Remember," he said, "just ring. I'm here if you need me."

"We'll see you soon," said Mavis. "Good luck tomorrow. They will love you for sure." Edith's eyes filled with tears as she hugged them before leaving to join the long column of passengers waiting to board the ferry. "You'll be in Dublin in no time. It's a high-speed ferry!" Mavis called out.

Edith settled for a window seat in a booth on the crowded lower lounge deck. She was squashed in but comfortable and exchanged smiles with the woman who sat next to her. "Jaysus," the woman said, "it's always crowded like this! Isn't that God's truth?" Before Edith could respond, the woman had turned away and was laughing with a youth seated opposite her in the booth.

As the ferry got under way, Edith was grateful to be alone at last with her thoughts. She had felt sad saying good-bye to Mavis and Leon. Already she missed them. Dear Mavis, who had faithfully steered her through the worst of times—which, she hoped, were now behind her. And there was Leon, her new father, full of love and hope, someone she could now rightfully claim as her own. Her thoughts turned to Irene, as they always did when Leon came to mind. Had they really loved each other, Leon and Irene? It was a question she pondered for the umpteenth time. Had she, Edith, been the result of a frivolous fling, as Ruby would likely have maintained? What is Irene really like? And her husband and children, three boys and a girl—what of them?

The ferry gave a sudden jolt. Edith inhaled sharply and felt a little nauseated. She fumbled for her handkerchief. "Are you all right there?" the woman next to her asked. "You look a bit pale."

"Yes, I—"

"Don't worry now, love. It'll be calmin' down."

"Right," said Edith. She tucked the pink-and-yellow wool scarf that Lil had crocheted for her into her coat collar. "She picked them colors special like, just for you," Reg had said. Edith smiled to herself and turned to face the window. She looked out at the roiling sea and the gray storm clouds above. Somewhere out there, somewhere up there, she imagined Ruby, her finger wagging, her head shaking. "God rest Ruby's weary old soul," Lil and Reg had said. Ruby's soul I never reached, Edith thought. Were my efforts enough? Did I really try? I think Ruby tried hard to be my mother, she thought. "Our mothers are our only anchors," Edwin had bleated, "linked by a chain never to be broken!"

"What about the rust?" Edith had retorted. "What about the barnacles that will not budge?" She pondered Edwin's paltry soul. Poor Edwin, she thought, I hope you have found some solace in your Sybil-ruled world. At least you were honest, unlike Saleem. She wondered what would happen to the other wife and her children. And what of Millie's rude awakening? Just more fodder, she thought, for Bogmire's wagging tongues. A slap of hands on the booth table startled her. A pack of cards appeared. "I'll get yer this time," the woman said to the youth opposite.

"'Struth, yer won't! No cheatin', Ma." He laughed and dealt the cards with a flourish.

Edith yawned. Shaky music dribbled from a speaker above her. Somewhere a whining child was being reprimanded. Guffaws and cheering came from the bar at the far end of the deck. "Goal!" was shouted in unison.

I'm moving at last, she thought, far from Slattery Street. That life is gone, it's all gone. Is this the change that Ruby, with all her good intent, tried to shield me from, keeping me tethered to her old ideals? Have I stopped chasing that something, that something I felt I'd never catch? I have it now, she said to herself, and closed her fingers around the photograph in her pocket. I think I have finally caught it. With a soft smile on her lips, she closed her eyes and dozed. The patter and the chatter of the card game faded as the vessel's engines throbbed steadily beneath them.

Sleep came to her in fractured bouts as the ferry rolled and pitched its way across the Irish Sea. One senseless dream followed another. In one dream, she met her Irish mother, who shouted at her, "Go away, you are not mine! The nuns made a mistake!" In another, she was in a plane en route to Australia with Reg and Lil. People were singing "Waltzing Matilda."

"Now," someone said. "Now!" Edith woke up. A voice on the sound system announced, "Last call for the duty-free shop. Last call, now!" She shifted forward in her seat, rubbed her eyes, and looked out the window. The Irish shoreline was just visible through a bank of gray mist. She placed her left hand on her chest and breathed deeply, closing the fingers of her right hand over the photograph in her pocket. Passengers moved about, fussing with bags and packages. The youth whistled as he scooped up the playing cards.

"Go tell yer da to drink up now," the woman said to the boy. She turned to Edith. "Them fellas can't watch a game without a jar in their hand," she said and gestured toward the bar. "Feelin' better now, are yer, dearie? Stayin' in Dublin, are yer then?"

"Yes," said Edith.

"Visitin' family, are yer?"

"Well, yes I am." Edith stood up and gathered her belongings.

"See yer then," said the woman. "It's drizzling out there." She laughed. "What's new, right?"

"Right, 'bye," Edith said, and joined the line of passengers at the exit. She wound her scarf snugly about her neck and joined a second line on the dock to wait for a taxi.

The taxi dropped her off at Coogan's Hotel. It was located in central Dublin, two blocks from the River Liffey. Rhonda had booked the reservation. "It's a fine old place," she had said. Edith paused for a moment at the entrance and held on to the door's brass rail. The motion of the ferry was still with her. When she entered the hotel, she stopped abruptly and then took a step backward. A young woman stood directly in her path. It was the woman's red curly hair that commanded Edith's attention before their eyes locked. "Excuse me," Edith said, stepping to one side. The woman made no effort to move. "Jaysus!" she said, stepping in the same direction as Edith. "Fer Christ's sake!"

"Sorry," said Edith.

"Oh, fuck it," the woman said, casting Edith a look of distaste before stepping back. She hunched up the collar of her black pea coat and headed for the door. What did I do? Edith thought. She turned to watch the bobbing red curls disappear among the street crowd. Maybe I am still disoriented. Am I that dizzy? Cautiously, she approached the clerk at the desk in the center of the hotel lobby.

"Morning, miss, welcome to Coogan's," the clerk said, patting a gold-embroidered C on the pocket of his green blazer. "I'm Bernard. How can I help you?"

"I have a room booked. Edith Sharpe."

"Indeed you have," he said, pulling a card out of a file. "A single, is it?"

"That's right," said Edith.

"Would that be fer one night, Miss Sharpe?"

"I, er, think so. Well, maybe two."

"Fine, then. Just be letting me know if that's so," he said. "Come far, have you?" he asked as she completed the registration form.

"Bogmire," she said, "on the Lancashire coast. Do you know it?"

"Can't say that I do. Welcome to Dublin," he said, beaming as he handed her a key. "Would you be wanting a hand with your bags?"

"I'll be fine," she said.

"Oh, I almost forgot. There was a lady here earlier, around 10 a.m. She was asking after a Miss Sharpe. She chose not to leave a message or her name."

"Really? Perhaps it was my aunt Rhonda?"

"Perhaps. She was on the young side. What does your aunt look like?"

"I don't know," Edith said, realizing how stupid she sounded.

"Well, then, I'll let you know if she comes back."

"Ravenswood, is it far from here?" Edith asked.

"Not far. Nice drive, though."

"Thanks," said Edith.

Her upper-floor room looked down on a busy square. She lay back on the big, soft bed, only to be disturbed minutes later by a ringing phone. It was Bernard from the lobby. "Miss Sharpe, a lady to see you," he said, "the one that was here earlier. She says she's a relative."

"I'll be right down," said Edith. It puzzled her that Aunt Rhonda hadn't phoned first as promised. She entered the lobby from the elevator and looked over to Bernard. He raised his eyebrows and nodded toward a woman who stood a short distance from the desk. She had her back to them, with her feet apart and arms folded, red curls spilling over the collar of her black coat. It was the same young woman that Edith had almost collided with earlier.

"Miss," Bernard called out to her, "over here, miss." The woman spun round, and her large brown eyes scanned Edith from top to toe. "Well," she said, "this time around I'm getting a damn good look! And I don't bloody believe it, that's fer sure!"

Edith gasped and held out her hand. "I'm Edith Sharpe. I—"

With her hands on her hips and a toss of her curls, the woman said, "Sure! I know just who you are. I knew earlier! God's only truth, you look just like her!"

"I, er, look, I—"

"Aunty Rho told me everything," the woman said, "but I didn't bloody believe it. Been waitin' since early this mornin' I have. I had to see you for meself!" she said with a sneer. "I'm Brigid! The eldest. Or did you know that already? It's quite a story you dug up!" She spat out her words as if they tasted sour. "Don't be bringing a mess back to our house, for God's sake. We've fuckin' trouble enough."

"Well, I don't know—" said Edith.

"No, you don't know!" Brigid said.

"Look, I—"

Bernard interrupted, "Call for you, Miss Sharpe."

"Thanks," Edith said, and stepped away to take the phone. Bernard raised his eyebrows and shuffled papers about the counter.

"Edith, love, it's me, Rhonda. She's there, isn't she, Brigid?"

"Yes."

"Are you all right, darlin'?"

"Well, I am, yes."

"I'm so sorry, Edith. She promised me she'd behave. She's a hot-head—she has a mouth on her like, well, you'll have had a taste already, no doubt! Always spoilin' for a fight, she is. The girl has spent too much time up north. Thinks she can save us all! Believe me, Edith, it's not what I planned. Let me talk to her. I'll call you tonight, pet, I promise. Don't be worryin' now."

"It's Rhonda," Edith told Brigid. "She wants to talk to you." She held out the receiver and Brigid grabbed it. Edith heard snippets of the conversation. "Sorry, I had to, Auntie Rho, I had to! … I know, I will … Yes, 'bye." She handed the phone back to Bernard and looked at Edith. "I can't help meself," she said in a low voice. "Anyway, don't take any notice of me; nobody does. See yer." She hurried off toward the door.

That afternoon, Edith walked beside the River Liffey, dragging her tired feet. The water was murky, the streets crowded, and the traffic noisy. Her head was saturated with new problems. *I'm already resented! What if the others feel the same way? What if I am asked to leave?* After a light supper in the dining room, she went up to her room and placed calls to Mavis and Leon. They wished her luck the next day. "A nightcap will help you get a good night's sleep," said Mavis.

"Who knows what tomorrow may bring? I could be stepping into chaos!" she said to Leon.

"Edith, you are strong. You are going to be fine. Put your trust in Rhonda. Take her hand. I'll be holding your other hand," he said, "at least in spirit, with all the love I can muster." She missed them both and wanted to cry. "You always feel better after a good cry!" Lil would say. "Split open an onion. It'll get you started—never fails." Edith laughed to herself. *Ah well, crying takes energy,* she thought, *and I am already spent.* Besides, she wanted to look her best for her mother, not cried out with red, swollen eyes. She took a miniature bottle of Bailey's Irish Cream from the room fridge and lay on the bed.

Rhonda's call came later that evening. "Leave the family to me," she said. "We'll weave peace amongst the lot of 'em!" She apologized pro-fusely for Brigid. "That girl has always felt left out. Irene dotes on those three boys, Michael, Colin, and Liam. She dotes on Brigid too, but the girl doesn't see it. She's just two years younger than you, Edith. Perhaps it's all a bit too close for comfort yet, the shock an' all that. You see, I was the only other person Irene told. She even lied at confession. I'll never forget it. Oh my, she cried and cried. 'The church is no comfort; my baby's gone!' she said. 'What's the point of confession, Rhonda,' she said to me, 'talking to a hole in the wall?' She's never been to church since.

"Irene joined up with Sean a short time after that. He took good care of her, he did. He'd had his eye on her since grammar school. He's a good man, Edith. He's a good father to those children. Irene tried to phone you after we first talked. 'I'll hold your hand,' I said to her, and I did, but her tears were flowing like the River Liffey. She gave up in the end."

"I think I understand that," said Edith. "It's all a bit frightening."

"That it is, that it is! Are you okay just now?"

"I'm sipping on a nightcap."

"Good for you, Edith. It'll be just the three of us tomorrow," she said. "You won't be wantin' an audience; there'll be time enough for that. I can't wait to see you, love. It's a nice drive to Ravenswood, to their farm, if it's not pouring."

That night, Edith prayed. Please let her love me, like me, she said. Let Brigid and those brothers love me. She prayed for sleep, for a simple peace, for happiness. They were floating prayers, and she repeated them over and over as they wafted from her like feathers. They have to land on somebody, she thought, they have to.

27

Mother

- - - - - - - - - - - - -

dith heard the gentle clatter of a tray being placed outside the door of her hotel room. She had ordered room service, as the thought of breakfast in the dining room overwhelmed her. She had slept fairly well, waking only once in the night to the sound of noisy revelers in the corridor. Lying awake, she watched the shadows on the ceiling of the unfamiliar room. She was inundated with thoughts of the Monahan family rejecting her, seeing her as a troublemaker, as Brigid obviously had. She imagined the sons viewing her as an interfering outsider. It wasn't until she placed her hands in a prayer position and reflected over and over on Leon's words, "You will be fine, Edith, you are strong," that she drifted back into a dreamless sleep.

Bernard's call came from the lobby at 9 a.m. "Your aunt, she is here for you, Miss Sharpe. Will I send her up?"

"No thanks, I'll be right down." Edith held her mother's photograph against her chest. "This is it! This is our beginning, the day we meet," she said, before placing the photo in her jacket pocket. She finished her coffee and brushed the toast crumbs from her lap. She checked herself in the mirror. Navy pantsuit, pink silk blouse, jacket left open. She lightly dusted the lapels of her jacket with her fingertips. Stepping back from the mirror, she fastened the jacket buttons; then, with a shake of her head, she undid them again. Steadying one hand with the other, she applied a final touch of lipstick. She teased and touched the dark curls that framed her face and felt that she looked too pale and thin. Maybe she was just tired. Mavis would scold her now and tell her to get a move on. Mavis was usually right, she thought, heading for the door.

She decided to walk the three flights of stairs down to the lobby. She assured herself as she did so, I am going to be fine; take it easy. She paused on each landing, attempting to still her thoughts and slow her breathing. She could hear the rumble of voices and clatter of footsteps growing louder as she approached the final set of stairs, the ones that circled down into the lobby. Before reaching the last steps, she stopped, held on to the banister rail, and looked about her. An endless stream of people exited and entered the hotel through the main door. Suited men holding briefcases stood around in circles. A maid straightened newspapers on a table; another flicked a duster across some chairs. Bernard soon spotted Edith. He nodded and gestured toward a slender, silver-haired woman who was standing beside the reception desk. Edith took a deep breath, buttoned her jacket, and approached them slowly.

"Good morning, Miss Sharpe," Bernard said. "I was just telling your aunt here—oh, pardon me." He quickly turned from them to answer a ringing phone. The woman stood about four feet away from Edith, smiling.

"Hello," Edith said, aware that she was blushing and visibly shaking. Rhonda took a step forward. Tall and elegant, she was nothing like the matronly figure that Edith had imagined her to be. Her hair was swept up in a chignon. A silk stole matching the blue of her eyes was fashionably draped about her shoulders.

"Hello, Edith, love," she said. "How are you?"

"I'm—I'm fine." Edith stared at the set of Rhonda's eyes, her cheekbones, and her soft mouth, readying to smile. They were her mother's features, ones that had become so familiar to her from the photograph.

"Sorry, I ..." said Edith. They laughed nervously.

"It's all right, darlin'," Rhonda said, her eyes glistening with emerging tears. "It's wonderful to see you at last, Edith, love." They moved closer together. Tears slid down Edith's cheeks. She felt as if she were melting with relief and wanted to say, "Thank God you are nice! Thank God you are here," as she almost tripped into Rhonda's outstretched arms. "Rhonda, I—"

"Bless you, dear child," Rhonda said. They hugged each other long and hard before stepping back to stand at arm's length, their hands clasped.

"I don't know what to say," said Edith. "I didn't mean to stare. It's just, your likeness, the photo I have of her. It's amazing."

"Oh, I know," Rhonda said and laughed. "We were often taken as twins, Irene and me. There's just over a year between us." She shook her head. "As God is in heaven, there's no mistakin' whose child you are. Look at you! My, you're lovely!"

"Oh, I'm a mess," Edith said, wiping her cheek with the back of her hand. "Really, I—"

"Ah, hush now, pet." Rhonda said. "It's enough for me that you're wearing our Irene's smile. She lost it somewhere along the road. For sure, you'll be giving it back to her, Edith, love." They hugged again, rocking together, laughing through more tears. They turned to Bernard, who was watching them. "This is my niece," Rhonda said, and linked her arm through Edith's.

Bernard nodded. "Fer sure, family's a wonderful thing," he said. "It's a grand morning for a drive, ladies."

"That it is, that it is," said Rhonda. "C'mon, Edith. Our Irene's waiting for us."

They drove through the center of Dublin and out through the suburbs before reaching open countryside. Talking continuously, Rhonda and Edith paused only to marvel and sigh at the circumstances that had brought them together. Rhonda frequently interjected their conversation with "Thank the good God in heaven! Who would have believed it?"

"I have never had so much to say to someone I just met," said Edith after relating an abridged account of her thirty-six years. "I wanted my life to be so different," she said. "I never ever imagined that it would turn out this way! I knew that Ruby would die at some point, of course, but this! Her death was a shock, it was so awful! Believe me, no one should die alone like that, no one."

Rhonda reached over and gave Edith's arm a squeeze. "You are not to blame for all o' that. T'was God's will," she said. "You suffered as well, pet. The cruelest lies are told in silence. A lie is like the cut of a knife. The wound may heal, but the scar can be stubborn. Well, let me tell you, Edith, love, when Ruby died, the scars went with her, and that's the truth!"

"The thing is," said Edith, "I never knew, really knew, what I wanted. I do now."

"And what would that be, Edith, love?"

"Well, when I say the word 'mother,' I want to know in my heart what it means. That I belong to her, just as I know now that I belong to Leon." Edith covered her eyes with her hands. "I'm sorry, I'm getting so soppy about him."

"Ah, don't be worryin', pet. Nothing dries sooner than a happy tear. And there'll be more o' them before the day's done."

"He's a fine man, Leon, my father, a good man," said Edith.

"Ah, I know that for sure," said Rhonda. "I remember Irene's eyes smiling every time she mentioned him back then, and mention him she did, even after she wed Sean."

"And Sean," said Edith, "what does he think now?"

"Well, like I said, I was the only one who knew about you," said Rhonda. "It's three years now since our mother died, and our dad five years afore that. 'They can't hear me now,' Irene said to me after Ma passed. She decided then to tell Sean everything. He was mighty angry—not with you, Edith, but because she had kept it a secret. He claimed that she didn't trust him, and he was hurt. The kids knew something was up, Irene crying all the time. I had to keep quiet because it wasn't my place to say anything. Finally, she told the kids herself. I just wanted my sister to feel better, as did Sean when he calmed down. They soon sorted themselves out. I know there are people you contact now about adoptions, people who find people. I offered to help her with that, but she was scared, she said, that Ruby would turn you against her and make trouble."

"How is Sean, now that he knows I'm coming?"

"Fine," Rhonda said. "He's relieved and happy. 'The sleeping dogs have slept too long,' he said to me. 'Irene is all at sixes and sevens,' he told me last night. 'She's crying one minute and laughing the next!' He is the nicest fella you'd ever want to meet, Edith, stable as they come."

"What did she say when you told her where I was, that I wanted to visit? What did she say?"

"Well, she worried me at first. She sat on the back steps with the dog, ever so quiet she was. 'Leave me, Rhonda,' she said. 'Let me get used to this.' It wasn't long before she had a smile on her face and a zillion questions. 'I'll have to tell the boys and Bridgey,' she said."

"How did they take it?"

"Colin said he was happy for his mum. He's set to go to Trinity this autumn; he's a clever lad. Liam went to the pub. When he came back, well, I'll be honest with you, at first Liam reckoned you needed money, showing up after all this time. I heard there was a bit of a tussle. Sean sorted him out, and he apologized to his mother. He didn't mean it, he said. Michael, the sweet soul, said it was exciting, and he was sorry he couldn't meet you. He's away in London, lookin' to be an actor. Brigid went off the deep end! Well, you know now, that's Brigid. More brains than common sense. She spends a lot of time up in Belfast—says she needs to, with the troubles an' all. She'll come to peace with it at some point. You know, I love 'em all. They are the kids I never had."

"Well, I suppose … ," said Edith.

"Suppose what?"

"I am the 'it' in the story, right?" Edith said. "I just hope they'll be at peace with me."

"Of course, and nonsense! You are not, and never were, an it!" Rhonda laughed. "You are part of our family," she said. "Look now, we're here." She patted Edith's knee.

They turned in to an unpaved lane, passing fields of grazing cattle before coming to a sign at the entrance to a driveway that read, "Monahan and Sons. Prize Dairy Cattle." At the end of the drive stood a double-fronted brick two-story house. A dog was barking. Rhonda slowed down. "Here comes Sam," she said. A golden retriever bounded toward the car, his feathered tail waving. The car crunched to a stop on the gravel. "The boys are with Sean at the sale yards," said Rhonda. "They'll turn up later, I'm sure. Who knows—maybe Brigid will show her face."

Edith looked in the visor mirror; she frowned and pursed her lips. "You look a treat," Rhonda said, "come on."

With the dog galloping ahead of them, they walked up a paved path that divided a small lawn fronting the house. "She has left the front door open," Rhonda said. "She does that sometimes." The dog sped up to the door, banging it wide open.

They entered a hallway and were greeted by a sweet smell of fresh baking. "Mmmm," said Rhonda. Edith followed her into a large sitting room. A wood fire burned in the hearth. Sam's tail slapped against Edith legs, and she bent down to pat him.

"'Reen! Irene! We are here, love!" Rhonda called out. "She's fussin' in the kitchen with something. I'll go and see." Sam trotted out behind her.

Edith heard voices and pots clattering. She looked around the room. There were gleaming brass ornaments by the fireplace and embroidered cushions on the chintz-covered couch and armchairs. She eyed numerous silver trophies in a corner china cabinet. A door slammed and Edith jumped, dropping her handbag. She bent down to pick it up.

"Well, here we are," Rhonda said. Edith looked up, and there, standing together, were Irene and Rhonda. The dog bustled past them back into the room. A smiling Rhonda had her arm around her sister's shoulders. Irene appeared to be thinner and a little shorter than Rhonda. She wore a print blouse with tiny lilac and blue flowers, tucked into a gray pleated skirt that flared out from her narrow waist. She gazed at Edith with an expression of wide-eyed bewilderment. Edith gazed back. The only sound in the room was Sam's panting and the occasional clink of his collar as he settled himself down on the hearthrug.

Edith opened her mouth to speak, but her breath caught and she could not form a word. Irene covered her mouth with her hand. "Can this be? Can it be?" she whispered.

Edith's pulse resonated strongly through her body; it was as if she could hear it. "Hello," she said. "I, er ..." My words have no place here, she thought, feeling helpless and awkward. She looked at Rhonda, then at Irene. The fire crackled; the dog scratched himself. Rhonda cleared her throat. Seconds passed before the reality of the moment struck Edith. This was her mother, standing before her. She was real. This was happening. This was love. She had reached it. She felt the aching pressure of welling tears. Her mother was beautiful. Time had respected her lovely face. Her clear, pale skin was unadorned by makeup. Silver strands of hair mingled sparingly with her short, dark curls. Delicate lines enhanced her blue eyes as her face relaxed into a smile.

"Is it?" Irene said. "Is it really you?" It seemed to Edith that the only thing distinguishing her mother from her earlier photograph was a graceful maturity. "Yes, yes it is," said Edith, and her joy felt naked and raw as tears began to stream down her cheeks. Irene cupped her face in her hands and closed her eyes. "The good Lord be praised!" Rhonda said, and crossed herself before stepping between them. She took Edith's hand and then reached over to take Irene's hand. She placed their two hands together, palm on palm, mother and daughter. "Bless you. Bless you both," she said, and crossed herself again. "I'll make tea," she said softly and left the room.

Irene and Edith stood stock-still, expressions of joy alternating with disbelief on their faces. Irene looked down at their joined hands. "The last time I held this hand," she whispered, "you were five days old!" Tears filled her eyes. Edith drew her mother to her, gulping back her own tears. With their heads nestled and arms enfolded, they held on to one another tightly. They shed tears for the pain of what life had denied them, what each had missed, and their joy of reconciliation. It was a scene that would be repeated many times that morning until, eventually, they sat down to the lunch that Irene had prepared. They simply picked at their food, their appetites overridden by excitement and their heightened sense of one another.

"Who can eat at a time like this?" Rhonda said.

"They can," Irene said, pointing to the window. Two men were stepping out of a large truck that had pulled up to the house. They were slapping each other about, joking and laughing. Sam barked and bounded out of the room. Irene groaned. "Oh dear!" she said. "It's Sean and Colin. I told them to wait till suppertime. Those lads smell my scones a mile away. Edith, love, this isn't the way I planned things. Would you look at them now? They're not washed. They're filthy!"

"'Reen, darlin', they are fine—there's no plannin' to a day like this," said Rhonda. "God love 'em. They couldn't wait to see you, Edith." The front door slammed open, followed by the clumping of footsteps in the hall. The men tumbled into the room, all boots and bustle, their open, flushed faces grinning. Edith stood up, and Rhonda stood next to her, resting a hand on her shoulder. I'm really on display now, Edith thought. Why did I jump up? Her legs trembled, and she sensed perspiration beading on her forehead. Irene went to stand beside Sean and linked her arm in his. She beamed and nodded to Edith. There she is, Edith thought, my mother! She is with me; she is for me. Everything is going to be all right. She took a deep breath.

"Welcome," said Sean. He was shorter than Colin, who shared his father's blue eyes and wide cheekbones. Strands of gray hair barely covered his scalp. He clasped Edith's hand in both of his. "Welcome to our family, Edith," he said, a look of genuine pleasure on his face.

"Likewise," Colin said, stepping forward. "It's nice to meet you." He shook her hand vigorously.

"So much for our quiet lunch!" Irene said, and they all laughed.

The day so far was nothing like Edith imagined it would be—none of the strained conversation she had dreaded, nor embarrassment or scrutiny. She watched as Sean and Colin quickly devoured the remaining scones that Irene had fetched to the table.

"Well," Sean said, looking at his watch, "we must get back to the yard. Later we can all—" There was a screech of brakes outside. They turned to the window. The dog barked and headed for the door. "I knew it! It's Bridge," said Colin.

"Fer goodness' sake, she's drivin' that old car into the ground," said Irene.

"Lord help us," muttered Rhonda.

"She was at the pub," said Colin, "I know it. She's been hangin' out there all week. Where does she get the money, Dad? She doesn't do a stroke o' work!"

"Enough of that now, God only knows," said Sean.

"Don't start now, please," Irene said.

Edith looked through the window to see Brigid walking toward the house. Brigid looked up; she pulled a face and stuck out her tongue. Then, with a flick of her finger, her cigarette butt landed on the lawn. She thrust her hands into the pockets of her black pea coat and looked down. "I wish she wouldn't do that," said Sean.

"Do what, Dad?" Brigid said, entering the room. "Do what? You don't want me to smoke now? That's it, isn't it? Same old stuff, don't do this, don't do that!"

"Bridgey, you reek!" said Colin.

"Really now! Looks like you are having a party of your own here," she said.

"Have you eaten anything?" Irene asked.

"Who cares, Mum? I see you all have." She put a hand on the table to steady herself. "Well, well! I've already met our honored guest just yesterday! We got one up on the lot of you. Didn't we, Edith?" Brigid said. "All settled in now, are we, Edith? Fuckin' looks like it!"

"Bridgey, that's enough," said Irene. "Edith, don't listen to—"

"No, don't listen to me, for God's sake!"

"Brigid, please," said Irene.

"I'll clear the table," said Rhonda.

"Oh yeh! We don't want a mess. Edith's here, Edith's here!"

"Knock it off, Bridge," said Colin.

"I mess up the place, don't I, Dad?"

"Bridgey, come on now," said Sean.

"You know what I think? I'll tell you. She thinks she's somebody, Miss Edith! Waltzing in here like she knows us all. What the hell! Who's she fooling, for Christ's sake! I think—" Brigid's hand slipped off the table, and she slumped forward but quickly pulled herself upright.

"Stop," said Colin.

"Wait, wait!" Edith said, stepping away from the table. "Brigid, listen, please listen to me," she said calmly. "I don't expect anything. I don't expect anything from you or anyone else. I am simply here to meet my mother, and no matter how you care to interpret it, she will always be my mother and our mother. Our mother! So Brigid, we are related, like it or not—that's a fact!"

"Yeh! Did you get that?" said Colin.

"As God is in heaven, it's true," Irene said quietly.

"Love grows," Edith said, "if you give it a chance. It finds its way through the rotten stuff in life if you let it in. I'm proof of that!" She looked around at everybody in the room. Sean nodded and put a steadying arm around Brigid's shoulders. Her lips were quivering.

"It's all that matters, really," said Edith. "It's all that matters, that love!"

"Oh Christ!" Brigid moaned. She was hanging on to the table. "I think I'm going to be ..."

"C'mon now, Bridge," said Colin. "Let's go." He took her arm, steering her out of the room and up the stairs.

"She gets so mixed up," said Irene, shaking her head. "There's no reasoning with her sometimes, but I think she heard you, Edith, love, I do. I'm so, so sorry. She can be so rude."

"It's all right," said Edith, "really."

"That was good, what you said, Edith," said Sean. "We have to get back now; Liam is by himself holding the fort."

Colin came down the stairs. "She's away, gone, she's out for the count," he said. "I don't know about her sometimes, I really don't. She won't remember most of what she said. Honestly, Edith," said Colin, "she doesn't mean half of what she goes on about, believe me! Anyway, you stood up to her," he said with a smile.

"We'll celebrate tonight," said Sean, winking at Edith. "Liam plays his flute a treat," he said, "and Colin doesn't need an excuse to flex his tonsils!" He laughed, cuffing Colin on the shoulder. "We'll see y'all later, then," he said, and kissed Irene. "We're glad you're here, Edith." He gave her hand a vigorous shake.

That afternoon, with Sam leading the way, crashing in and out of the bracken, Rhonda, Edith, and Irene walked thorough the woods nearby. Edith listened to stories of their young Catholic lives. Irene spoke of her dreams of a wild freedom in England. "I worked at the mattress factory, for God's sake!" she said, a remark that triggered her tears. "Who did I think I was? I was seventeen! I was as green as these trees. I don't think I had a lick o' sense!"

"Don't fret, Irene," Rhonda said. "It's all turned out for the best. God is lookin' down on the lot of us!"

"Edith, tell us about Bogmire these days," said Irene.

"Well, not much to tell, really," Edith said. "The sand hills have eroded. The shrimps are gone. Plenty of red herrings, though; we have our share of scandal." She told them about the chaos of Alice and Jimmy's wedding. She talked about Mavis, Lil, and Reg.

"Bless their darling hearts," Irene said. "They were good to you as a child, then?"

"Oh yes," said Edith, feeling that was all she needed to say. This was not the place to speak of her childhood struggles. This was not the time to speak of Ruby and their endless acrimony. There would be moments, she knew, when she would speak of these things to her mother. And the occasion would arise when she could speak of Leon, beyond what had already been said. Edith was sure that he had truly loved her mother and perhaps still did. All of this would be carefully weighed and measured in its own time, Edith thought.

For now, she simply wanted to stay sealed in her happiness, to bathe in it and let it wash over her. Warmed by the spring sunshine, the three of them walked, Irene on one side of Edith, Rhonda on the other, their arms linked, elbows pressed together. "Who would have thought?" Rhonda kept saying. "God is looking down on the lot of us."

ABOUT THE AUTHOR

Brenda Foster was born in Lancashire, England, in 1939. After qualifying as a registered nurse and later as a midwife, she emigrated to Canada, where she met her husband. In 1978, after ten years in Northern California, she moved to Australia with her husband and two daughters. Widowed in 2002, she now lives in Tiburon, California. She is working on her second novel.